Fanning the Flames

A Flaming Rogues Novel

Fanning the Flames

Alexa Whitewolf

To Steven, for the happily ever after I never knew I needed, but feeds my soul.

Glossary

This book will have a few hard-to-pronounce names, and words, because Romanian isn't the easiest. But I wouldn't have been true to the story if I'd removed them soooo here's my little phonetic trusty guide.

Legătură, or the binding - leh-guh-tuh-rah

Împerechere, or the pairing - ihm-peh-reh-ke-re

Frate, or brother - frah-teh

Da/nu, or yes/no - dah/nuh

Zmeu/zmei, or Romanian dragon shifters - zh-mehu

Balaur, another type of shifter - bah-lah-uhr

Vasilisc, the Romanian type of basilisk - vah-sih-leh-sc

Ileana and *Făt Frumos*, or Prince Charming* - E-lya-nah and Fuh-th Fruh-mohs

*They're heroes of lore in Romanian folklore :)

Happy readings,

Alexa

"We came into the world like brother and brother.
And now let's go hand in hand,
not one before the other."

- William Shakespeare -

Prologue

Declan

Once upon a time, two brothers existed. Born to a zmeu clan, they were heirs to a legacy much older than they knew. Their father proved the wisest, the justest, the kindest... until he was no more. So, each brother grew, raised by a Council with antiquated views, well apart from the human world that despised their kind.

Each one was meant to be king. Each one was meant to be grand.

Some say the eldest took a shine to the spotlight. Some say the youngest could not stand the shadows. One became Light, one became Dark.

And this? It's the story of the Light one. But it is also *my* story. Because I will be damned if I let my brother take it all away from me again.

Everything I do, is to ruin him. To make him pay. He has stolen millennia from me and now... I have finally set up the pieces to ensure he loses everything. All that he holds dear in the past, present and future. All that he cannot see coming, but that I have foreseen.

Tytus will lose it all, and I alone will be left standing victorious. The one, the only, the truest king.

Revenge is a dish best served cold, humans say. My brother has come to love their kind... Thus, his ending is only fitting.

Chapter 1

Inceput
"Every new beginning comes from some other beginnings end."
- Seneca -

Fiona

How unlucky can one person get? I've been wondering that myself for the last few years. It's funny, when I think about the life I was meant to have, and the one I ended up with. Because of one simple mistake, I enslaved myself to a being far more superior than I, far more cunning than I, all of which culminated into a lifetime of misery.

I'm a witch. One taught to respect nature, do little spells, and the whole bit about the gods and my Gaelic heritage. Not that I know much about it, other than snippets. Eons and eons ago, my people lived somewhere in the northern part of Scotland, and were pagans. That's as far as my parents ever taught me and I was too busy to attempt further learning.

From a young age, I showed promise in magic. It was in me, spoke to me. And then came my teenager years, and my idiotic arrogance. By the time I got into my twenties, well, let's just say nothing was challenging enough. Not for the great Fiona, the perfect A student, the popular queen of, well, everything.

Until something was.

A powerful someone.

Declan.

A zmeu, born millennia ago in the Carpathian Mountains. A human who can shift into a dragon-type creature yet still walk and talk like a regular person when it suits him. Someone with fantastic magic, driven from the skies themselves… Someone whose sole purpose, once upon a time, was to seduce young maidens so he could eat them.

Well, I wish he'd eaten me. Maybe then I would have an easier life, rather than being coerced into acting as his middleman. His errand runner. Never seduced, never truly acknowledged, but used to get Declan's will, Declan's orders, to whoever he wished.

As it is, I still can't believe I've survived. If you can call it that.

Rain falls around me in thick curtains, and my only shelter is a massive tree in the woods near Rockland Creek. A wolf pack lives here, one who just won an important battle. It's thanks to them I've gained a reprieve from my jailer, and for the first time in ages, I can sit and hear the rainfall, without worrying of what it will cost me.

And with sitting, with not doing anything, comes the never-ending wave of thoughts and memories. Of how I got where I did, all my stupid choices and mistakes, wrapped up with a neat bow.

My independence, my ability to be my own person, were my post prized possessions. Declan took all that away from me. Had me at his beck and call, day and night. It started at first with that stupid connection, with his voice in my head. I didn't know he was a zmeu, I couldn't even fathom that kind of creature existed.

Not at the time. Now, I know better.

Back then, though, all I cared for was the next challenge, the next magical high, the next job well done. And Declan offered me that and more. I remember his words, hinting I could try this one other spell, that I could do that one thing differently... And then came offers of more magic, more power.

He channeled his own brand of supernatural into me. That, on its own, was addictive enough. Zmeu magic is potent, linked to weather and a zmeu's core energy. It's impossible to wield for humans. Impossible... unless one such creature gives you permission. Uses you as a conduit.

Which is what I became. Through me, Declan wanted to create an army. Through me, he hoped to escape the prison underneath the earth he'd called home for centuries. And by listening to him, ruled by my own ambition until it was too late, I ended up giving him exactly what he wished, and more.

In the end, Declan ruled me with an iron fist. I became his, day and night. Passing messages to the rival packs of wolves he controlled as much as me, making sure they focused on the plans he outlined. Their every movement brought him closer and closer to that elusive escape.

But his name alone no longer needs to bring me shaking to my knees. He is gone, imprisoned by powerful immortals who just happened to keep watch on Rockland Creek. And I was there to see it happen. A tale as intriguing as the world of shadows I was pulled into… and one I have no wish to dive deeper into.

In truth, I desire nothing more than to put everything behind me. To learn how to live, again. Perhaps a part of me would return home, but I'm not the girl who left years ago. Back then, I had stars in my eyes. Back then, I saw myself doing great things under the tutelage of a great spirit.

How foolish I have been...

And even so, some good has come out of it. Declan may no longer be in my head, ordering me to find the strongest villains for him to control. To be fair, he's not ordering anyone, anywhere. Yet the magic in him, the one he used me as a conduit for, still flows in my veins.

I want to refuse using it. It's as addictive and alluring as its master. But perhaps another way exists. A *better* way. And perhaps, in this better way, I can put the zmeu magic to good use.

As the rain keeps falling harder now, I glance at my fingertips. The skin is pale under the olive tone, almost translucent. Nails bitten to the bone. My clothes are soaked, my white locks so tangled even the purple streaks are nowhere to be seen. If anyone looks inside this tree, all they will see is an old woman... Until they see my face.

And that is yet another mark of Declan's. The white hair. Punishment for using magic not meant for me. My regular human body cannot contain such energy, not when it is so weak. The more I give in to the zmeu magic, the worse it will be for me. But I cannot just set it aside, not when I can do so much more with it, than with my own magic.

So, how can I use it, but for good deeds only?

I've spent the last years in captivity, under different creatures. At their mercy. Mainly because Declan spoke to them, seduced them as easily as he had me with promises of power and a better life. And I ended up their pawn, time and time again. Used and abused.

Now that I'm free, I don't know what to do. Rain continues to pour around me, and I shiver in the cold. I have no one left. My entire life became Declan's wishes. Declan's will. Declan's orders.

That is all I have known, and without it, I am....lost. Untethered. In desperate need of a purpose.

In the night's cold, something moves. A man. I freeze, fearing he'll notice me. But he passes right by me, head bowed, his stride determined and powerful. I know those shoulders, and in the bare dimness of the moon, I can make out a familiar profile.

Tytus–Declan's brother.

What is he doing here?

I'd helped him, just days ago. When he faced Declan, I was by his side in a futile attempt to save a young girl he cared for–Elisandra. Not that we succeeded, at least not at first. But I was there, even flew on his zmeu back as he squared off against his brother. As he lost….and got injured in the process.

A shiver runs through me. Yet, just as suddenly, a crazy idea builds in my mind. And before it's even fully formed, I'm getting up and following in his footsteps.

Tytus

Millenia I've lived, and for the first time I feel connected to something. To more than something, to some*one*. Elisandra, my last descendant. And I've just left her behind in a small town filled with secrets, because I have something more important to do.

I told her I needed to heal, but it was not the full truth. The real thing would be too much to explain, take too long, and already time is not something I have much of. Declan is imprisoned, and I would wish no less for that cunning bastard. He has hurt too many, and it's obvious there is nothing good left in him. Nothing of the boy I grew up with, of the young brother I nurtured.

Harsh judgment? Perhaps. Or, perhaps not so harsh. Declan was first imprisoned millennia ago, when our kind still existed. Our Council–elder zmei who wished to protect us–determined he had broken our most sacred law by drawing humans' wrath onto us. They tried Declan and found him wanting.

And when I learned of it, I did nothing to stop it. I had seen darkness rise within him for months, years even. Now, last of my race, I cannot go by pretending I do not see the evil he has wrecked.

I fought him, sensed that same darkness roll off him in waves. I saw it first hand when he went after me as wildly as an unhinged psychopath, as soon as he was released from his previous prison. And I still carry the mark of his wrath in the wounds he inflicted upon me.

Absentmindedly, I rub my chest as I walk. It stings, losing to my youngest brother. But that is the least of my concerns right now.

In the mountains of my youth lies a dark, dark secret. One my brother rediscovered, and one I must hide from humans at all costs. I know not what it is, only that Declan has messed with it. And I cannot allow it to fester. Like an infected wound, it must be cut, destroyed... Before it is too late. Before it fractures the supernatural world in a way no one has foreseen–no one except Declan.

Deep in my thoughts, I've made it as far as the meadow. After months of living in the area, of watching over Elisandra, I know it now as well as the valleys of my home. Countless times I've been here, turning to my zmeu form, and taking off into the skies.

Zmei are part of the draconian family, but unlike true dragon shifters, our real form is human. When we transform, we maintain our consciousness, our will. Whereas dragons masquerade as humans, their true appearance is the monster itself, and they lose themselves to it with every change. Zmei also have a rare type of magic, and can use the weather elements at their disposal in battle. That, and the magic in us, the true core, is... Well. Powerful, one could say. Much more than dragons, whose only ability is to breathe fire.

Not that it matters, the differences. Until recently, I thought I was alone, a remnant of an obsolete legacy. I still wish I was–my brother's return was not welcome in the least. Still, I have kept the humans ignorant of my existence, at least until Declan resurfaced.

Now, I must be more careful with the transformation. I dig inside, accessing that raw, primal energy, ready to let my zmeu loose. And then I catch the sound of footsteps–slow, timid. A scent I recognize. The flames licking my skin pause and wither as I turn around. My gaze finds the witch emerging from the trees.

"Looking for something?"

"I..." The witch–Fiona–only stares at me, unable to finish her thought.

I don't have time for this. My body is still weak from my fight with Declan. The fight I lost. I need to get back home, to heal. To find out what he messed up. To undo it.

And yet, the hunch of her shoulders, her drenched clothes–I must have spent too much time around humans. With a sigh, I step towards her. She backs away, not even realizing what she's doing. Her obvious discomfort has me slow down my approach, trying to think through my next moves.

This is a woman who was captive until mere days ago. Someone under my brother's thumb, who has lived through who knows what at his hands and his various men. Is it any wonder she doesn't trust me? Our only interactions were helping the wolves in Rockland Creek, specifically Lucas' pack, the leader. And when we spoke, I acted like an arsehole.

A second sigh escapes me, and I stop moving. Instead, I turn a palm towards her.

"You seem cold. I will not harm you, but this rain is rather annoying. For myself, I prefer dryness. Do you mind?"

Fiona looks at my palm, then back up at my face, and a small nod escapes her. She seems surprised that I ask her permission. Something akin to pity fills me, but I try to push it aside. I need not take in a stray right now.

I clench and unclench my palm, and fire rises from it. The flame burns through the rain, expanding until it becomes a circle that surrounds us both. Then, from the ground, a blazing dome shoots upwards, cutting off the downpour and surrounding us with dry heat.

Fiona stops her shivering and looks around in awe. "This is amazing."

Her childlike wonder gives me pause. What's amazing is the fact she can still walk around, still enjoy the simple things, after everything she has been through.

I try to see what she sees, everything I take for granted. My gaze shifts around the dome, the flames, the magic surrounding us. Zmeu magic. Perhaps all the millennia alive have jaded me, as I see nothing of worth.

Fiona is still staring, rubbing her hands to warm them, and turning in a circle. The fire reflects off her violet eyes and onto her oddly colored hair. A reminder of her past ties to my brother. Of the magic she used, when it was not hers to use. For a moment there, she seems almost unburdened.

While I hate breaking that, I also cannot continue to waste any time. "Was there something you needed?"

My blunt question is the wrong approach. Fiona moves backwards, almost into the blazes. I reach out to catch her wrist, and she freezes under my grip.

"You're walking towards the flames," I say as softly as I can manage. Then I force my hand to release hers, trying to shake off the feel of her soft skin. *How can someone be so soft?*

Fiona peeks upwards, darting a gaze behind, then inches a little away from the edge. I move backwards, giving her more space. "I didn't mean to scare you."

"You didn't," she replies automatically.

Instead of arguing, I let my silence speak volumes. And wait. And wait some more. Fiona shifts from foot to foot, rubbing her hands. One moves up to her tangled hair, and she tries to sort it out before giving up.

"I was looking for you," she finally says, not meeting my gaze. "Are you leaving Rockland Creek?"

My head tilts to the side. "How did you know?"

"The way you were walking... Away from where the wolves are. I thought you'd be there, celebrating."

I think back to Lucas and his rogues, and shrug. "They probably are, but I have things to do. Things that have nothing to do with them."

"Such as?"

My eyes narrow on her timid form. Something tells me her question isn't all that innocent. "I'm going back home for a while. To heal and check on things." It's the best I can give her, not knowing if she's trying to find this out for herself, or for Declan. He may be imprisoned, but he was always crafty. And if he still has access to her mind...

Fiona looks up at me then. Her eyes are even more ethereal than I thought. There's a stubborn grit in her, something equally surprising and... attractive. It's not the first time I noticed, but it is the first time I let myself think it.

A murmur rumbles in my gut. *Da...* My zmeu agrees with my assessment, apparently.

I shake my head, and with a sweep of my hand ensure the surrounding dome is no longer covered in flames, yet equally effective. "If there's nothing else..."

"But there is," Fiona says.

More silence follows her announcement. I could leave now. There is nothing keeping me here or glued to find out what she wants. And yet, something has piqued my interest. Will the little witch surprise me?

After another two beats where she avoids my gaze, our eyes connect again.

"I want to come with you, wherever it is you're going," she says.

That... I didn't see it coming.

Fiona

I'm probably crazy, signing up for something I'm nowhere prepared for. But I've lived the last of these years in captivity. At the mercy of powerful shifters, all greedy and aiming for more than they were given, or had a right to. I was a tool, an easy shortcut to that power–through Declan.

And the bastard enjoyed it. He relished every human and shifter that fell for his tricks, every moment where his choices forced me to side with the bad guys only to keep myself alive. I did things I wouldn't have thought I'd ever do–things I'm not proud of. Kidnappings, coercions by magic, attacks on innocents… And I spent nights upon nights begging for death to take me, to end my suffering.

Not anymore, though. I have a choice now, a second chance.

And despite his hard exterior, Tytus is a good man. Or, at the very least, he's not like the ones I've known.

I've seen his patience with the wolves, though he could have wiped them away with one hand. I've witnessed his protection of their various females, expecting nothing in return. Granted, they were all mated, but I strongly suspect he is not the type of man to take advantage of a situation.

Of course, I could be wrong. And this could turn disastrous. I could end up at another zmeu's mercy, one who has already made it clear I'm not his favorite person on earth. If I misread Tytus, it will mean the loss of a freedom I fought too harshly for. One I only regained through a stroke of luck.

But if I'm right... he is the one person who can help me. Through his quest, whatever it is, I can find my redemption. I can find another purpose. A way to forget what I did, and focus on something better.

Given the havoc I helped cause, and everything else that happened as a result, I need to do some good. Maybe I'll fail. Maybe I'll lose my life. But... I have to try. Otherwise, my entire existence is a failure, and I cannot live with that.

With a deep breath in, I meet those gray eyes of his and say, "You're wounded.

Surely your quest will be long, but with a witch on hand, well, it wouldn't hurt, right?"

He frowns at me, as though he sees right through my bullshit. He probably does. "And what's in it for you?"

"I only ask… that after I help you, you drop me somewhere with as few people as possible."

"Few people? That doesn't seem like a normal request, for a human. Aren't your lot social creatures?"

A tiny shrug escapes me. "Maybe. But not me." His frowns deepens, causing me to blab. "I'm done with this world, with being used. I… You saw what happened, how I ended up helping Thiago, then Cade. I don't want to worry about that anymore. What's the point of wasting years trying to figure out if a person is worthy of my trust? I just need to be alone, to live in peace."

More moments pass, and then he nods, those stormy gray eyes seeing way too much. "I can understand that. Eons ago, I would have wanted the same thing as you."

Silence lingers between us, extending

and expanding, like it has its own life force. My chest constricts, fearing he will refuse me. And through it all, I'm aware of his gaze on me, of my ratty clothes, my unwashed hair... And I think how pitiful I must appear to him.

"Trust is hard to earn," Tytus agrees. "You are correct to worry about who you give yours to, next. That being said... You must realize nothing about this will be simple, right?"

"I do."

"And some of it may bring back memories... Triggers. We are both zmei, after all. Declan is my brother, no matter how much I wish that was not the case."

I shrug, pretending like I'm not afraid, when inside I'm falling apart. "I can handle it."

"No, see–" Tytus moves closer, not enough to make me bolt, but enough to make me think about it. His hands are massive, his broad shoulders even more so. If he reaches out to me, I could break with a sure snap of his fingers.

And yet his voice continues to be soft, gentle. Unlike the angry zmeu I've been around. "This won't work if you don't talk to me. Tell me your limits. For as long as we're traveling together, for as long as you help me out, you cannot be afraid of me."

I gulp then, and whisper, "I can't promise that."

He pauses for so long, I fear he'll deny my request. Finally, he says, "Can you promise to try?"

"Yes."

"All right." His hand moves towards me, and I stare at it. Little by little, I reach for it, letting it engulf my own.

And then I look up, and up, into those hypnotizing gray eyes. "All right," I repeat, wondering what the hell I got myself into.

Chapter 2

Introducere
"The key to growth is the introduction of higher
dimensions of consciousness into our awareness."
-Lao Tzu-

Tytus

After Fiona agrees to my terms, I don't waste any time. I lift my hand up to the dome holding us dry and allow the air to whoosh out of it, right into my grip. The energy travels up my arm, then the barrier is no more and rain is once more falling on us. I step back a few paces, gesturing for Fiona to do the same.

"Keep in mind, my real form–"

"I've seen your real form already," she snaps. It startles me–and her, judging by the widening of her eyes. "I'm not scared," she repeats, like it's a mantra and if she says it long enough, she'll finally believe it.

I stare at her for a beat longer than necessary until she shifts her gaze away. My zmeu rumbles in appreciation–he needs that submission. Yet I wish for more of that spunk. Part of me wonders if it'll arise again, and the other part reminds me that is not the purpose of my mission.

With that in mind, I toss my head back and let the flames consume me. They travel over my human flesh, burning it away until it no longer exists. Until only my essence, my core energy, breathes on, surrounded by impenetrable fire. Only then does my zmeu take over, rising from fire like a phoenix out of the ashes. Powerful muscles bunch together, wings unfurl, canines grow, until I am much, much taller, and all I see are vivid colors.

Once the change is complete, I'm panting, several heads taller than Fiona and covered in scales the color of blood. A glance down shows my six-inch long claws, my wings unfurling as large as the meadow itself–even bending some trees backwards. My tail sweeps from side to side, the burgundy diamond-shaped tip glinting dangerously. Rain drops fall over my scales, making them shine in the light we have.

Finally, I glance at Fiona. She stares up in awe and fear, and I sincerely hope this isn't the worst decision we've both made. After another beat, she approaches me slowly.

I move equally slow, placing my head on the ground and inching one of my scaly hands towards her. She eyes the massive claws doubtfully, then purses her lips and climbs in. Little by little, her hands move over me as she makes her way all the way on my back, nestling between two raised spikes. Her movements are slow, but sure– like she knows where she's going. Which is not that surprising given she flew on me, once before. When we fought Declan.

The memory is loud in my mind–I shake it off, instead drawing a rune in the air. My claw moves with sure strokes, and fire sizzles around my design like I've scratched the surface of something that should not be tangible. Within half a second it shimmers and parts as a wool blanket floats through. I duck my head as air takes over, carrying the blanket over my back to Fiona.

I turn enough so I can see her. She hesitates, then mumbles a thank you and grabs the wool cover, wrapping it around herself. The shades of burgundy and black only make her white hair stand out even more, and I force myself to look away.

I want to tell her to hang on. But, recalling the battle from not that long ago, I let it go. Instead, I push my powerful muscles off the ground and take off in the air. The entire time, I'm focused on the little witch, and making sure she doesn't fall off me.

It's odd, but I don't recall this being the focus before. When we were facing off against Declan, my entire being was aimed towards him, towards besting him. And I still failed. Now, though...

I focus instead on getting us up, and up... Past the clouds and beyond. And then I let my mind go blank, enjoying the pull of the wind against my wings, and the acrid scent of human-permeated air disappearing below me.

¥

If anyone had told me I'd cross an ocean to find my descendant and cross it again with a witch, I wouldn't have believed them, yet here we are. I can feel her dainty hands on my back, holding onto the scales for balance. I've been keeping to the clouds high up in the sky, avoiding the contraptions humans call planes. We have a long way ahead until we reach my home, and the less attention we can attract, the better.

Even as my focus remains on flying, I'm also wondering about Fiona, and what her goal here is. Is it really to repent and feel better about what she's done?

Declan had her stuck, da, but she had the choice of what she was doing. Or did she? After all, he was always very good at warping minds, especially human ones.

I recall my initial aversion to her, when Fiona was helping Declan and almost harmed a human I was protecting. I wanted her dead, back then. And even more recently... But she came through, helping me with information when she had nothing to win, but everything to lose. *Surely that's worth some trust?*

My zmeu sure as hell seems to believe so, given he has chosen to ignore everything I wish. Normally, his will is in tune with mine. We are one full entity. Not in this case, apparently. Rather, he acts instead like Fiona's presence on our back is perfectly normal. Even more, like she... belongs.

I push the thought away, annoyed. My zmeu thinks in raw emotions, impulses. It's a good thing I master both of us while transformed, given I've always seen the world in black and white. And that won't change now. Not when it's imperative that I remain without distractions. One human witch cannot become my sole center of focus, nor will she.

And yet, no sooner do I think those words, that I'm proven wrong once again. This time, it's not by Fiona's words, but by her lack of action. Specifically, her grip on my scales slackens, and that's my only warning.

The second after, she slips off my back and falls into the abyss below. With an inward curse, I dive after her, wings flattening against my back. There is nothing beneath us but the ocean's harsh welcome, and a hint of panic spreads in my chest. I catch her body before it slams in the unforgiving waves, then with a burst of my wings, I shoot us back to the cover of clouds.

It was stupid. So fucking stupid, putting myself out of cover like that. Humans hunted every single one of my kin before, and they'll do so again if they catch wind of my existence. And yet, I didn't think twice before saving her. *Being around humans for so long must have muddled my mind.*

A glance downwards confirms Fiona's still unconscious. I must keep her in my grip for now, though her tiny body seems infinitely more fragile between my perilous talons. Did she have a coronary? Perhaps flying at these heights... I didn't think it was dangerous, but... *Fuck.*

I could keep flying. Push us where we need to get, while holding her. My zmeu does not agree, tossing me images of the way she'd looked, standing in the rain. So frail, despite her strength. So vulnerable, despite the fire in her eyes. And even so, she answered my questions and forced herself to make sense.

For me. To ensure I take her on this journey, and help her find the redemption she seeks. I am an old soul, and that measure of grit deserves some respect. Coupled with her previous help, it makes my zmeu unwilling to continue carrying her like a load of human junk.

Already, I'm scanning for a proper shelter. It's another half an hour until I spot land, and some more precious moments until I find a peak of a mountain far removed from civilization. A cave on the side attracts my eye and I drop Fiona on the cool ground, then shift to human next to her.

The change is more painful this way. It doesn't help that I'm injured, thanks to my brother and his keen fighting skills. A glance down at my bare torso reveals no wounds, but I know they're there, sapping at my inner strength. *If only I could get rid of them.*

With a shake of the head, I conjure a set of clothes. A rune in the air, magic fills my fingertips, and I relish the comfort it gives as much as I do flying. I've done it so many times before, I barely have to think. Tug in my core, a whispered thought, and the items I wish for appear on my body. I've opted for jeans and another black shirt, at least in the meantime.

A glance at Fiona's clothes, falling apart, makes me reconsider and I conjure some items for her, as well. With a bit of luck, the humans whom I'm taking from will not find them missing... And if they do, that they will take the payment my magic leaves behind. Soon enough, a small pile forms by her unmoving form, containing some jeans, undergarments, and sweaters, and a skirt or two. She will probably hate my fashion sense, but at least she cannot get sick on me.

My next course of action is lighting a

fire. Even unconscious, Fiona is shivering in her wet clothes. She'll be unhappy–and even more scared–if I try to disrobe her, so I don't even attempt it. Instead, I figure out another way to dry her up, kneeling on the cold stone and drawing two more runes. A sizzle, a burn, then flames jerk to life, crackling and roaring.

Fiona's body is unmoving, so freaking light as I pick her up and move her closer. I'm keenly aware of her fragile state once more and wonder how in hell Declan could hurt someone so... precious.

I stare for a second too long at her face, then move my attention to the flames. A tug of magic here, there, I use them to conjure more furs for her comfort and unwrap the soggy blanket from around her. While I cannot catch a human disease, Fiona is at risk for whatever her body cannot withstand.

I could leave her here... yet the thought repels me the minute it forms. Perhaps the journey started off on the wrong foot, but perhaps it would not have, if I had taken more time to ensure she was all right before flying off.

My gaze gets lost in the flames as I sit next to the fire. How long has it been since I've worried about someone else's comfort? And to think, without Declan's meddling, I wouldn't have known of her existence.

I reach a hand out, wiping her moist forehead, before moving to her throat to check for a sign of life. Even unconscious, Fiona flinches away from my touch. Yet there is a pulse, steady under my hand.

I watch over her for a while longer, then drop on the furs next to her and try to catch some sleep. It's been a long time since I flew such distances. They used to be the joy of my life, back when I had no ties to any human city.

And then I found out about Elisandra, feeling an unspeakable pull towards this town in the middle of nowhere. The minute I saw her, I knew she was tied to me, and I to her. My last descendant. She has her mate, but I know our paths will cross again. There is so much I must teach her, to master her magic and more. Too much…

My eyelids blink slowly, and an odd

fatigue descends on me. My weakness annoys me. *Damn Declan and the harm he inflicted.* Brothers should watch out for one another, not attempt to destroy everything they hold dear.

We both failed at that. And while home will help me heal, it is not truly home, not anymore… Not when there's nothing there to keep me, except for the mountain peaks and sacred walls of my ancestral palace.

My thoughts ebb away, and the crackling of the fire is the last thing I hear before falling asleep.

Fiona

I wake up feeling like a train ran me over. Despite the battered sensation I'm so used to, I'm also very warm. And, comfortable. Nestled against something hard. That, more than anything, rouses me out of sleep. Only to notice furs, and Tytus' body wrapped solidly around mine.

In sleep, I've turned to him, seeking his heat, and my head rests on his chest. A myriad of emotions runs through me, all of them resulting in my body being unwilling to move. Even unwilling to breathe. *This is dangerous. This is unsafe. He could have... But he didn't.*

At long last, I glance up, and the emotions within me only slam harder against my chest. My breathing comes out shaky when my eyes collide with Tytus', finding him watching me. He's making no move, giving me space, although I'm practically glued to him.

His gray eyes are darker than usual, and there's something almost primal in his gaze. It warms me up, albeit in a completely different way. In a way I haven't thought of for ages... And suddenly I'm aware of just how hard, how unyielding, his body is against mine.

"What... What happened?"

Tytus says nothing, still staring at me. My tongue slips out to moisten my dry lips, and his eyes zero in on the movement. His hold on me tightens. I freeze. He freezes. The air crackles.

Then, he lets out a breath and shifts, slipping out from under me, and the blanket. I'm relieved to see he's dressed, then shame replaces the relief. I chose to come along with him. Surely that means I trust he'd at least... That he wouldn't... Or am I losing it?

I must be, judging by the way I can't tear my eyes from him. Dressed in jeans and a shirt, he looks almost... normal. A façade, I know, hiding the creature inside. Nonetheless, it's a very hot, and alluring façade.

I watch as he steps to the edge of the cavern we're in, taking the moment to gather my thoughts. What the hell happened? Last thing I remember is the wind against my face, the rain soaking the blanket, and my internal berating at the fact I didn't think to shield myself from the elements. I was trying to remember a drying spell–if I'd ever been taught one– when everything went dark.

And then I vaguely remember more wind, more cold, and finally the dryness of a shelter. And heat. So much heat... I must've sought him out unconsciously in sleep, drawing comfort from his presence, but none of that means what I did is safe.

Tytus may be good, but he is still a zmeu. And a man. I cannot understand his way of reasoning, let alone what makes him feel. Or why he's not yet gone, although I have delayed us on our barely begun journey.

He interrupts my thoughts when he walks back to me. "You passed out mid-flight. I had to find solid ground while you recuperate."

"I… I'm sorry. It won't happen again."

"Yes, it will. And we had a deal, Fiona. You need to tell me when your human body reaches the limits of its endurance. Anything else will only delay us."

I look down, playing with the furs and trying to change the subject. "I've never felt something so silky."

"I conjured them to keep you warm," Tytus says softly. "I wasn't sure if the passing out was due to cold, or weakness…"

A sigh escapes me. "It was a little of both. Fatigue catching up with me." *Because I'm afraid to sleep. Because I fear Declan will be there, pulling me under again. Because I do stupid things when I sleep, like try to cuddle with you.*

I don't say any of that out loud. Nonetheless, it's all over my thoughts.

Tytus frowns my way. "Will sleep help, then?"

"I... I have a hard time sleeping fully."

"You seemed fine just now."

"You were watching me sleep?"

He shrugs. "I need little of it myself. So when you rolled into my arms–"

"I didn't! I..."

Tytus arches an eyebrow, daring me to contest it. I can't. Because I probably did as he accuses me, desperate even in my sleep for some kind of love. I break all eye contact before he can read any of that on my features.

"Is there food, too?"

Tytus is silent for a bit, then he says, "Sure. I'll go hunt us something."

Panic fills me at the thought of being alone, in a cavern on a mountain top isolated from civilization. "Don't leave!" When he turns my way again, I try to amend my tone. "I... Can't you conjure something?"

"It doesn't work that way. When I conjure items, they disappear from someone's possession. Usually, within the vicinity. I always leave behind a token of my appreciation. Clothes and furs, I take from my own home. But food, well, it has to come from the closest village."

"And what's wrong with that?"

He tilts his head to the side, smiling. "Nothing. If I don't wish for humans to hunt me down, that is."

"Oh."

"Yes. I would expect they aren't as open-minded as the ones back home." Another pause. "Will you be all right? I won't be long."

I nod, forcing myself to be brave. At least for the time being.

Tytus

Easier said than done. The land I've chosen is sparse and devoid of any humans for miles. It takes me over an hour to track down a pack of seals at the edge of the island, and by then my mood has passed annoyance.

Why is this witch so contrary? One minute she's afraid of me, the next she crawls into my hold in the middle of the night like she belongs there. Makes my zmeu all riled up and appeases him within the same touch.

If she wants my bed, all she has to do is say so. I will not deny her, nor think twice. But despite having her in my arms, the moment she woke up she dismissed me. Again.

Humans.

With a heavier hit than normal, I claw a seal off the rocks and rip its head off, then fly back to the cave. By the time I'm back, dumping the animal at the entrance so its smell does not invade our sleeping spot, Fiona has reanimated the fire.

I watch her melt some ice in a pot and use it to rub her face and neck clean, hissing at the coolness slipping under her top. While I was gone, she changed into a new pair of jeans and a sweater, and the sight makes me smile. At least she's comfortable.

A second later, she feels my eyes on her

and drops her hand, then turns to me. Wariness fills her movements, the slight relaxation now gone, replaced by an unreadable expression.

"You're back fast."

I jerk my thumb towards the outside. "Caught a seal. If you can keep the fire going, I'll skin it and prepare the meat."

Fiona makes a face, then nods.

I gesture to her clothes. "I'm glad they fit, and that they're comfortable."

A blush creeps up her neck and she ducks her head, a quiet thank you floating back to me. To avoid her further embarrassment, I head over to a corner of the hot blaze and reach for a flame. My hand doesn't burn, instead it grips the fire like it's tangible. It shivers and resists, then gives in to become a dagger. The handle is all black leather, with a curved, jagged blade that looks deadly.

When I stand with it, Fiona pales and crawls backwards. Her wide eyes are glued to the new weapon I'm holding. "How...how did you do that?"

I frown at her, not understanding the

fear. "This? It's primordial magic. Only zmei can wield it, and immortals."

Her gaze finally detaches from the dagger. "Pri...mordial?"

Her lips part, and that sneaky tongue comes out once more to moisten them. I'm a red-blooded male, a zmeu whose last lay was so long ago I cannot remember her face, let alone her name. I cannot be faulted for my reaction to her–but I do snap to my senses enough not to jump on her. It's the last thing she needs, and judging by the way she's blowing hot and cold on me, she's even more confused than I am.

Instead, I keep my tone low and calm, just on the verge of hypnotic. Fiona is not used to my full power, and I don't want to scare her. Or have her compare me to Declan, knowing how powerful we both are. I've given her my word she can be safe with me, and I will not break it.

"Primordial," I repeat. "The energy of the divine, back when they first created the worlds. It's raw, pure magic, since before humans came to know the weakened magic they do, and way before other shifters existed."

"And it belongs to the gods?"

Her eyes are so wide, I sigh heavily, telling myself to keep being patient. But how do I explain exactly how powerful I am, without having her run off? In the end, there's nothing I can do but give her honesty. And if she runs, perhaps it's best that way. Less headache for me–and my zmeu.

"Da. Back when the worlds were created, gods had their divine energy. Each creature they brought to life received a little of that energy, in various bursts. Humans, as they were the last created, had the weakest bit."

"Probably for the best," Fiona mutters.

"Perhaps."

"So what made zmei so worthy of more?"

I shrug. "The gods created us to protect them. Thus, it only made sense that we were powerful. It is why our core energy reacts to the elements, and why we can change things. Turn a flame into a dagger, conjure items from far off, create portals to transcend time."

Fiona's wide eyes get larger still. "How then did your kind go extinct?"

This time, my tone is less gentle. Elisandra asked me the same thing, and the answer is just as idiotic and a letdown. "Because we became greedy, and arrogant in our might. Once the gods no longer needed us, locked up in their own pantheons, they left us to our own devices. Unfortunately, it seems the longer some of us stayed on the earthly realm with humans, the more we lost the wisdom that made us so powerful to begin with."

Fiona must sense the bitterness in my tone, as she glances at the fire, silent for a bit. Her next question is a clear desire to switch the subject. "Can it only be done with fire?"

"Fire, earth, air, water, lightning– anything that has a beat, a life and core energy to it, something to draw on."

"And how does it work?"

It's my turn to be wary of her questions, and their implications. Zmei created powerful mages by sharing secrets of primordial magic with humans. The last thing I want is to make the same mistake. Fiona herself is already affected by Declan's machinations... In a way, perhaps she still is. Either way, my gut no longer wants to stay on this topic.

"Humans cannot wield it," I say harshly.

"Really? Doesn't Lucrezia?"

Images of the redhead with blue eyes from Rockland Creek snap me into focus. She was a human, originally, that much is true. I'd taken her under my wing, by accident and not aware of what my protection would unchain.

In the end, a long string of events led to her becoming a powerful sorceress, albeit completely unaware of her full powers. She became a Solomonar–a gifted human whose purpose was to help a zmeu in battle. Like much of my kind, they were eradicated. Until Lucrezia...

My expression must be furious at the impertinent question, as Fiona backtracks. "I... I meant nothing by it. It was only curiosity."

"Let's keep it that way."

My tone comes out even more biting, and I stalk to the outside of the cavern, leaving her inside. It only takes me moments of skinning and slicing the seal to realize I've been unfair, and perhaps a tad too snappy. *Great. Now we owe the human an apology.*

Fiona

This was a mistake. I don't know what I was expecting from this journey, but sticking around a being way more powerful than me, who can play me like a fiddle, is obviously the stupidest idea I've had in a while. Even more than what dumped me into this never-ending cycle of servitude.

The fire catches my eye, and I move closer, lost in the flames.

Fiona! Fiona, show them what you can do! Echoes of the past come back to me, taunting me.

I had been young and foolish, so I showed the people of my village. I didn't know someone was watching, listening closely to my conjuration spells. Didn't know Declan was searching for exactly the stupid human who would fall under his spell. I wanted power, and then he led me to his burial site, and it doomed me.

Declan searched far and wide for something leech on to. First it was Thiago, then Cade... And finally, me. Still. Always.

Like a shadow I cannot shake. I lift my hand to the flame, angry. Maybe I can burn him from my flesh, this connection I cannot escape.

You will give in, Fiona, he taunts me even now. I don't know how much of it is real, or my own fear. But it's enough to set me on edge. It may be fainter in my dreams, but still very much there.

A firm hand wraps around my wrist, stopping me from reaching the flames. "What do you think you're doing?"

Tytus' voice snaps me out of my thoughts, and I jerk away. His hold only tightens, and I react. I lift my other hand to attack, already drawing a rune in the air. He smacks at the magic with his free hand, dissipating it into thin air. My panic only rises, choking me, and I try another rune.

Tytus grabs my other wrist and pins them both behind my back.

The movement draws me flush into his arms, and we both freeze. He could do anything. He's strong enough–male and magic. Despair threatens me, but Tytus surprises me yet again.

He releases my wrists, and in the same movement wraps both arms around me in a...hug. I freeze completely.

And then he drops his mouth to my ear. "Now, I don't know as much as I'd like to about humans, or understand them enough to consider myself an expert. But I do believe this is a hug, and its aim is to comfort when someone is feeling particularly... unsettled." He pauses. "Which, unless I'm mistaken, sweetling, is you right now. Will you speak with me, without barriers or look of fear?"

I open my mouth into his chest–and sobs pour out.

Chapter 3

Emoții
"The degree of one's emotions varies inversely with one's knowledge of the facts."
-Bertrand Russell-

Fiona

There are tears that come from one situation, and then there's sorrow that has followed an entire lifetime. That's what comes out of me in Tytus' arms, in all its unholy, ugly glory. Part of me tries to staunch it, but the tears flow only harder.

Tears of exhaustion. Tears of anger. Tears of fear. They have been building up with every moment in captivity, always suppressed, always ignored. They are everything, all that I see, all that I feel. All in the comfort of his embrace, something as incredible as it is wearying. This is the same man–dragon, entity–that wanted me dead not so long ago. And then I saved his descendant, helped his wolves, and joined him on this quest.

What the hell was I thinking? I sure as hell didn't have all my wits. If I did, I would have known that no matter what I tell myself, I'll be vulnerable with him. That he'll see me at my worst, see what Declan did to me, and realize I am weak. That I don't belong here. And if he realizes that, then I cannot in any good standing continue, because I'll have lost my chance of redemption.

By the time I'm done crying, we're no longer standing, but kneeling on the furs. The fire is dwindling. Aroma of fish comes from the outside. And Tytus' arms aren't wrapped around me, instead they're resting by his sides.

Despite the sobs having quieted, I can't quite look him in the eyes. I also can't help my nose from wrinkling. Tytus' chest moves, shaking–he's laughing.

"What is that smell?"

"Seal, sweetling. Can I leave you alone while I cook it?"

I nod and let him move, my eyes traitorously glued to his lean body as he stands and goes over to a pile by the fire. As he prepares the bits to cook on sticks, Tytus talks as if my crying never happened.

"I was preparing it when I saw you standing much too close to the flames. Why was that?"

I busy myself with tidying furs that need no fixing. When I next look up, Tytus has some meat bits cooking on the fire. Despite myself, I feel I owe him an explanation, if only to show him I'm not a nutcase. But how to explain the utter allure of the fire?

In the end, I settle for, "I was lost in thought, and didn't realize how close I got."

"Are you sure that's all it was?"

"Yes." My voice is weak, and I hate it. Hate how whenever he comes near, I want to curl into myself. It has nothing to do with him being intimidating on purpose, but more with how I perceive him. As this all-powerful being, who could snap me in two if he wished it.

Yet, in complete contradiction, more and more I'm aware that he's also a man. And nowhere in my decision to join him did I factor that bit in. If I had, I wouldn't be so thrown off by the comfort he provided, or by the way he looks at me sometimes. And yet, I am. More and more.

"If you say so…"

He lets his words trail off, and stupidly, I catch onto the bait. "What else would it be, if not my inattention?"

Tytus sits back on his heels, the flames glittering in his gaze. "Perhaps you were trying to purify yourself. From past deeds… Or other things."

Uneasiness spreads into the pit of my stomach. My first impression of Tytus was that he was aloof, yet just. I had counted on that ability of his to keep himself detached, uninvolved. Yet now, I notice his fairness actually comes from being so perceptive. From seeing everything. Which is bad news for me… the worst.

Instead of voicing any of that, I

whisper, "It won't happen again."

His gaze is sharp on me. "You feel this was a failure, somehow, on your end?"

"Wasn't it?" I'm hesitant to admit as much to someone so powerful. After all, he could always use it against me. Wouldn't be the first time.

His jaw clenches in time with one of his fists. The movement draws my eyes in fear, and my entire body freezes again. Tytus mimics my move, glancing between me and his closed fists. An odd reaction passes his features, and I stare in amazement as this powerful creature forces himself to backtrack, unclenching his fists, relaxing himself–for my sake. His words are at odds with his actions, not harsh, but brutal in their truth.

"Fiona," he says, using my name, "let us get one thing clear. It was you who asked to come on this journey. I did not force you, nor do I force you to stay. You have complete and utter free will for yourself, to do as you please."

"I understand."

"I don't think you do." He assesses me

for so long, I squirm under his gaze. Then some kind of decision comes over him, and he stands, towering over me. "May I come closer?"

"Yes," I mutter, looking anywhere but at him. No way do I feel comfortable with him being close to me. Whether because I'm afraid of him, or my own reaction, I don't feel like investigating further in that moment. If I could make myself invisible, I would, but there is nowhere to run in this blasted cave.

Yet despite my acquiescence, Tytus doesn't move. His inaction causes me to look up at him. I frown when I notice he's simply... waiting. "Why aren't you moving?"

"Because you did not give me permission to approach you."

"I did, though."

He shakes his head, and something akin to sadness crosses his expression this time. "No. You told me what you thought I needed to hear. Not because it was true. In fact, I'd wager it is the farthest thing from the truth. My very presence makes you afraid."

"It doesn't!"

"It does, and it should. I am a thousand times stronger than you, Fiona. I hold the wrath of the skies in my hands, and I can transform at the drop of a hat into a feared monster of legends. It is wise to keep your distance from me. But," Tytus takes a stick with cooked meat and holds it out for me, "I swear I will not turn that power against you. When you joined me in this quest, you became my partner, under my protection. That does not take away your free will. You have survived much, perhaps much more than anyone realized back in Rockland Creek. But we are not there anymore. And whatever you do from now on, is entirely up to you." He holds out the food again. "Would you like to try some?"

I glance between the fish and his neutral, kind eyes. Taking in the magnitude of the words, of what he is trying to communicate. My hand is shaking when it reaches out, but it's a step in the right direction. I think. "Thank you."

He waits until I take a dainty bite before sitting back down. And this entire time, he hasn't approached me, despite my so-called permission. I don't really taste the food, barely realizing I've devoured most of it until Tytus hands me another. I stare in shock at the empty stick.

"When was the last time you had a proper meal?"

"I... I'm not sure."

"Since they freed you?"

I shake my head, shivering at the memories of his wolf friends risking their lives to save mine. "Maybe. I've been living off what I could find in the woods, near Rockland Creek."

A heavy sigh escapes him, and as he hands me more food, his other hand reaches for the fire. The flames climb higher, and heat pours over the cold stone, heating the furs and everything around us. Heating *me*. Because he noticed I was cold. I don't know which of his thoughtfulness or perception warms me more, though.

"Why..." I stop myself before I can get the full question out. My captivity screwed me over. They might not have broken my spirit, but I'm no longer the young girl I used to be, either. And planning what I want to ask is harder than I thought, to the point I almost give up, not wishing to be the target of anger. Of humiliation. Even though I know, or at least I'm realizing, that Tytus is different.

He says nothing, instead munching on some food. But his gaze is on me through the flames, and that alone feels like a challenge. So I swallow the fear in my throat and look up. "Why are you so nice? How can you be, considering what you know?"

Tytus tosses the empty stick away and tilts his head. "And what is it you think I know?"

"That I was imprisoned by two villains you fought. First Thiago, then Cade. Did their bidding, at the behest of your brother. My actions directly affected the wolves you watched over–hurt them."

"And you believe it's your fault?"

"Isn't it?"

He nods, as though considering my words. "Yes, I can see your reasoning. After all, you let Declan corrupt you. Allowed him in your head, fell prey to his temptation. And then you were his to toy with, to do with as he pleased."

I want to lower my head, to escape that piercing stare, but I cannot. Instead, I keep our gazes locked, nearly holding my breath.

"I thought as much, too," Tytus admits. "When I first ran into you, I wanted to kill you. Or use you to find out more about Declan and his plan. Even when you came of your volition, I did not see you as anything other than a vessel to be sacrificed, if it meant saving the wolves, their mates, and Elisandra."

His words are harsh. I tell myself I deserve them—that I asked for them. And yet he surprises me once more. His tone gentles, and he says, "But I was wrong. I realized it the moment I protected you, over my own blood. There is a reason Thiago and Cade were drawn to you. There is a reason they wanted to break you. And that same reason is why I wanted to give you a chance to find redemption. You have an innate ability to take the darkest experiences and turn them into light, Fiona. And it is something that others may wish to destroy, but I only wish to treasure. This world has too little of it left."

All I can do is stare at his admission. Tytus says nothing, instead dipping his head and devouring three sticks of his own, leaving another two for me.

Tytus

This will not end well. The witch makes me more truthful than I want to be, and it is unnerving. Even as I stuff my mouth with the rest of the food, I feel her uncertain gaze on me.

Yet I did not lie. I have seen strength and resilience in Lucrezia, and the other two females in Lucas' pack, Daniela and Elisandra. One is a half-wolf, half-witch who came seeking help, unaware it was Declan himself who turned her pack crazy. The other is my descendant, blood of my blood, and the whole reason I was in that town in the first place. All three of them have grit, and an uncanny ability not to shy in the face of danger. To be resilient, to survive.

I see the same in Fiona. She was dealt a bad hand by her own choices, but her life is nowhere as close to its end as she seems to believe. And I can help her see that while she's with me –

What am I even thinking? My focus should be on healing. On finding out what Declan meant, what he did.

As if on cue, Fiona speaks again. "Can I ask you something random?"

"By all means."

She hesitates, as if afraid to offend me. Now my curiosity is really piqued.

"The Romanian…. I mean, you're Romanian. Born in the Carpathian Mountains, right?" She blushes. "I heard the wolves talk, before."

"Da," I nod.

"But aside from *yes*, I haven't heard you speak much Romanian. How come?"

A snort escapes me, followed by a full chuckle. *This was her pressing question?*

Fiona blushes further, but doesn't back down, so I give in. "Having lived as long as I have, I've learned the less things that set me apart from humans, the better. Especially as I want to blend in. So the real answer to that question is, I've trained the Romanian out of me."

"But you still speak it?"

"I do, yes."

She munches on some more food, then switches topics again. "And what makes you think Declan messed something up, in your home?"

I settle on the ground, relaxed and relieved she's more comfortable to engage with me now. "I may not know my brother as well as I did growing up, but some things do not change. When the immortals caught him, he taunted me, saying our house is still standing. Ileana–the immortal witch who imprisoned him at my behest–thinks he meant the objects within the house. But I know Declan, and if he brought that up, it is because he prepared something much, much worse than making sure some magical objects fall in human hands."

Fiona gulps audibly and sets aside her food.

"I've ruined your appetite, haven't I?"

She shakes her head, then stops and nods. I'm surprised at the honesty. Perhaps my own brought this on.

"A little, yeah," she says. "But I need to

hear this. Declan has been in my head for so long, I should know more... But in truth, I know very little about him. About the man he used to be."

Her unspoken question lingers in the air. Will I tell her more?

With a sigh, I grab a stick and start playing in the flames. "As you know, a zmeu–what me and Declan are–is human first. We are ancient shifters, and our chosen form from eons and eons ago is a creature similar to a dragon. Yet we are less greedy, less temperamental, mainly because even in fully shifted zmeu form, we still keep our consciousness."

"And you can shift as much as you want?"

A short laugh escapes me. "You would think so, but not always. If we're injured, the more we shift, the more our human form suffers. And if it is injured beyond hope, there is no way to save our soul." The flames dance with my next exhale. "Declan... His ability to get in your head, I'm afraid it was cultivated from a young age. We both hatched within months of each other and were extremely close as children. So close, that particular game was our favorite one."

"You mean, getting into each other's heads?"

I nod. "It may seem odd, but we used to fly and hunt, and play at being in the other's head. With zmei, such a thing does not leave lingering effects. It's different with humans."

"Right."

There is an odd note in her voice, and I look up at her. Fiona holds my gaze, and I'm oddly glad to see less of the fear in those violet eyes of hers. "I'm sorry."

"What for?" she frowns.

"For Declan. For the way he invaded your mind, controlled you... Made you an accomplice to his bad deeds." I search for the right words, but they elude me in the face of her vulnerable expression. "Most of all, I'm sorry that the games we played as boys are what trained that particular skill of his. If I could make sure he pays for it more, I would. Believe me."

Fiona gulps, then gulps again. After clearing her throat, she says, "Thank you.

You cannot apologize for something he alone is guilty of, but I appreciate it. Will you tell me something?"

"Anything." Stupidly, I mean it.

"Where is he being kept?"

"Not even I know the location," I say truthfully. "The immortals who took him–Ileana and Făt Frumos–they're protectors of my part of the world."

"That's who the guy in a suit was?"

I nod, recalling she'd seen both of them mere days ago. I'm still not sure how Ileana, an immortal, came to be entwined with the wolves of Rockland Creek. Elisandra said she was there because one of the wolves was her godson, and perhaps that is the case. Either way, she must have a bleeding heart rather than the usual iciness of the immortals, since she stuck around and guided the wolves through various adventures, going so far as to dragging her consort in the middle of it.

Whatever the reality of her presence there, it was Ileana's plan we carried out to entrap Declan, and it was their magic that sealed the capture.

"Yes, Ileana and Făt Frumos are their names." For Fiona's sake, I enunciate, knowing she'll be unfamiliar with the pronunciation. *E-lya-nah* and *Fuh-th Fruh-mohs.* "His name is the equivalent of Prince Charming, if you will. But as for Declan's new prison location, I do not know. Wherever they imprisoned him, though, I can assure you he will not reach out to you. You are safe now, Fiona."

She picks at her jeans as if not quite believing me, but says nothing else on the subject. Instead, her next question is another deflection. "And you think what Declan did, in your home, it also has to do with these games you used to play?"

"No, but I sure hope it's fixable. Knowing my brother, it is nowhere that easy."

I can tell she hesitates to ask more, but the silence prompts filling. "How did you two fall out?"

Fiona

Tytus stares into the flames for the longest time at my question. Just as he opens his mouth to say something, he jerks his head to the cave entrance. The next moment, he's dashing across, plastering himself to the side of the wall as if to keep hidden.

I want to call out to him, but his form alone pauses that knee-jerk reaction. His back is tense, fists by his side, and his eyes are glaring daggers. Then, even scarier, he freezes. Whatever he sees out there is enough to make him snap from his silence.

Though his voice is low, I catch it when he returns briefly to my side. "Fiona... Stomp out the fire. Grab whatever supplies you can."

He holds out his hand and the air shimmers, before releasing a steel blade in his palm. Just like with the dagger, it seems he's playing with air itself. The handle of this new weapon is black, also leather from what I can tell. The blade curves into a dangerous-looking type. I've seen these weapons before—in museums and old movies. A scimitar. And it looks even more deadly in Tytus' grip.

Without looking at me, he adds, "Do you know how to portal out of here?"

"Yes, but Tytus–"

He meets my gaze then, briefly. "Just do it. If I don't come back." Then he's gone, swooping outside like some avenging angel. I can't understand what drew his attention so, but some instinct of self-preservation outruns my curiosity.

Rather than go see, I follow his orders and use one of the furs he conjured to pack the other supplies, while stomping out the fire. Once that's done, I stand on wobbly feet.

Should I go look? Before I can decide, a clash of swords draws my attention, followed by the unmistakable sound of agony–men crying out in pain, gasping for their last dying breaths. And then Tytus is back, panting. Slashes cover his shirt, and a gash shows through the cut skin. Another bleeds profusely on his face.

His relieved gaze finds mine. "Come on!"

I grab the pack of supplies, then his outstretched hand, and follow him uphill rather than down. When I try to glance back, all I can see is the snow, painted an ungodly shade of red. "T-Tytus?"

He throws me a dark look over a

shoulder, enough to make me shake in my boots. Gone is the man in the cave who'd opened up to me and said exactly the words I needed to hear. This is the zmeu, in all his glorious and ruthless glory.

As we reach the pinnacle of the mountain, he lets go of my hand and turns away. Flames surround him, burning the human and replacing him with the zmeu. The scent of sulfur and cinnamon suffuses the air, even at these altitudes. My grip on our supplies tightens.

I remember what he said about me having a choice. To leave anytime I see fit. And yet... I glance at the blood-stained snow, and the outlines of bodies. Tytus hasn't given me an answer. I have no idea if this was murder or self-defense. Yet part of me wants to believe in good, where he's concerned.

Regardless of the reason, when he holds out his massive wing, I consciously decide to follow him. Whether or not I've signed my death warrant remains to be seen.

Declan

I stir awake in my prison–the cavern the immortal left me in. The gold underneath me is a reminder of the irony. A zmeu, as powerful as me, stuck within a human contraption.

What woke me? I have had pleasant dreams of date, but this was not it. I glance around, expecting to see my latest visitor, with no luck of her golden hair.

So what gives? I give in and do something I have stayed away from and probe mentally to the outside. Ileana may have imprisoned me here, but not even she can stop me from connecting with my own kin. The last of our kind, still roaming free.

Envy courses through my veins. Why should Tytus be the one out there, flying wherever he sees fit, achieving whatever he wishes? I should be there. I *would* be there, if it weren't for one inconsequential error of judgement... Which will thankfully be corrected rather soon.

I focus on our bond further. Since we were kids, perhaps because we grew up together, Tytus and I had an easy connection. All it took was me thinking of him, or him thinking of me, and that connection materialized at the forefront of our consciousness. All we had to do was dive mind-first into it, and it would connect us, making it possible to travel upstream into the others' head.

And now, when I try, it is not so different. Harder perhaps, but once we click, his emotions swirl everywhere. A rush of fear and anxiety swims back to me. Before I can focus on it further, figure out what's going on, I'm yanked back and slammed into my own consciousness and shaking my head to clear it.

Blasted Ileana and her tricks...

The damn witch must have known and added something to the prison defenses. No matter, it will not last long. And what's more, I've felt enough. Tytus is being chased, and if it's any indication, it's not by anything I've set in motion. Which begs the questions... What else would we fear out there? Or has my brother softened so much, he can no longer take care of himself?

A snort escapes me. *That would be Tytus.*

I should be happy. If nothing else, I've received confirmation he is in pain. He is definitely not leisurely sitting by in Rockland Creek, and has taken the bait I tossed his way. Before too long, he will be exactly where I need him to be, doing exactly what I need him to do.

Now all I have to do is wait. Patience has never been my virtue, but it is never too late to learn.

Chapter 4

Dușmani
*"You have enemies? Good. That means you've stood up
for something, sometime in your life."*
-Winston Churchill-

Tytus

As soon as Fiona's on my back, I push off the ground, for once damning my large, cumbersome body as it takes me a few extra flaps before I can get us all the way up. I could have left her behind, but that damned protectiveness gripped my zmeu again, and he was unwilling to leave without her.

Perhaps it's better this way. It's not Fiona's fault the Cavaleri Serafim found my trace. I didn't even know this fraternity dedicated to eradicating my kind–any dragon-based shifter–existed still. How could I ignore it? And how did they sneak up on me? Could Declan be at fault for this?

If only I could see my brother, talk to him... But then what? He wouldn't tell me what it is I seek. On the contrary, he would only laugh at my expense. Tytus, zmeu grandiose, taken unaware and nearly killed.

I thought I was hallucinating when I heard them nearby. The perks of heightened senses–in our case, hearing– and their human clumsiness alone saved us from an ambush. And in that cavern, it would have been one. It was the main reason I went out to meet them, knowing full well it would be dangerous.

The four knights had been scouts. Which means they will return... They will track me. The knights themselves are devoid of magic– it is why they call themselves Cavaleri Serafim, or the Serafim Knights. As with most hypocritical humans, this does not stop them from using a sorcerer in their midst. It is how they trapped my kind, before. It is how they will, again, if I am not careful enough.

All that implies is this journey just got more interesting–and dangerous. Especially for Fiona. She did not sign up to be chased halfway across the earth by a band of fanatical soldiers.

As soon as I find us a safer spot to land, I'll explain everything, including how me and Declan fell out. For now–

"Watch out!" Her useless tug on a scale is enough to send me to the left, as she's been trying to signal. Just in time to avoid an arrow coming after us. *Shit.*

I look down, noticing a regular human truck. Only, in the back of its cargo is an old-school arrowhead weapon, and it's pointed right at me. Two men on either side are taking aim, preparing the arrows. The silvery hue of their tips mocks me, and real concern washes over me when I realize the truth.

Fuck. Fuck!

These are no copycats, as I had hoped. It's the real Cavaleri. Only they would know titanium-pointed arrowheads could pierce through zmeu scales.

"Again! TYTUS!"

I follow Fiona's signal and zoom out of the way. I can't tell from where the arrows are coming, as they're too swift, and emerging from my blind spot. Luckily, she can. As soon as we're away from their reach, I flip around, pointing my muzzle downwards.

Fire coils in my gut, roaring and demanding freedom. I feel it rising in my throat, then open my muzzle and let it loose. It rains down on the humans, and I'm aiming to stop the truck from following us.

It doesn't work. Once the sulfur smell clears in the air, and the smoke parts, I see the human contraption has avoided my fire, instead switching lanes. I duck more arrows and burst back into movement. If I draw on lightning and the elements now, we will alert more humans in the region.

I can only hope to escape—to *run*, much as I loathe the thought. Without another choice, I increase my speed, trying to put as much distance between us as possible. Soon as I'm far away, I can portal out of here—and hope they cannot follow past there. Something tells me that hope will be dashed sooner, rather than later.

A gust of magic off my back warns Fiona's on the attack–to defend me. One moment she was hesitating to follow me, the next she is quick to toss out magic– Declan's magic–to protect us. I've fought with her before, against my brother. Out of necessity, mainly. At the time, there was a disconnection between her actions and mine, and it never felt... whole. This time, perhaps because of the moment of peace we had, I feel more connected with her. My zmeu does, too.

Fiona is no Solomonar–no witch born to ride a zmeu into battle. Lucrezia alone holds that title, now. I never expected to be chased across the skies without backup, but I also never expected having Fiona watching my back.

Blasts echo below, and I slow down enough to check on our enemies. Fiona's magic found a target and the truck blows up, turning its occupants into ashes and smoke. I don't hesitate. I push forward, using the wind to propel us, and send us straight into a portal.

Just before we dive in, I hear a whoosh–

and an arrow embeds in my wing. *Must've been a stray one.* Despite my roar of pain, I manage to stay on course, through the opening, but end up toppling into the skies of the Swiss Alps. Without a way to balance myself, we go rolling downhill, crashing into the snowy peaks.

Fiona's cries echo in my ears, but her words get lost amid the chaos. I'm too focused on my massive body rolling over and over, afraid of crushing her. *So close. So far.* With a huge effort, I dig my claws into the snow and manage to stop our fall. My body gives out then, turning to human.

"Tytus! Tytus!" Fiona's voice comes nearer, panting as she makes her way through the powdery dust. "Oh, shit! You're bleeding everywhere. Tytus!"

I force my eyes to open. The sky itself is blurry, the shimmering portal closing above us. Despite the reassurance no one followed us through, frustration weighs me down. My body is too weak to properly warn her, but I get out the basics. "Find... shelter. Hide...our tracks... my blood. They... can follow... zmeu... magic."

Panic flashes across her expression. I want to stay awake, to explain. Fiona deserves more than this, and I am duty-bound to provide it. But sleep is already pulling me unconscious. And for the first time in millennia, I leave my fate in the hands of a human.

A witch, no less. *If Declan knew of this, I would never hear the end of it.*

Fiona

I glance again at Tytus, check his forehead for fever, and sigh. When he first fought Declan back in Rockland Creek and was hurt because of Elisandra, I took my knowledge of zmeu biology from Declan. I could tell the wolves he would heal in his own time, that his human body had to first, and his zmeu form would take over from there.

Now that I don't have that anymore... I'm not even sure how much is truth, and how much is fiction. What's causing this? Is he weak because of the one arrow, or weaker still because of the injuries Declan inflicted? How long will it take him to heal?

I followed his instructions and found us a spot to hide, then went back out and covered our tracks. I made sure none of his blood remained in the snow, and that nothing could trace us here. Even more, I racked my brain until I remembered some long-forgotten defensive spells.

It took me a while of muttering incantations and placing myself just so under the skies, but I managed to add some protective barriers. And I was rather proud of my efforts and my own magic, since the zmeu one was apparently trackable. *Who even heard of such a thing?*

Tytus groans in his sleep, and the fur I covered him with slips as he moves. I go to pull it up, feeling the heat of his half-naked torso. I only know human first aid and with his clothes all wet and bloody, I couldn't even see where he was hurt. So I stripped him to the bare minimum and found his wing wound actually manifested under his shoulder blade as a human.

Which was tricky in itself, since I depleted a lot of magical energy to close the gash. I didn't realize until the fourth time I had to restart the muttering and the focusing of my magical healing, just how much zmeu magic had been... easy.

Kneeling next to him, I glance down at my hands. It felt great using them for good, of my own choice. In battle, I'd used the zmeu magic from Declan, almost on autopilot. It still courses through my veins, as addictive as the first few times I gave in. But, after, and taking into account Tytus' own warning, I couldn't make myself do it.

Instead, I dug deep inside myself for the well of magic I was born with. The kind that's been on earth for ages, as old and ancient as the man I used it on, perhaps. Either way, when I used my core, my own magical essence, and poured it into healing Tytus, it felt good. It's the first real sign I've had that this journey isn't a waste.

An odd sound escapes him, and I lean over him. "Tytus?"

His eyelids flutter and those gray orbs stare into mine with a glazed look. "Where...?"

"We're safe," I whisper. "For now."

His eyes close again and I fully expect him to pass out. After a groan and shifting under the blankets, he blindly reaches for something. It takes me a moment to realize he's reaching for my hand–so I give it to him, allowing our fingers to intertwine.

"I'm sorry," he breathes on a soft exhale.

"For what?"

"Declan... For his actions."

I duck my head, staring at our joined fingers. An odd heat has settled in my gut. "We are all responsible for the choices we make. Some have bigger implications than others, it's all."

"You're... kind. Too kind." He speaks haltingly, like every word is painful. After another beat of silence, he asks, "How bad... was it?"

I hesitate, wondering how much to tell him. It's a fair question–how bad was my captivity under his brother. "The worst was not being able to be alone with my own thoughts," I admit. "The beatings, the starvations from Cade and Thiago, those I could take. They wanted results, and Declan wasn't providing fast enough. But my mind was the only space I had to myself... Declan took even that away."

He stares at me again. "Sorry. He... will... pay."

Unsure what he needs me to say, I squeeze his hand. "It's fine. I'm done with him now."

"How... did... he... get..." He trails off, a frustrated frown on his face.

I duck my head again, unable to meet his gaze. "I was ambitious, as a child. As a young teen, I grew arrogant. As an adult, well, none of that improved. I started reading on world myths, trying to call onto creatures I had no business calling. Declan answered. It was my fault, really."

"Not... your... fault." Tytus squeezes my hand again, and I stare at him. Noticing his long lashes, the curve of his mouth. Like this, so vulnerable, he could almost be human. Almost.

The moment after, his hand goes slack, and he passes out again. I curl up next to him, keeping a distance between our bodies, my mind churning with the short conversation. Before I know it, I fall asleep.

Tytus' groans wake me up what feels like hours later. This time I see a distinct sheen of sweat on his face. I step outside, grabbing some snow to melt, and use it as a cooling cloth. It's meant to be a quick stepping out, something that would require very little effort on my part.

Luckily, the newer developments and my history of villains have caused me to be wary and aware. It's that same awareness that makes me notice them.

They're farther down, at the foot of the mountain. It has to be the same men Tytus fought earlier, only those were dead. And I killed the ones trying to give us chase. Which means these are new threats… and there are more of them.

Shit. I force myself not to move. My defenses should hold, but what if they have ways of seeing past them? What if they come after me, and Tytus in his injured state? Mighty zmeu that he is, he wouldn't stand a chance if they attacked right now.

And yet… We seem to have gotten lucky. Mutters travel on the wind, but I can't make out the language, let alone the words. Then another portal appears, and they're gone.

I wait a little longer before heading

back in and melting some snow on a cloth for Tytus. I wipe his brow, noticing he's clenching his jaw even in his sleep. Does the man never relax?

Still, it's a rare moment that I'm allowed to enjoy. I lean closer, inhaling his scent of fire and something so... Tytus. His cheekbones seem more pronounced this close, and I can't help my fingers from reaching out and tracing his jaw, all the way to the strong chin. His frown only deepens, the sensual lips parting. I want to run my fingers on those, too, just to feel if they're as soft as they look.

And then Tytus jerks—and his stormy eyes open, catching mine with an intensity that steals my breath. "You... stayed. I thought I was dreaming."

It's all he says, but it's enough. He expected me to leave him as soon as the going got tough. Maybe we're not so different, after all. Mutely, I nod.

The intensity in his expression smolders, and I inch closer. Part of me doesn't know why, but the other part is drawn like a magnet to its opposite. Before I fully realize what I've done, Tytus reaches around and cups my cheek. His thumb traces my lower lip, then my upper. "So fucking soft. Just like I thought." Then he pulls me closer, his eyes never leaving mine, allowing me enough time to pull away.

When our mouths are practically touching, he breathes, "May I?"

I stare at him, uncertain for a beat. What is this line we're about to cross?

"I shouldn't..." My whispered words echo between us, and Tytus makes no other move. I should follow my own advice, and pull back. Yet as I meet his stormy eyes, I don't see a menace, or pity. There is no fear coiling inside my body, only a fire that's growing ever hotter.

It has been a while since a man has looked upon me as a woman, rather than an object. And that, coupled with the ability to make the choice, is a powerful, heady drug. In the end, the pull is too much, and I'm the one crossing the last bit of the distance, claiming his lips.

That brief touch is explosive, and all the control I'm allowed. With my next breath,

Tytus groans and pulls me closer, angling my head and taking over. His kiss overwhelms me in the best way possible. My mind shuts up, all my senses focused on the feel of his mouth against mine, his hand on my cheek, and his body under mine.

He is steel where I bend, and with another groan he tugs me away from his lips. His eyes are dark, darker than I've ever seen them. "Fiona..."

Whatever he's about to say is lost, as in the next moment his hand drops from me and he passes out.

I quickly check him for injuries, but the bandages I had prepared hold steady. Something else is wrong with him, but I don't know what. And we're stuck here until I do.

Tytus

I wake up disoriented. A cavern. But where? My last memory is of the snow, the chase...

I jerk up, but a hand claims my chest, restraining me. "Easy," Fiona whispers. She comes into my field of vision holding a goblet. I drain it in a few gulps, then hand it back and wipe at my mouth.

"What happened?"

She hesitates, an odd look crossing her expression. "What's the last thing you remember?"

"Landing in the Alps."

Again, that look. Fiona sets the cup aside, then says, "I followed your instructions. Hid our tracks. Found a new cavern to lie low in. I also put up protective barriers."

"Using zmeu magic?"

Her lips purse. "I'm not a novice. Of course I didn't, I used my own."

I frown then, noticing the darker circles under her eyes. "When's the last time you slept properly?"

"Not since we landed here. You and your friends kept me busy."

I freeze in the process of sitting up. Part of me registers her words, the other is focused on the fact I'm almost naked. And bandaged. My body screams for more rest, but I need to get us going. Even as all that crosses my mind, flashes follow–of feather-like touches on my forehead, a cooling cloth, whispers of comfort.

I focus on what makes sense. "You're saying they followed?"

"Yes," Fiona admits. "Now will you tell me who they are?"

I sigh, running a hand through my hair. A disgusted groan escapes me when I sense the oil and stickiness of the strands.

"There's a small waterfall further in the cave," Fiona adds. "A little piece of heaven, hidden within. If you want to clean yourself, I mean."

I glance up then, but she won't meet my eyes. Despite my best efforts, I can't figure out what I did to upset her. At least, not consciously. "Did something happen while I was out of it?"

"No," she says, too quickly. "You should wash up. I have a lot of questions, and I have a feeling we have to limit our time here."

With a nod, I get up and stumble towards the area she pointed out, grabbing some clothes on the way there. Good thing she had the foresight to save some of our supplies.

A few moments later, I have to admit Fiona was right. There is indeed a small waterfall. Damn witch didn't mention its icy temperature, though. I hiss as the arctic liquid batters my skin, then force myself to push through and wash off. Ten minutes later, I storm back in the main cavern with a scowl.

"Thanks for the tip about the water. Could've mentioned it's icy."

"Could've mentioned you're being hunted by extremely skilled trackers," she shoots back.

Fiona's still seated on the ground, her long hair now braided neatly. I notice she's got a change of clothes, too, from the ones I conjured for her before. Which means she also used the waterfall. Somehow, the thought of her naked body in the same space completely derails my anger–and more than that, if I'm perfectly honest.

"Tytus?"

Her voice provides a welcome distraction from my thoughts and I resort to pacing, so I can shun away all fantasies of her. This is not the time for my body to remember it has needs, fuck it.

"Tytus!"

"My apologies. Da, you had questions."

She gives me an odd look, but thankfully

lets it go. "Yeah. First and foremost, what's going on with your wounds? Why are the ones from the fight with Declan not healing?"

"How do you know that?"

"I noticed them when I bandaged up your new ones. Speaking of, come here so I can fix you up."

I hesitate. Something about her behavior from earlier, not meeting my eyes, is enough to make me wary. Am I missing something? Something right under my nose, perhaps to do with…

No. I won't think his name. Declan has long tainted Fiona, and if I see her like that, as one of his victims, I am not doing her any good.

In the end, I sigh and join her by the furs. Within moments and with efficient movements, Fiona has more bandages ready and starts fixing me up. "Well? I'm still waiting on answers."

"The wounds aren't healing because my brother's claws have venom. We were each blessed with an extra gift, if you will, and his was the ability to kill without fault. Hence the venom."

"What's yours?'

I smirk. "Let's just say I can be extremely persuasive."

Fiona's hands freeze on my shoulder blades, and I realize how that must sound to her. "It's not what you think, I cannot force people to do things they wouldn't do on their own. But I can persuade them to lean one way or another. I'm careful with how I use this ability, I swear it."

When she still doesn't answer, I chance a look over my shoulder. She's staring down, biting on that full bottom lip, and my thoughts go haywire again. Why is it I can practically taste a kiss I've never had?

"Fiona?"

She looks up then, a faint flush on her cheeks. "I heard you. I don't know what to say, Tytus. It's not... usual, this gift you have. And yes, it makes me wary." She sighs, and her breath tickles my skin. "But it's not like I can do anything about it, is there? At least, not until you give me a reason to doubt you." Her hand caresses my wound, and then she whispers, "Is there a way I can help with the venom?"

I'm getting tired of her deflections. Still, I push aside the annoyance. If Fiona wants to deflect, to avoid the issue, I should let her. She's been through enough. Besides, we'll have plenty of time to dish it out when we get to my castle. Once we're out of danger.

"No," I answer her. "Once I'm around my mountains, it will help with healing."

"What about flying?"

I turn away, holding back a groan as she wraps another bandage around my wound. "I can do it."

"You seemed weaker last time. Why not use a portal?"

"They will only track us faster." I grit my teeth. "I said I can do it."

"Tytus, if you're going to be stubborn, neither of us will survive this. Those guys… They seemed determined."

"They are. They're called Cavaleri Serafim–Serafim Knights. Their order has been around for as long as my kind has. And they have hunted us, even more so after my brother messed up and provoked them."

She tilts her head to the side. "Was this around the time you both fell out?"

"Yes. There is not one single incident I can blame for it, though I am sure Declan has his own reasoning. I could say it started as kids. We were the last eggs hatched from the original lineage, what you humans would call royalty. Our parents died in a hunt early on, and it was only me and Declan. We were inseparable, as children."

"But?"

Fiona's quiet prompting makes me realize I've fallen into a daze, almost seeing those times again, but not quite. I shrug it off as best I can. "But, nothing good lasts forever. Rumors began of a Dark and Light zmeu, who were to face off. Because I was the rule-follower, and Declan the mischievous one, the Council watching over us quickly made up their minds."

Fiona's mouth parts in surprise. "That's harsh, for such a young age."

I shrug. "We were well into our third century, but yes. It impacted us, though we did not realize it at the time. But with each passing century, Declan was less focused, more prone to take off on his own. It was hard to keep track of him. I couldn't protect him when the

Council chose his punishment. He deserved it, as his constant attacks on humans had driven the Serafim to our gates. But Declan sees it as a betrayal, and it is why he hates me so."

"Siblings are both a blessing and a curse. They're the only person you would happily kill and kill for." Fiona says nothing else for a long moment, then she sighs. "I'm not sure what to make of all that. It wasn't the story I expected. It almost makes Declan sound... not like himself, I guess. But these Serafim, they're human?"

"Of a sort. They always have a dark mage with them, and each one I have come across uses some version of my ancestors' bones for power."

"Necromancer?"

I nod. "And the reason they can track me is that they drink the blood of a zmeu. It cements their connection to us, to any portals we open. And if they have my blood specifically, it would be like giving them a homing beacon to light their way."

Fiona seems shocked. "That's why you warned me about your blood, and to dispose of it."

I nod again. "The same will go for everything here. Once I am home, I can take them on. It is why they're trying to catch us now, unawares, while I'm far from my own land. Sadly, in my weakened state..."

I trail off, loath to admit it. I'm used to providing protection, and right now I cannot. I've let myself fall at the mercy of a human. As if sensing my mood shift, Fiona finishes wrapping me up and steps away.

The loss of her presence at my back is both a relief and an annoyance I do my best to dismiss. Instead, I turn to her. "Why did you stay? You could have gone anywhere."

She shrugs, more at ease with me than before. "Because I choose to be here and fight this fight. Danger or not, Tytus, I made a commitment and I intend to stick through with it."

Well, I can't say I saw this coming, either.

Chapter 5

Dorință
"Curiosity is the lust of the mind."
-Thomas Hobbes-

Fiona

Why did you stay?

My, but he's an infuriating zmeu. One moment telling me I have all the choice in this partnership, and when I do make that choice, acting as if I've chosen wrong. There is no mistaking the insulting surprise in his tone, and I barely hold back a huff.

As we stare at each other, all I want to do is smack him. And violence is definitely not an ideal way of dealing with conflict. "Does that answer your question?" I bite finally.

Tytus nods and adjusts his pose on the

ground. "Forgive me, I didn't mean to offend by it. It's been a while since I've trusted humans."

"You seemed fine with the wolves." I don't know where the accusing tone comes from. I guess I expected more gratitude than this suspicion after saving his life.

As though sensing this, Tytus sighs and reaches for my hand. "I'm sorry. You are right. I owe you for saving my life, Fiona. Thank you."

Embarrassed now, I pull away, blushing at his touch. Everything reminds me of the kiss from last night, one he obviously doesn't remember. Part of me tries to point out that's probably the reason for my annoyance, more than his suspicion. I tell that nagging voice to shut up.

Perhaps it's best he doesn't remember that particular kiss. It was folly of the stupidest kind, an irrational move on my part. One I still don't understand. What would entangling myself with Tytus lead to? Sure, he's easy on the eyes. And evidently my hormones are not scared of him. But the better part of me, the wiser part, is very much aware of how much more powerful he is. How dangerous.

And even if he's acting very vulnerable now, and completely at my mercy, none of that changes the fact he is a ruthless zmeu. I've seen it, just as we escaped that last mountain. And I cannot forget it. Which means there's only one thing left for me to do, and that's getting my head back into focus.

"Whatever. Let's just move on. The guys, the Serafim, or whatever you call them. How do we evade them? My geography lessons may have been a while ago, but I do know the Swiss Alps are nowhere close to Romania."

"No, but I can make sure we get there safe. If I rest one more night, I'll be able to make the journey home."

"But you said morphing is not something you can do at the drop of a hat, especially when you're injured. Matter of fact, if I recall your words exactly, repeated transformations when injured would make your human form weaker, thus putting you in jeopardy because of the powers involved and you losing strength."

Tytus' expression hardens. "Da, those were my words. I must admit, I did not expect my honesty tossed back in my face. However, I will not fail, Fiona. I know my strength well enough to promise you this."

I let the matter drop, going back to the fire and warming some dried seal meat from our last trip. When I chance a glance at Tytus, his gaze is lost in the distance. My annoyance drops. I don't know why I care, when he can obviously take care of himself, but something about his loneliness calls to me.

I know it so well, though under different circumstances. And while it was his brother that contributed to that, Tytus is as different from Declan as day and night.

At war with myself, I still end up asking, "What's wrong?"

His response is surprising in its honesty, and heavy with emotion. "I worry about... Elisandra. The Serafim shouldn't find her, but if they're back on my trail, it may lead them to Rockland Creek."

I recall the young woman, his descendant, and her gentleness. When I'd met her, she was warring with her own inner demons, but her resilience proved key to imprisoning Declan. "I'm sure the wolves will protect her."

"They will, as will her mate. That's not what I'm worried about."

"Then what?"

"Whether they can fight off a full assault. Declan messed up Rockland Creek, badly. If the Serafim get wind of it, and go back to investigate, I'm not sure Lucas' pack can fight them off in numbers."

I say nothing this time, leaving him to his thoughts as I munch some dried meat. There is nothing to say, really, especially when his concern only makes him appear that much more approachable, that much more... human. I fight off the thought, instead focusing on a different one. "Are you not hungry?"

Tytus glances over at my snack and wrinkles his nose. "Too old. I'm craving fresh meat."

I shrug. "Suit yourself."

Moments later, I go to sleep, making sure my furs are set up away from Tytus. After that first morning when I woke up in his arms, I made sure to sleep far, far away. Temptation cannot cross distance, surely?

Besides, after watching over him while he was recovering, my body is beyond exhausted. With a full belly, I pass out at once…. Only for Tytus' trashing to wake me up a few hours later.

I stand up, rubbing my eyes and trying to pinpoint the sound of the movements and groans of pain. My eyes fall on Tytus. Furs are tangled around him, and sweat soaks his bare torso. It must be the groans that woke me up. But are they because of the venom? Is it causing him more pain, what with his recent injuries?

I jump out of my makeshift cot and crawl to him. "Tytus?"

When he doesn't answer, I rush to the outside for snow, hoping the coolness will help his heated body–and that's when I sense it. The air is filled with dark magic.

I peer down the slope, pitch dark except for the mountain and nature. But… No, that's not true. Something's moving out there. And I have a feeling I know who.

Hastily tossing another defensive barrier,

I grab a handful of snow and rush back to Tytus. Kneeling by his side, I dump most of it on his chest. It melts with the sizzle of his skin heat, turning into more water, but doesn't wake him.

My hands are trembling as I search for something, anything, I can use to stir him. How could they have found us again? Are they tracking us with something? Tytus said his blood, the zmeu magic, that they're trackable. Maybe...

Someone's watching me. I glance towards Tytus again, and my hands stop their incessant questing. He's awake now, and his full attention is on me.

The slowness of his breathing is what I notice first. His nostrils flare when our eyes lock, and his eyes drop to my mouth, as if pulled by a magnet there. Heat spreads through me, something almost magical, alluring. I don't know what this sensation is, but it's not a rational one.

Tytus seems to be under the same spell. His hand lifts slowly, slower still, and reaches for me. Fists a handful of my shirt, tugging on the material until it makes me lean further, closer to him. We freeze, gazes locked with heat, tension palpable in the surrounding air.

Just hours before, I was rebuking myself for my folly. And now, I'm about to give in once more. It's a pull I have no defense against, something that removes all manner of control. I don't understand it. It's beyond anything my mind can comprehend, but a deeper, rawer, more primal part of me does. My limbs are lazy, and already I lean towards him. I cannot describe it, but I need his lips like I need water. A touch. Just one touch.

There is no fear, no doubt, no wariness. My body craves his in a way I've desired no one else. It's basic, primal... raw. Completely unlike me, yet also completely... me. The old me. The impulsive me. The Fiona who didn't care about boundaries and was fearless.

I'm already moving closer to him, and then he's pulling my head to his, nose nuzzling mine, kissing the corners of my mouth. My rational mind wants to ring the alarm bells, warning that we're under attack, but all I really care for is his touch, and making sure none of it stops. Ever. It's irrational.

When his lips finally meet mine, I pounce on him, earning a chuckle from him. He mutters something in another language, but I don't even register it. My hands are tracing his torso, nails digging into his skin, and it feels like the temperature skyrockets a couple more degrees. His heated skin scorches my palms, not that I care.

Tytus stands then, me in his lap, and grabs a handful of my braid instead, twisting it around his wrist. The gesture leaves me vulnerable to his kisses, and he pauses, hovering, waiting... I let out a soft, mewling gasp, and he drops his mouth to mine once more. He continues down my throat, to my collarbone, his free hand on my hip, pressing me down–*oh*.

I'm incensed, burning against his touch and begging for more. The flames are fanned, and I desperately want what I've never had.

Flames–smoke fills my nostrils. *My barrier!*

Eyes snapping open, I push off Tytus, crashing to the ground and sending our possessions in the fire. He freezes, then blinks and stares at me as if seeing me for the first time.

"Fiona?"

I don't have time to ponder the question in his tone, like he wasn't aware of his actions. "They're coming!" I shout instead.

Tytus doesn't bat an eyelash. One moment he's on the ground, the next he's up and reaching into the flames, materializing another flaming scimitar. He doesn't even bother putting on a shirt, instead he scratches a rune in the air and more flames engulf the supplies we'd left.

Then he holds out his free hand. "Follow me!"

We rush out–right into an ambush. And for the first time, I get a good look at our faceless enemies.

A dozen or more knights face us, dressed in black from head to toe. They have no old-school armor, as I expected. Instead, they have guns strapped on their hips, swords drawn in their hands, and dark motorcycle helmets obscuring their faces.

They move in unison, as well-trained

as any human soldiers could be. And as they've cornered us with their crescent formation, Tytus and I find ourselves backed against the flames burning hotly in the cavern behind us.

Then Tytus moves with a curse, straight in their midst. I call forth magic–zmeu magic, since there is no point hiding it–and draw runes in the air. Fire escapes one and hits a knight in the chest, and air escapes the other, swooping two men further downhill.

That's when I see the second wave inching closer, hidden by the first. Another dozen knights. "Tytus!"

He follows my gaze, and his jaw tightens when he sees what I do. Tytus digs his bare heels into the snow and swings the sword, slashing and cutting through his opponents. I keep a distance, trying to watch his back and eliminate anyone that gets too close.

I'm not able to protect him from the slashes of the blades he faces, but Tytus alone is a master of his sword. As I watch him move and parry, cut and slash, his body golden in the light of the flames, something burns inside me. It's more than desire this time, though there's a heavy dose of that. It's also admiration for his skill, awe of the man–not the beast.

So lost am I in my contemplation and my defending him, that I don't immediately notice what he's doing. He's not trying to eliminate all the Cavaleri Serafim. Instead, he's cutting us a path through, not bothering to finish them off.

When he's made enough of a hole in their midst, Tytus grabs my hand and tugs me after him. We escape thrown swords and I even hear a few guns going off, with none hitting us. When I glance behind, I see everything tossed our way being diverted by strong gusts of wind. *Tytus. He's doing this.*

My focus returns to the devil himself, and wherever it is he's leading me. Past his shoulder, I notice we're about to run out of ground, inching closer and closer to a cliff.

Not that it stops him. Rather than slow down, he speeds up, dragging me with him. I scream as we dive off the edge, as if getting ready to take a swim in the deadly depths of the mountains below. Mid-air, though, Tytus' body is engulfed by flames, and he dives beneath me. I grip his scales, slippery at first, then I catch onto the raised ones lower on his body. Though my palms are raw, I find enough support to hang on.

Soon, we're flying away, and leaving the rest of the Serafim behind. Something tells me it won't be the last we see of them.

¥

We're surrounded by clouds and cool air, having once more escaped the clutches of those fanatics. Whatever they've got on us that's making them able to track us, I really hope we destroy it, and soon. Because if we die mid-way to reaching the Carpathian Mountains, then I'll never find that redemption I seek. I'll never make up for the bad deeds I contributed to. And something tells me I don't want to meet my maker without achieving that.

If nothing else, the frigid air serves to cool my mind and my body. How could I lose it like that? Again! And with Tytus, of all people? Just as I'd talked myself into behaving responsibly... I made peace with myself, knowing he is beyond my league. Knowing that nothing good could come of it.

And then I wake up, and all it takes is one look from him, and I'm a mess all over. This isn't me. Unless there's some kind of magical reason for this, I never... Even before my stupid life choices, I never just dropped everything for a guy.

And now? I thought I had control, but obviously I don't. I'm powerless against... With a sinking realization, I remember what Tytus told me about his powers of persuasion. Same as Declan's ability to kill. An innate gift, something he bragged he was very good at. Could that be the reason?

He wouldn't have...

But it would explain why I'm acting unlike myself. Why not even the fact he's the brother of my captor is enough to deter me from wanting to kiss him. I said before I couldn't understand this need rationally, and maybe it's because it has nothing to do with being rational. Not if it's someone else's idea...

This is Tytus I'm talking about. He said

himself he'd never use this power against me.

The defense sounds weaker now, in my mind. Before I can further convince myself, I hear his voice loud and thunderously clear in my head.

Care to explain what that was?

Tytus

My heart's still racing. That's twice now I avoided the clutches of the Serafim, and so close to my goal. If I wasn't sure of Fiona's inability to do so, I could have sworn she's leading them straight to us. Only she couldn't be... *Could she?*

I duck a particularly close cloud and sneak a glance under me. Mountains only. No soul that I can see. Perfect. I focus back on Fiona, on her hands on me, picturing her features, her white hair streaked with violet blowing in the wind.... The connection clicks, and I ride that wave to her consciousness, more determined than ever.

Fiona, answer me!

Her grip on me slides, then she catches herself. Her mental probe is shy, tentative as she tries to reply. *How… How can you do this?*

It was a guess. I didn't really think I could reach your consciousness, but I had to try. There are too many questions left unanswered, and we've got a while to go before we get to my home. Plus, I assumed Declan already pried open the defenses of your mind, and you're obviously not recovered from it.

I can practically see her cringe from my words, and I want to stop and shake some sense into her. Make her see they're not meant to hurt her. But we have no time, and it's imperative we sort this out.

Either way, it benefits us. What happened back there?

Your knights came back, she says. *Obviously.*

There's more to it than that, though, isn't there?

Just because you can link telepathically doesn't give you the right to dig around my mind!

A dart of Fiona's anger travels through the connection, and I shake my head at the pinch in my own mind. I should have warned her to keep her emotions in check, but I let it slide... until her words sink in. Is that what she thinks I'm doing?

It doesn't work like that, Fiona. I'm not in your mind. Rather, I'm only able to catch the words you project towards me, specifically. Emotions that you feel, like anger, can cause me harm—psychically. Like little darts. So unless you want us to crash, please keep them in check. Realizing the harshness of my tone, I add, *Any inner thoughts are still yours alone, Fiona.*

She's quiet for a long moment. *I'm sorry,* she finally says. *Only, I'm still rattled.*

From the battle?

No. Her reply is quicker this time, and I risk a glance behind. She's staring at her hands, her cheeks aflame.

Then what?

You ... How do you not remember! The anger in her tone takes me aback, and I cringe again at the darts attacking my consciousness.

Remember what?

You kissed *me! Twice now, waking up in the middle of the night.*

I nearly drop us out of the sky, but catch myself in time. *What?*

Fiona looks away, still wringing her hands, and I force my gaze forward. Obviously, she's a distraction I really cannot afford now. But her words... Like a rollercoaster, the images hit me back. The feel of her in my arms. The taste of her on my lips.

How could I have done so, tasted her, and not remember? Unless I was not in possession of my own faculties. And if that's the case, only the witch atop me could've enchanted me. *Fucking hell of all hells!*

The more I try to ignore the memories, the more they assail me. Her little moans... A growl tears from my muzzle, and I sense her grip clutching me tighter.

Tytus? Are you hurt again?

I'm fine, I snarl and glance her way again. *What sorcery is this?*

Sorcery? You can't seriously think I had anything to do with it!

Then how do you explain me losing these memories?

I don't know! She shouts. *Maybe it's another thing you conveniently hid from me.*

Whatever it is, I'll get to the bottom of it. No one's magic lasts long around me.

Hurt flashes in turbulent waves towards me through the connection. *That wasn't my doing. Nor did I ask for your confusing kisses, dammit! All I wanted was a chance to atone for my sins, to help save the world rather than destroy it. I never asked for your attention, or advice. Nor for your persuasion skills to be focused on me!*

Are you seriously accusing me of trying to hypnotize you into my bed? In case you haven't noticed, witch, I don't need to force women to be around me.

Well, maybe if they knew your true form, the reality would be different.

The jab stings more than it should. Up until now, though I've seen wariness from her, not once did I catch repulsion. Does she really think that? Does it mean my zmeu form revolts her, too? It's an odd thought to cross my mind, and it lingers, making me care more than I'd like.

A retort becomes impossible, rather

fortunately. An arrow passes my right wing, followed by another that barely misses me. I dive the other way, and this time Fiona's shout is unrelated to our drama.

"They're back! Below!"

I glance underneath and see one of those human contraptions their soldiers use–a chopper. Its outside is painted black, and it looks able to carry multiple men inside. Only instead of military, it's filled with Cavaleri Serafim and a hell of a lot more arrows.

Hold on! I yell back inside my head. *It's about to get bumpy.*

As for our conversation, we'll have to finish that later. If we survive these guys a third time... And if she'll still talk to me.

Chapter 6

Vulnerabil
*"Being vulnerable is the only way to allow your heart
to feel true pleasure."*
-Bob Marley-

Tytus

Blast it all to hell! I can't shake them. Even with Fiona's help, I spent the last thirty minutes trying to outrun the blasted metal bird, only to fail time and time again. And with each passing second, their aim is improving.

We can't survive this much longer! Fiona warns.

I catch the exhaustion in her tone. She still hasn't recovered from her other ordeals, and now here I am, putting her in even more danger. Zmeu magic is easy for me to use, to an extent, because my body was made for it. Fiona is still human in her core, there is no way she can continue overusing this way. The price she'll pay will be too steep.

Despite our previous fight, I want to make sure she's safe. That we both are. Because I think I know what the cause of my getting frisky is, and if I'm right, the Cavaleri are not the only ones she needs to fear.

When I still can't shake the Serafim, and my zmeu grumbles in frustration, I realize it's time to be reckless. In a desperate–and stupid–move, I dive towards the mountains below us.

We emerge into the bright sky and almost collide with a snowy peak. I avoid it last minute, but continue to lose altitude and drop on the snow, Fiona next to me. One smooth shrug of my shoulders and she slides off me, staring in confusion.

I shake my head and face away from her, staring at the skies. Once I get rid of these knights, home is the last push. *I have to do this right.*

When the caped idiots start dropping from the sky, as I expected, I take a step closer. Open my muzzle and allow fire to churn, to pounce on them. The flames worm their way from my belly and straight above me, charring their bodies and parachutes until chaos alone remains.

Behind me, I sense Fiona getting closer. *Find somewhere to hide!*

I want to help!

Turning to her, I bare my fangs right in her face. *HIDE!*

I'm not used to being disobeyed, and she stands staring at me for a moment before backing away behind some massive rocks.

Good. Finally, some sense got knocked into her.

I turn my focus back to the Serafim. Until now, I've fought them in human form, not wanting to risk them collecting my blood as I'm in full zmeu form. But now… It's no holds barred.

With a roar, I inch closer to them. The ones that survived my fire have fanned out on the ground, some with swords and others with bows and arrows. A few brave ones train their human guns on me, not that it matters. Their bullets will only ricochet off my scales.

I open my jaws and shoot more fire, incinerating two unlucky ones. That only leaves me a dozen or so to dispatch... They swarm me, using some strategy they think will win them points. I lift my back legs and swoop with my tail. Its razor-sharp point cuts through four of them, and their gutted bodies drop on the ground, staining the snow with their blood.

Taking advantage of their surprise, I snag the closest ones to me and rip their heads off with my talons. Then I stomp on two more. That's four more down.

The remaining ones face me, black masks covering their facial expressions. I don't need to look them in the eyes, though. I can almost taste their fear in the air, acrid and sweet all at once.

Time to deliver the last blow.

I inhale deeply, knowing I won't get another chance like this once I switch to human form. I have to maximize every attack, especially this one. With a rush of satisfaction, I let loose the fire and watch as it burns them.

One of them–the farthest one–drops his sword and tries to back away, but something blocks his escape, like a shield. His cries of pain echo until nothing's left of him and his brethren except charred corpses.

I turn to Fiona then, finding her standing by the rocks. She's lowering her hand–her magic is what prevented the knight from leaving.

Thank you.

She nods, her expression inscrutable. "Now what?"

I incinerate the remaining carcasses around us and toss my head back. *Now we go home.*

I bow low enough for her to hop on again, and wait. She could decline. After everything else, she could choose now to leave, to continue her quest separately. And before, I might've let her go. Technically, I still could. But my zmeu has other ideas, and he's trying to make me understand that what's deep in our bones, the certainty there, cannot be changed.

Fiona won't understand any of this. I don't, even, and it's *my* zmeu causing it. So I bide my time, hiding the emotions from her, and wait. After a beat, and another, Fiona moves through the snow and climbs back on me. Once I feel her securely perched on my scales, I head back to the skies.

¥

After a few hours of flying, the sun goes down and Fiona's grip on me keeps slipping. I could carry her, but truth be told, all the evasive maneuvers from earlier have taken their toll on my still-recovering body.

I dip lower, near the peaks, and make sure the elements, the clouds and mist, envelop and hide us from any human eyes. This is not an area I'm familiar with, and it's better we don't take any chances in our weakened state.

Still, as I seek a refuge, Fiona tugs on a scale. *Tytus,* she says in my mind, *something's happening below.*

I try to see what she does, but more

clouds block my vision. A snort escapes me, just enough to clear a path, and I stop moving, instead only flapping my wings and holding us immobile in the skies.

Below us is a human village—or town, I can't quite tell the size. Buildings are sparsely laid out, and humans are running from spot to spot. My sharp hearing picks up on screams of agony, pleas of mothers to save their children, and gunshots. Executions. A closer glance shows fire rising in one spot, then another. I can even make out the muted explosions causing the bursts.

They must be at war with each other, or some other idiotic pastime.

Disinterested, I move again, but Fiona tugs on my scale. *We could help them!*

You don't even know what's happening down there.

Maybe, but we could find out. For us, it would be a quick fix. We'd probably save innocent lives.

Not happening, Fiona.

Her fist beats against my scales. *Why not?*

Better question is, why do you care so

damn much? We've only just escaped our own set of problems. Now you want to dive into another?

She's quiet for a bit, and I take advantage of it to put more distance between us and the village.

You know why, she says finally, faint in my head.

I do. Not that I'll admit it to her. But I know her redemption means a lot, and I'm also aware it makes me a selfish bastard to stop her from doing good. She's right—it would only take a moment of our time. But I won't risk it, not with the Serafim so close on our tail.

Regardless of your wishes, we won't be stopping. I'm the one flying, and we're both too weak to deal with any of this. Let it go.

She grows quiet, and I go back to scanning our surroundings. Another hour later, I find a fissure in a mountain. I land and drop Fiona, then shift to human form. My knees wobble and before I know it, I'm face-down in the snow. Weakness unlike anything I've known courses through me, and I let the cool powder reinvigorate my skin.

Soon. I'll get up—soon.

Fiona kneels next to me, pushing me on my back. Her hands move fitfully, but when she sees I'm conscious, all worry leaves her. Face impassable, she gets up and heads to the cavern, leaving me alone in the snow.

I suppose that answers whether she'll speak with me now that we're out of danger.

With a groan, I stand and go about inspecting our new lair. Since the Serafim will pick up on my zmeu magic, I can't even set up defensive shields. *No matter. We won't linger for long.* Despite not having a real reason, I take my time outside. Been around this world for millennia, fought humans and monsters alike, yet none of that matches to dealing with Fiona's wrath right now.

Eventually, the sky grows even darker, and the fire inside pulls me in. Fiona is lying on the bare ground, her hands lifted up to the warmth of the flames. I raise my hand and, like before, conjure us the furs needed to sleep on, setting them up by the heat.

The silence grates on my nerves, so I

finally break it. "Will you not speak to me, witch?"

When she raises her eyes to mine, the violet hue in there is full with emotion. "Not afraid I'll *spell* you again?"

I cringe at the sarcasm in her tone. "It is deserved, I won't deny it. It was an idiotic accusation."

She simply stares at me, so I sit next to her, the fire our only light. It makes her gaze appear otherworldly, almost Fae-like, and the hue of her skin so soft. I dig my fingers in my thighs to stop from reaching out.

Now that I know what's pushing me to touch her, I should be able to control it more. Instead, I find I'm even more aware of her than before. And I have to keep reminding myself that she was hurt–badly– and until recently, she was captive. Under my brother's thumb. There is no way she'll take what I have to say lightly. And I don't know how to explain everything, when I've never faced this before.

"Forgive me, Fiona," I end up saying. "I spoke out of confusion, because I have not had this happen to me, ever. It is my fault."

She frowns. "What do you mean? You know what's been happening?"

How do I even explain this to her without scaring her further... With a sigh, I hold out my palm. "I need you to hold my hand and not let go. At least not until I'm done speaking."

She glances at my outstretched hand, but hesitates. "Why?"

"Please." *Because I can't have you running off.* I should have realized what was happening. Should have foreseen it. Should have stopped it... somehow.

With a sigh, Fiona places her palm in mine, and I intertwine our fingers. For a long moment, I simply stare at our joined hands, trying to gather my thoughts. To explain this to her in a way that she will not feel obligated, or misunderstand. In a way that she realizes she has a choice... of sorts.

"This will be hard for you to hear, never mind grasp. I need you first to understand I would never use the power of my persuasive skills on you, Fiona. I know what you've been through. At least from what you told me, and from the way you act around me. I do not want to add to that trauma, please believe me."

She searches my expression, and I do my damnedest not to let my gaze drop to her mouth. When she finally squeezes my hand in understanding, I continue.

"That being said, when I was injured the first time, you were there. Remember that?"

She frowns this time, trying to see where I'm going with it. "Yes. It was your showdown against Declan, and your descendant was siding with him."

"Exactly. I protected you, going against my own blood–Elisandra. And I do not regret it. It was the right choice, the *only* choice. However, it created complications."

"What complications?"

"Do you remember the redhead in Rockland Creek, Lucrezia?"

"The Solomonar witch, yes. The wolves were saying there hasn't been another one in centuries, that those types of witches are what kept your kind alive."

"Right. Well, that's not what's important

to this particular conversation. Rather, *how* she became a Solomonar, is."

Fiona frowns, and there's an odd emotion in her gaze this time. I wish I could read past it, but it's hard enough figuring out the right words, *caring* enough not to hurt her. My zmeu grumbles in frustration.

"Lucrezia was a regular human, before I got involved. When our paths first crossed, she was looking for her mate, and I knew where he was. The bond between them intrigued me–especially knowing what he was, and the fact she was human. Long story short, I protected Lucrezia against some wolves. In so doing, I did what zmei do best and began a long bond between us, one that practically guaranteed she would become a Solomonar later on."

"I don't follow." Fiona searches my gaze.

Fucking hell. Who knew explaining this to a human would be so hard? Another deep inhale later, I say, "You have to understand, it wasn't on purpose. There is a reason zmei stayed away from humans, from all the emotions they can stir in us. Protectiveness.

Jealousy. Love. The more my kind was around humans, the more we got in idiotic messes. Declan was skilled at it."

"Did that also contribute to your fall out?"

"Not entirely, no. It's more complicated than that. But Declan's hate towards humans, and the crap he pulled, caused the Serafim to come after us. To hunt us down. They went after the Solomonari first, destroying entire generations. And then, little by little, the zmei fell." I shake my head. "But that's not what I'm trying to tell you, Fiona."

"Then what *are* you saying? You're not making much sense."

I shift under her gaze and finally admit, "My zmeu imprinted on you. I'm not sure if it was that exact moment, or before, but the end result is the same. It was he who saved you, when my mind and heart at the time were all for Elisandra."

"I don't understand," Fiona says.

I take a deep breath, diving into the last of it. "You know how wolves have the mating process?"

Fear slips in her expression then. I'm not explaining this right, because it's not the reaction I'd been hoping for. Still, it's too late to pull back, so I just barrel through.

"Zmei have something similar. It happens in two stages. We call the first phase the *legătură*, or the binding. It's a step chosen by the zmeu part of us, not the human. Completely out of our control. Unfortunately, that's what you've been witnessing. The midnight kisses–when I woke from fever-induced dreams, it was with your name on my lips. Craving you at my deepest, rawest, most primal core. It is also why I could speak with you telepathically. Not because of my shitty excuse. It is... a link, a connection between us. And it leads to... Well, the next stage involves the human, and it's called the *împerechere*, the pairing–basically, it's an eventual mating."

Fiona is gaping at me like I've grown three extra heads by the time I finish. The hand in mine has grown slack, then she tries to remove it. I hold on to it.

"You promised," is the only reminder I give her.

She bows her head and stares at our joined hands. I wanted us to maintain some contact to ensure full communication, but now I'm not so sure. The more the silence lengthens, the more I'm aware of her pulse, the curve of her neck, the bow of her lips, the air between us...

This thing is primal, raw, and it will pull us together whether or not we want it. And I know she definitely doesn't.

As if hearing my thoughts, Fiona looks at me, her eyes filled with tears. "Is this some kind of sick game?"

I'm shocked enough that my hold on her hand loosens, and she shoots to her feet before I can stop her.

"Is this your way of teaching me a lesson? By playing with my emotions?" She shakes her head, wiping furiously at her cheeks. "You're no better than your brother."

I jerk to my feet. "Need I remind you Declan destroyed an entire city within minutes of being brought back?"

"And *you* flew away from another in need of salvation."

"Human wars have nothing to do with me!"

She clenches her fists, anger filling her expression. "You could have helped!"

"I didn't see you going."

"Because I was stuck in the sky!" She looks away. "I should have, though. I shouldn't have listened to you. It's yet another missed opportunity."

I wipe a hand on my face. "How do we go from talking about mates, to this? Tell me."

Fiona only shakes her head, and I don't get it. I move closer, and on impulse touch her shoulders. She flinches but doesn't move, not even when I drop the barest of kisses on the corner of her mouth.

"This cannot happen," she whispers. This close, I can see the true agony in her gaze, the pleading–the fear.

"Why not? Does it feel wrong to you?"

"No, but it doesn't mean that it's not."

"Fiona–"

She holds up a hand, stopping me mid-sentence. I've never in my entire existence taken orders from a human, but I shut up at her gesture. Even more at her words.

"We have our separate goals, Tytus. You need to figure out what Declan did to your home, and I'm seeking redemption for my past sins. So let's just get there, do what we have to, and then go our separate ways, yeah?"

I grasp at her hand, desperately trying to hold on to a connection I feel slipping between my fingers. "And what if I don't want that anymore?"

Fiona warned me at the very beginning that once this is done, she wishes only loneliness–away from anyone and anything. That's not workable, not with this connection between us.

Fiona moves back. "You promised you'd respect my choice."

"I did."

"Well, this is it. I don't care if it's you, or your zmeu, or whatever, deciding this. I do not want this, *any* of this."

Her words, said with such determination, are what I've been dreading. Unable to go back over my word, I watch as she turns her back to me and slips between her furs. My ears pick up on a faint change in her breathing, like she's trying to hold back sobs. And I crave nothing more than to hold her, and show her this can work. That it will work. But she doesn't want me near her, as evidenced by her pretense of being asleep.

Not that I'm fooled. I know why she's pulling away, at least partly. And if I could get my hands around Declan's neck, I would make him pay for the harm he caused her. Yet I'm also detached enough–I hope–to realize a lot of Fiona's denial also comes from another source. Namely, her fear of something good, something worthwhile in her life. Will I ever be able to get past that shield? Show her there can be more, even past the physical?

Unable to sleep, or even pretend to, I stand up and head towards the exit of the cavern. If air can clear my head, then so be it.

Fiona

I sleep like the dead, too tired from the journey and Tytus' revelations. It's not even something I can wrap my thoughts around. Mates? He... Whatever he wants from me, it won't happen. I cannot allow it to happen. That certainty is the only thing keeping me sane.

In the middle of the night, I wake up alone in the cavern. Tytus is nowhere to be seen, and for a moment I fear he left me behind. But he wouldn't. Still, unable to fall back asleep, I stay up waiting for him. Without much of a choice, my thoughts keep going back to what he said.

To have the protection of a zmeu... I've been under one's thumb. What would it be like to see the other side, where nothing and no one can hurt me? Is it truly what I want? Won't it come with its own chains?

And why do I keep thinking about it, when I've already dismissed it to him?

It's almost dawn when Tytus comes back, smelling of fire and gunpowder. I jump out from my furs, finding his wobbling form almost collapsing on his.

"Where did you go?"

"Nowhere," he mutters. "Need sleep."

He turns away from me, burying his

face in the furs and passing out within the next minute.

¥

Fiona…

I jerk awake, having fallen asleep again next to Tytus. The heat of his body beckons me further, but something else has my psyche immobilized. Something that shouldn't be there… Some*one* I had thought to be rid of.

Fiona… I've missed you, darling.

Panic spreads through me, even as I crawl away from Tytus, curling into a ball. No! Not Declan, not again. He's supposed to be imprisoned, unable to reach me! Yet his voice in my head is powerful and alluring, same as always.

You've been bad, keeping me out of your head… And bad girls must be punished.

I try to fight it, but to no avail, and it happens the same as it always has. I sense a shift in my mind, like I've been smacked over the head, then everything goes black for a long, long moment after.

When I snap out of Declan's mental hold, it's too late. I don't know how long I was under, or what he made me do while he had control of me. But Tytus is gripping my wrist in his, inches away from the burning flames.

I gasp, try to remove it, and he lets me go. For a moment, I think I see conflict warring in his expression. But once I blink, I realize there is no warmth left in his gaze.

What did Declan make me do? And does Tytus realize what just happened?

Before I can even ponder the implications, Tytus speaks. And his tone is no longer kind and understanding.

"How ironic. Last night I opened to you about this bond between us, wanting nothing but honesty, yet you clammed up. Started a fight." He takes a step backwards. "Now I know why. I thought you were afraid of the power of the bond, of what we could be. But that has nothing to do with it, does it?" A bitter laugh. "It's not that you're afraid of what is between us. It's that you already belong to another–to Declan."

"What?"

"His scent is on you, as if he was here," Tytus growls. "That only happens when it's a strong bond. And he was in your *head*."

There's a note of possessiveness in his tone that he has no right holding. But it's the implication in his words that really gets me angry. "How *dare* you? Are you seriously implying that I'm working for him, being his Trojan horse?"

"Not *for* him, sweetling, *with* him."

The endearment has none of the usual warmth, and I push aside the odd pain in my chest. Tytus' opinion of me shouldn't matter. This fight shouldn't matter. But it does... more than I care to admit to myself.

Unaware of my internal turmoil, he keeps at it. "It now explains how the Serafim keep tracking us. It's *his* blood they're following, through his link to you. I don't know how, but it's evident you're the homing beacon lighting their way to me."

The harshness of his tone truly makes me shake, now. I've seen his ruthless zmeu side, even had it directed at me. For some idiotic reason, I thought what we'd shared would be enough to keep me in his trust. Not so, apparently.

On a whisper, I ask, "W-what are you

going to do?"

Tytus stares at me for a bit, then smiles coolly. "Use it to my advantage." He shakes his head one more time, muttering under his breath. "I've really gone soft."

With jerky movements, he grabs our stuff and tosses it in the fire. I can only stand there, half-dazed, internalizing my feelings. But through it, perhaps because of that bond he's so adamant about, I also see him differently.

Lighted by the remaining embers, Tytus' expression isn't angry. It's... hurt. Exasperated. Frustrated. With a sinking feeling, I call it what it truly is–*betrayed*.

The realization is so swift, so sudden, I can't help my intake of breath. Tytus throws me a glance before dismissing me just as easily. But I see enough, in that brief moment our gazes catch and hold. *Did I really....*

My gosh. Last night, then, I completely misunderstood what he'd been telling me. It wasn't about power or control. The bond, everything he'd explained to me... Tytus was being sincere. And I threw it all in his face, so broken and messed up from my experiences, that I shut the door on the one good thing being presented to me.

"Tytus–"

He gets up and walks to the cavern's entrance. His posture is stiff and I'm afraid he's about to fly off, disappear into the dawn. Instead, he stands there and takes a deep breath.

"The stupid thing is, I even listened and went to save your damn human village." Another rueful shake of the head. "Some mighty monster I am. You get your wish, witch. This will not progress any further, and I'll make sure not to mention the bond to you ever again. I'll be waiting outside for you."

It's with a heavy heart I follow him into the snow, and climb on his back. Have I screwed it all up so badly?

We fly out, and as if to drive the dagger deeper into both our hearts, Tytus does one pass above the human village. I can clearly see the humans are peaceful, and whatever he did fixed their turmoil. A zmeu who should be hell-bent on destruction, yet he fixed the same humans that would hunt him down if they knew what he is.

Knowing an apology would be useless now, I hold on to his scales tighter and let my mind wander to what could have been.

¥

Hours later, Tytus loses altitude. At first I'm worried it's his wounds again, but nothing apparent is wrong. Then we break through the clouds, and I gasp. A ripple in the air, and the beautiful landscape of rivers, mountains and valleys gives way to a white, fairy tale castle nestled in a groove of two mountains.

Unfazed, Tytus lands and switches to human form. I follow him on wobby feet as I stare around. "What is this place?" My wonder-filled eyes take in our surroundings.

"This...is home."

Declan

I stretch from my crouch in the cavern. A moment, two, later, I'm back as a human, with Ileana's annoying bangle bracelets around my wrists. There are no chains attached to the walls, as the prison itself is meant to keep me out of trouble.

If only they knew what I have planned...

A chuckle escapes me as I think back to Fiona. My, but she was frightened, this little witch of mine. It took me a while and some subtle pestering into Tytus' head, but imagine my surprise when I realized she was with him.

Of course, it wasn't that big of a surprise... Not that they need to know it.

I move around the cavern, stretching my legs. The torches up on the walls flicker when I get near them, the flames responding to my zmeu presence. Too bad I cannot use them. My glare falls on the heavy golden bracelets around my wrists. The first few days I was here, I tried everything in my power to destroy them, until I realized it was futile. If anyone would know how to imprison a zmeu, it would be immortals.

Thus, I gave in... for the time being.

Now that time is nigh, I will truly enjoy watching as the final pieces of the puzzle fall into place.

Tytus knows I still control the little witch. It was his hold on her that jostled me out of her consciousness, and my, he was angry!

Which means it will be only a matter of time, now...

Chapter 7

Acasă
"Home is where love resides, memories are created,
friends and family belong and laughter never ends."
-Unknown-

Tytus

All the miles I've flown here, I imagined what it would be like to return home. When I wasn't busy avoiding fanatic knights and old magic entanglements, that is. Still… It's been half a millennium since I last set foot here, cutting the place off from the world, including myself.

At first, I'd only meant to roam around, see the rest of what is out there. Escape the memories of the past and the loneliness that follows me around like the plague. The more I was away, the harder it became to return.

I told myself the castle was better off without me attracting attention to it. That by staying away, by keeping it hidden, it would be better. Less odd occurrences to explain, fewer humans likely to come sniffing around, fewer chances of the magical weapons within falling into their hands. In short, it was self-imposed exile. And now...

I watch Fiona's awed expression as she takes it all in, trying to see through her eyes. The massive towers, same as a fairy tale castle, glint white in the sun like a million diamonds. The round windows with many rainbows shooting off them–the crystal within acting as a conductor. A stone bridge leads to a pont-levis, which now stands lowered, waiting for its true occupant to return. White oak doors tease me with their open invitation to enter.

Da, it is quite a sight. To Fiona, it must be overwhelming. To me, it's simply home.

"Come. It is best we go inside." Her uncertain gaze meets mine, and I'm reminded of what transpired before all this.

When I woke up and felt Declan all over her...As zmei, everyone we come into contact with, we leave our scent on. Whether the contact is physical or mental, a shred of our magic lingers. And I would know Declan's particular signature anywhere.

Needless to say, I saw red. Especially as I'd spent the better part of the night unable to sleep and ended up in the human village she had seen ravaged by drama. I used my persuasion skills to get them in line enough so it worked. Within hours, the conflict was resolved.

I thought coming back, telling Fiona of it, would show her that I'm nothing like Declan. That I can care about humans– about her. I've never felt this need for someone, but it's obvious it has blinded me, and sorely so.

Instead of answering the unspoken question in her eyes, I say nothing and stride away. Anger still flows in my veins at my stupidity, at what I missed because of my attraction to her.

Declan.

My damn brother never liked parting with a favorite toy. Part of me balks at thinking of Fiona like that. The same part that remembers the taste of her lips, her soft curves against me. My body tightens uncomfortably, my zmeu not understanding the distance, and I will it away.

From now on, it's all business. I cannot be involved with her if Declan still has hold of her mind. There would be ways to help her break it, if she allowed the bond to continue. But given we've clarified that isn't happening, there is no point bringing it up.

Fiona clears her throat behind me as we enter the main hall. "I thought I sensed a barrier on the outside, something powerful. Is it zmeu magic? Won't it draw the Serafim here?"

"Da, you are correct. An illusion, to ensure no one sees what I do. No one, that is, unless they are a guest I allow." I run a hand through my hair, shrugging. "As for the Cavaleri, it doesn't matter. They will come with or without a reason, and I expect them to. But they'll be on my territory, and I will not let them cross my borders alive."

"Oh," is Fiona's only answer.

I turn to her, then. She's pale, shivering, and if the dark circles under her eyes are any sign, she's way past exhaustion. As am I.

My body wobbles and I lean against a massive column by the entrance of the white oak doors, hiding the weakness. *Strength. Portray only strength.*

"When you asked me to come, I explained to you it would not be a piece of cake, as the human saying goes. I did not expect the Serafim, but I dare say I have protected us both. At least, from the threats I knew we were facing."

Fiona opens her mouth as if to dispute my jab, to explain herself, but I don't give her a chance to. "As you requested, we will focus on the task at hand. Which, as you will recall, is to find out what Declan disturbed while he was here, and how big of a danger that is to the outside world. Now that we're here, I'll need your help to search the place, to discover what he did."

To my surprise, Fiona nods, no longer appearing in a mood to argue. I set aside the pang in my chest, and continue. "Since you have a link with him still, if we discover nothing at first glance, I'll need you to dive into that for a bit."

She pales further, but nods again. I would have thought the idea of reaching out to Declan would panic her, but it seems I've underestimated this witch by a lot. Either that, or I was right, and she's deeper in the trenches with Declan than I would like to admit to myself.

"As promised," I add, "once we settle everything, I will take you wherever it is you wish to go. Away from humans."

Once more, Fiona nods, this time avoiding my gaze altogether. Before my admiration for her grows and becomes delusional again, I start moving. "Come. I'll show you to your quarters."

We go up the winding staircase and I do my best to ignore the memories tugging at me, hidden in every corner. Laughs with Declan. Trysts with females. Meetings with Council members. It's harder than I thought, keeping it all at bay. In my long life, I've learned to compartmentalize, to keep everything in check. Yet this return affects me more than it should. More than I want it to. A glance at Fiona makes me wonder if perhaps she's the cause for making me feel something I never wanted, for drawing my zmeu to her.

Whichever the case, I tug my primal self back from the surface, and focus on what I do best. Which is keeping myself cool and collected. If she wishes, we will have a discussion about our recent argument–but later. However, given the way she's acting, I'm pretty sure this will be the last chance I have of getting through to her.

Instead of trying, instead of giving her an opening, I clam up and hurry my stride. Fiona struggles to keep up, and by the time we swoop down a long hallway and stop in front of a dark oak door, she is panting.

"These are your chambers," I say by way of introduction, and push open the door. A rune in the air causes the sheets covering the furniture to blow away, and the massive windows open to let in some cool, fresh air.

Fiona walks in a daze, taking in the large bed, the antique furniture, the shades of deep purple and burgundy, offset by the whiteness of the furniture.

"Does it meet your needs?" I ask, my voice a tad gruff.

"Y-yes." She darts a glance my way, then looks away.

So we're back to awkwardness now. Marvelous. With a sigh, I point to the corner. "An ensuite bathroom awaits you there, should you wish to wash up." Another rune, and I gesture to the antique closet. "And that should now have enough clothes to last you. Let me know if you need anything else."

Before she can truly answer me, I turn on my heels and walk away, further down the corridor. It's probably not smart to house her in the East Wing, right where I am, but there is nowhere else I can picture her.

As I enter my own chambers, I'm looking forward to dropping on my bed, relishing the feel of the white furs on my face, and passing out until the morning.

Only, my plans are dashed when I realize I'm not alone.

Ileana is standing at my windows, and by her side is Făt Frumos, dressed in a well-cut suit. I scowl. These immortals have a way of showing up when it most suits them, but not their host. Lucas, alpha of the pack of wolves I left behind, is more than familiar with that aspect. I've managed to avoid them—until recently.

It was the two immortals who helped us imprison Declan once more, in the crater from which they had released him in Rockland Creek. And it is they who hold the key to his freedom…. Which makes me even more wary as to their purpose here.

"I do not recall allowing immortals to enter my domain."

Ileana rolls her sun-filled eyes. Her dress made of pure spring flowers shimmers as she moves, as does the dark hair cascading down her back. Her expression is less serene than I am used to. "We are past that, zmeu. Read what is on your bed."

I don't move, torn between curiosity and refusing to take orders from an immortal, especially in my own home.

Făt speaks then. "Your pride has no place here, zmeu." Unlike Ileana's fairy tale attire, his modern suit is even more incongruent in my medieval-looking room.

I glare at him. "My pride alone has place here, immortal."

A closer look at both of them shows their façade cracking with a hint of fear. Curiosity wins and I inch closer and pick a loose sheet of paper. I recognize my brother's cursive handwriting, the angry lashes of the quill almost breaking the paper in some spots. It is only two rows of words.

You can search, but you will not find.
If you find, it will be too late.

The words alone are enough to bring back his betrayal. This is my *blood*, kin of my kin, and rather than safeguard the lineage of the zmei, he has chosen to taint it, to destroy it. As if causing the ending of our race was not enough. As if betraying his brother was not enough.

My hand trembles–waves of anger suffusing my body. I do not wish for these immortals to see me so, but keeping them at bay is even harder. After all this time, Declan loves to play games. I should've fucking figured.

I turn to the immortals, scowling. "I don't suppose you're here to help me solve his riddle?"

Făt arches an eyebrow. "You know we cannot intervene. Especially not with *your* kind."

"Right. And yet you are here, in my bedroom, invading the sanctity of my home."

I let the rest go unspoken, but it lingers in the air between us. Ileana and her consort share a glance, and again I catch that imperceptible hint of fear.

"Something has you two spooked," I accuse when they don't rise to my bait.

Făt moves closer to Ileana, his arm moving to touch hers. "Mind your business, zmeu."

"As you wish." I toss the piece of paper

back on the bed, and shrug. "So, Declan likes to play games. Nothing new, but I am not here for that."

"You lie!"

Ileana throws a warning glance to her consort, who returns to the window, trying to hide his seething. That makes two of us.

"No more than you do," I tell him. "Used to be you were too busy killing me and mine. Perhaps that's the reason for your inability to help—you'd rather everything happens as Declan wishes it to."

"That is not true, and you know it." Ileana steps between us. "Your zmeu dealings are beyond our control because you and Declan are the last of your race. Ying and yang, two sides of the same coin. The killing of one will bring about the death of the other. And the world needs the balance of all creatures... Even zmei." Another glance to Făt. "And while we cannot help, because we know not what Declan did, we can offer you one thing—a chance to speak with him. Face to face."

I freeze, trying to see past their angle. "Why would you do that?"

"It does no one any good if Declan wins and whatever he did here is unleashed," Ileana says. "Surely you see that."

"Not to mention, it makes you two look bad for sleeping on the job."

"I warned you it was a waste of time, draga mea," Făt scowls, using the *my darling* endearment. "Zmei are inherently selfish creatures, this one even more so. Let us leave him to his doom."

Ileana doesn't follow him to the door, instead stares at me with a pained expression. "Da, you may have a point. The gods assigned us to watch over this section of the world because of our own roots to the Transylvanian region. And in not seeing Declan's move, we failed. It is what we are trying to rectify. Thus if you get over your pride and change your mind, you have but to call my name."

"Not likely," I mutter and turn my back on them.

As I stare out the same window Făt previously occupied, I'm reminded of a time when everything was much simpler, yet equally hard.

Zmei have, since the beginning of time, cavorted with immortals, demi-gods and the like. Created to guard the gods themselves, we eventually became obsolete when the divinities isolated themselves from the ever-growing greediness of humans.

In the end, we were given territories to keep us happy. The dragons chose the northern areas, deep in the mists of Wales, whereas my kind chose Romania. All who met us prized our wisdom and abilities, as well as our homes. Each clan became the sole protector of one area of the earth, mine being the center for the Balkans.

Honor meant something, back then, and family was the most important to my clan. Echoes of the past bring more and more memories. Sword fighting by daytime, raids by nighttime–Declan by my side. We were brothers, once. Thick as thieves, with the same vision of a distant future.

When did it all go so wrong?

Fiona

I don't know what wakes me up. Perhaps

the unknown walls closing in on me. Or my racing heart.

Or perhaps the voice in your head, darling.

I freeze, hoping by some miracle if I don't move, Declan will assume I'm asleep and leave me alone. But, no, that would be too much to ask for.

Wake up, Sleeping Beauty. I have something you'll like.

My panting is loud in the large room. Shadows wink back at me, bathed in moonlight, and I burrow further into the thick furs, wishing sleep would take me over again, and show me this is all a nightmare. But the persistent nagging at the back of my head, so unlike Tytus' gentle probing while flying, is enough to tell me that won't happen.

Fiona... There is no use ignoring me. He sounds almost playful. *I know where you are. And what is hidden beneath...*

"And what's that?"

Good girl. A pause, just enough for my heartbeat to race more. *A cure for Tytus.*

I don't want to be stupid and listen to

him. But I remember the Tytus who was so kind to me, the one who helped those humans. The zmeu who held my hands and explained what the bond between us meant and gave me a chance to have more, from life. A chance I kicked in the gut.

And I recall my promise to myself, that I would find redemption, and figure out a way to use my magic for good. Well, what better way than seeking a cure for Tytus? We need more heroes like that around. So many more. And if I have it in my power to help, why not?

Plus, Tytus did say he wanted me to dig deeper into what Declan knows. Maybe this is the time to do so. And... to truly demonstrate how sorry I am.

"Fine. Show me."

A chuckle echoes in my head, then darkness takes over me.

¥

I snap to when my back collides with a cool wall. Harsh, the hit and change in temperature breaks the connection between me and Declan. It used to be I could at least see what he was doing with my body, but just like his first return, he now has full control.

Shivers race over my skin, and my teeth chatter in shock. All I sense is my terror, seizing my muscles and rendering me immobile. It grips my throat and makes it hard to scream.

Then, bit by bit, the rest of the picture comes through. Smoke in the air, suffocating and thick. A bare-chested man, his back to me, one hand holding me off and another facing an inferno.

"Get back!" Tytus shouts, then shifts to take the brunt of the impact.

Fire. Flames lick the walls. The antique tapestry depicting the Carpathian Mountains is half eaten by them, and the wall behind it looks charred. Under our feet, the thick carpeting is dirty with broken pieces of glass and other bits.

As I take in everything, Tytus shouts and scribbles runes after runes in the air, until an icy gust of wind breaks the windows across from us. It attacks the flames with a vengeance, led and controlled by Tytus, until nothing is left but silence, and our panting.

My breath escapes in puffs of white smoke, and I notice the thin robe I'm wearing, its edges frayed by fire. Tytus extinguishes the last of the blazes and turns to me, breathing heavily. His eyes are almost black in this light.

"Just what the hell are you playing at?"

"Me?"

With a sweeping glance, I take in the destruction. Tytus faces me fully, and my eyes slide down his naked chest, then rise back to his face. His cheeks are dark with soot, and his hair is sticking out at odd places. He looks like he jumped out of bed, present once more to save me.

Each breath makes his abs undulate, and something dark, primal answers in me. Just like in the cavern, that tug between us comes alive. Heat blossoms in my center, and a gasp escapes me that sounds more like a moan.

What the hell is happening to me?

I meet his eyes and we stare at each other. For a beat, maybe longer. Both panting, both unable to break this connection. I'm reminded of what he told me–the bond. The fire. That's what it feels like, as if I'm being consumed by something way out of my control. Something that makes me...

Without even realizing it, I move closer, my palm extended towards him.

"Fiona–" He groans, and then he's on me in a second, his chest flush with mine, holding my hand up above my head. "Do you even realize what you're inviting?"

I nod, though in truth I do not understand what he's talking about. But my small gesture seems to be enough. Tytus cups my cheek, hesitating. A second later he's kissing me, possessing my mouth. This time, I don't hold back. I give as good as I get, opening under him so our tongues can duel for dominance, my chest pressed to his, my breasts aching–my entire being begging for more.

Tytus' free hand lowers down to my side, igniting a trail of fire, and then it drops to my lower back, pressing me against him. I gasp in his mouth at the contact, heat blossoming further. Passion left my life years ago, and with my captivity it's not like I was meeting good guys. But in that moment, Tytus ignites my entire body, and I'm ready for everything else he's ready to show me.

His hand on my cheek also lowers, caressing my other side, swooping over a tight nipple–and then he groans and lets go of me, backing away until he's on the opposite side of the hallway, bathed in shadows.

His eyes glitter like diamonds, and I touch my lips, burning, humming, craving more.

"Why did you stop?" I ask, my voice hoarse.

"Because you're not ready for this."

I say nothing, only staring at him in accusation. In a deep corner of my mind, I realize my frustration is insane. No basis in reality whatsoever. But in that moment, I only want him to feel my anger.

Tytus' expression shifts into something else, almost a challenge. "Was it not you who wanted nothing to do with me? Strictly business, I believe you said?"

I gulp, then shakily wipe my palms on my

nightgown. Trying to collect my thoughts is useless, but I do my damnedest best. "I did, you're right. But it's obvious we both have an itch to scratch, no?"

A surprised laugh bursts out of him, and I take it as a sign of encouragement. Move a step closer. He freezes, watching me carefully.

"You want me, no?"

"Don't play me, Fiona."

Am I? Maybe without realizing it, I am. But I don't think I am. I also can't shake this burning, this need—it's making every thought harder.

"I'm not," I whisper, begging him with my eyes to see past this. To see *in me*, like he has proven he can. "But we both want this. Let's be consenting adults, then we can focus on the business at hand."

He stares at me for so long, I feel my cheeks burn. Then he shakes his head, and my stomach clenches in hurt and humiliation. It's only made worse by the fact he doesn't even reach for me.

"I don't think you understand what I said before, Fiona. A simple roll in a bed won't fix this."

"Whatever," I mutter.

He says nothing, and I walk away. Tytus clears his throat, stopping me in my tracks. "Before you go, care to tell me what you were playing at, nearly burning down my home?"

A petulant part of me wants to stomp away and not answer him, but I know I cannot. "You asked me to get in Declan's head. Well, he got into mine."

There's only silence for a long time, then Tytus' heat surrounds me as he hugs me from behind. He drops his head on my shoulder, tightening his hold. When he speaks, his voice is rough.

"Enough of putting yourself in danger. Forget what I said in anger, and let us start anew, hmm? I will show you the grounds tomorrow."

I nod, but he's already gone. And that night, I ache for him like I never have before for any man.

¥

The next morning, Tytus holds true to his word and shows me around. First, he takes me from top to bottom of the castle, making me visit all three floors with their mazes upon mazes of rooms and bathrooms and little side alcoves. Every area is decorated tastefully, yet richly. Old tapestries, plush carpets, silk bedding with fur blankets. Gold-encrusted or silver-lined lamps, door knobs, painting frames... Everything is opulence, luxury and taste.

They split the castle into the East and West Wing. The East Wing has always been Tytus', while the West–the same one I'd burned the other night–was Declan's. When he tells me this, I trip over my feet and nearly slam into a door, so shocked am I at the revelation.

"I guess that explains last night, then."

Tytus throws me a look, then runs a hand through his hair in agitation. "I didn't mean to upset you by bringing him up."

"You didn't," I hurry to reassure him. "Declan is your brother. You should feel free to speak of him, especially here. I can't even imagine the memories that keep you up at night."

Tytus stares at the carpet like it holds

all the answers. He's frowning so hard, I move closer and press my fingers to his brow, smoothing it out.

When he catches my hand, then intertwines our fingers, I smile. "I don't understand this, you know. Any of it. The bond. Last night... Why Declan lied to me, again. Why he won't let me go, even imprisoned as he is. But..." My stare falls on our joined hands. "I am also slowly starting to accept that not understanding, not knowing, is not all bad. When you have the right people around you, at least."

If nothing else, my little speech gets a smile out of Tytus. And so the tour continues, showing me the outside gardens, the land that spreads far into the valley and beyond. The vastness of the place feels at once humbling and majestic, and my gaze lingers on the skies.

"I can see the appeal. Of flying here, I mean, without a care in the world."

Tytus grins. "It's pretty awe-inspiring, but that's not my favorite spot."

"Really?"

He smiles in a way that makes my

stomach clench, then drags me to one of the rooms we haven't yet visited. When he pushes open the dark oak doors, my jaw drops. Tytus chuckles and moves inside, and I follow in a complete daze.

Bookshelves upon bookshelves line every wall in the room. They go all the way from the floor to the ceiling and are filled with what must be thousands–millions?–of books. In the middle is an area with three sofas, some armchairs, and coffee tables strewn around. The lack of dust means Tytus has already been here since we arrived, not that it surprises me.

Gone is the man who never relaxes. Here, in his element, his gray eyes glint with joy and mischief. It brings tears to my eyes when I watch him caress the spines of the books with such love, such devotion.

He pulls one out for me and brings it over. Its spine is worn, but inside are the most intricate designs of knights battling monsters, and beautiful maidens on quests.

"A compilation of local lore and legends," he says, watching my expression.

I don't miss a beat, flipping the pages and walking towards one sofa. Once I've already taken a seat, engrossed in the words, I'm not afraid to plead. "Please, can we stay for a bit?"

Tytus chuckles and nods, then picks up a book of his own, joining me in what's our most normal moment yet.

¥

After, we step into the massive dining room and he holds a seat out at the table. Food appears with a clap of his hands, and I jump in surprise.

"Do you have little elves running around, or something?"

He grins, and it looks good on him. Relaxed. "No, I simply borrow from the surrounding villages. By the time humans realize the food has gone missing, they also find some gold coins to make up for it."

I raise my eyebrows. "You do know gold is no longer the accepted currency?"

"Idiotic, if you ask me. But it is still valuable."

Feeling less guilty, I dig into the food,

loving how it melts in my mouth. The feast of cabbage rolls and lamb stew has never tasted better, and I lean back feeling so full.

"This... was amazing."

There's an odd glint in Tytus' eyes. "Satisfaction suits you," he says in that hoarse voice, and I gulp.

In an effort not to be reminded of last night, I peer around. The opulence of the castle bears on me, and I can't help but feel out of place. With its crystal chandeliers, silver cutlery and perfectly decorated ambiance, this castle is fit for a king.

Tytus, on the other hand, is right at home. The ease of his movements, the way he walks like he owns the place... Maybe my comparison to a king isn't so far off base.

Then he distracts me with his next words. "I had some visitors yesterday, when we arrived. I'll explain in a minute. But first, I really owe you an apology. For what I said, what I implied about you spelling me, and... for last night. I shouldn't have cornered you like that."

I turn my head away, taking another sip of wine. "You didn't." I finally meet his gaze. "We both said things we regret. You've had ample opportunity to hurt me and haven't. I think I'm starting to trust you, Tytus, despite it being your brother who has hold of me. I trust you so much, in fact, it was why I allowed him into my mind. He promised a cure to what ails you, and I wanted to get it, to heal you. Silly, right?"

He stares at me for a long moment, his gaze filled with something I cannot discern. Then he gets up and comes by my side, kneeling. "No more silly than me saving a village because your words got to this cold heart of mine."

My gut churns in protest at the vulnerability he displays. At the honesty he creates in me. This connection, this bond, it's tangible, all right. And in a way, I'm understanding Tytus' desire to have it be... more.

Just as I lean further, wanting to tell him my thoughts, the ground shakes.

Chapter 8

Apărare
"The best defense is a good offense."
-Proverb-

Tytus

One moment, I'm ready to kiss her again, cursing this need inside me that wants nothing else but to claim her as my own. Cursing the zmeu whose desire is affecting her own, not allowing her to see straight, to realize what we could be beyond the physical.

When the ground shakes, I'm both relieved and frustrated at the interruption. And then I'm up and heading to the closest window.

"Right on time," I mutter under my breath.

They fill the grounds outside my castle–Cavaleri Serafim, a few dozens. And they are not alone. A cloaked figure in their midst shows me they mean business this time–a dark mage. It is probably not their strongest mage, but he will still be a nuisance to deal with.

Fiona's footsteps echo in the dining room as she joins me. A soft gasp escapes her when she sees what I do. "They found us."

I turn to her. "Me. They found *me*. Their fight is not with you, so if I don't survive, remember that. Tell them I captured you, and they won't think twice about allowing your freedom."

"But it's not the truth."

"The Serafim don't care for the truth. If they did, they would take the time to realize not all zmei are evil monsters. But they have been stuck in their old-school beliefs for eons and eons, and nothing will change that now. Least of all, you." I grasp a lock of her hair, twirling it around my finger. "You are far too...unique, Fiona. And the last thing I wish is for you to end up in captivity, again. So if I fail, tell them I coerced you. Zmei are known for taking maidens. Feed into that belief, and you will be safe."

A flash of lightning crosses her eyes, but she lowers her gaze before I can determine whether she caught my meaning. Shouts outside draw my attention again, and I sigh. Gently, I tug on her lock of hair until it brings her forehead closer to me. I meet it with a soft kiss, closing my eyes and hoping I will have time for more, later. Then I head down the hall.

"Where are you going?"

"To show them the zmeu's true face." I shoot back.

Fiona's faster than I give her credit, though. She's by my side in a second. "What about Declan's plan?"

"I cannot allow them outside my gates and risk them catching us in our sleep. Declan's plan for world destruction will simply have to wait."

At her stricken expression, I soften my tone. "I know his reach scares you, and I promised to protect you. But I won't be able to do any of that, unless I eliminate these bastards off our plate."

"But you're not fully healed!"

"I will survive this."

"Tytus–"

I cup her cheek, resting my thumb on her lower lip. The softness of it, the darkening in her eyes, it hits my core. "I *will* survive this." Then, on an impulse, I drop my mouth to hers, stealing the kiss that had been lingering in the air.

When I pull back, Fiona's eyes are glazed, her mouth parted and begging for more. I intend to take her up on that, propriety be damned. But first...

"Seal the door behind me and let no one else in."

With each step away from her, I force my mind to focus. *Ignore the witch. Your lives depend on it.* I have to forget that I have something to care about now. If we're to survive, there is no other way.

So by the time I exit through the front white oak doors, I set my face in a neutral expression. I step all the way to the barriers, taking in the nameless faces that are so ready to give their life, only to have mine in return.

In Romanian, I ask them, "I suppose your brethren's deaths were not warning enough, da? You want to add to the count?" I shrug and open my arms. "You have come to the right place, then. Welcome to my humble abode."

Silence greets my words until one person moves forward. A cloaked man–the mage. "It is easy to talk, yet your actions show your fear."

"Fear?" Anger sizzles at my fingertips, and the clouds above reflect it, becoming darker, swirling in an unnatural circle. "Do I seem afraid?"

He removes his cloak, revealing a shaved head and white irises.The scar cutting his face in half is repulsing. "You hide behind a shield, do you not?"

I laugh, and cross over said barrier. "Not anymore, mage. Come get me, if you can." Before he can toss the hex I foresee towards me, I'm already shifting and pushing off the ground.

On my way to the skies, I grab the two

closest soldiers, and rip their heads off midair. Blood sprays down the rest of the Cavaleri, and I spin into the clouds until they cannot see me any more.

They want to play? Let us play.

By the time I swoop down again, the mage has recovered from his shock. He's barking orders at the Serafim. Three of them move into position with bows and arrows and start shooting them my way. When I avoid them all successfully, the mage walks to the arrows and bursts of dark smoke escape his fingertips, coating the arrow tips.

Dirty magic. All right.

Two can play that game. I fly closer to the clouds again, this time letting the sizzle of static crawl over my skin. Fire roars ahead at my command, and I use their inability to multitask to swoop down close. Lightning hits more than a few of the Serafim, and shouts of pain echo all around.

My mistake is I get too arrogant and stop watching out for the mage. When the first bolt of lightning hits me, I jerk in surprise. One wing is momentarily frozen, causing me to drop from midair. An arrow pierces it, and my howl of agony echoes next.

Then my gaze settles on the human, and his satisfied expression. *The little shit.* Before I can go after him, more arrows come at me. At first, it confuses me, as none are heading my way specifically.

Then the air moves, and I catch on to the trick. Each arrow strikes and doesn't fall, causing a net to be formed. If I fly in its midst, the mage will drag me down, causing me to be ground level and easily attacked.

I avoid it, still trying to figure out where he's getting the power. One glance down finally answers my question—he's holding a bone in his palm. A zmeu bone, I would bet my life on it.

Before I can do anything, a bolt of magic shoots the mage from behind. He whirls around, shocked, and the blast he'd prepared for me escapes his hands—and heads straight to one of my towers.

White streaks of hair catch my eye at the window of said tower, and I lose it. I swoop down on the Cavaleri Serafim, burning the rest of them to ashes, including the mage. When I'm satisfied with their deaths, I take half a second to draw a quick rune in the air to aspire their ashes, then cross the barrier without a glance behind.

¥

"Fiona!" My roar echoes amid the dust and collapsed bricks. Damn this witch! Why didn't she listen and stay out of it?

I make my way up to the tower that got destroyed, but is still somehow standing. Crumbled pieces of cement fill the area, with bits of broken furniture and papers scattered around. The place is a mess, and I have no blasted idea how it's even still standing.

There is no sign of Fiona. I push everything away, not even bothering with magic.

"Fiona!" I yell again. Why did she have to intervene..? I know it was to protect me, but I *told her* it was all under control. And still she didn't listen. I should be happy she went against my words, especially that she feels comfortable enough around me to disobey me. But I cannot. My heart is cold, frozen at the thought I might have lost her. How fragile are human bodies?

Then my ears pick up something in the distance, a faint cough. I head in that direction, and sure enough, the cough gets louder.

"Fiona?"

"In here."

Her voice is weak, but it's there. *She's alive.*

My hands tremble with relief as I remove the last of the rocks, and I help her up gingerly. We're too close to a part of the Wing that completely caved in, causing a crater of sorts. The only thing that saved Fiona's life was she got stuck in a corner and another boulder caught the brunt of the other rock, leaving her with enough room to breathe and not get crushed.

At the thought of her body smashed like a pancake, a shudder runs through me and I pull her tightly in my arms. It takes me a moment to realize she's struggling against my hold. Has the near-death experience changed her mind again, and she wants distance?

Luckily, it's nothing of the like. When I finally allow enough space between us, Fiona wipes out her dusty cheeks and wrinkles her nose. "I found something."

Fiona holds on to her treasure with one hand, the other clutched onto my shirt, right near my heart.

"Forget that." I dismiss it, not even chancing a glance towards whatever it is. "What were you thinking?"

"I was in the area because the Serafim worried me. And when I saw what was happening... I didn't want you dead."

"I wouldn't have died."

"Right. As if I'll believe that," she scowls.

I take in the fire in her eyes, the determination in her features, and the last shred of control snaps in me. Relief fills me at her being alive, in my arms, and without a second thought about our previous night or anything else, I push her into the wall. The moment after, I'm claiming her mouth and not holding back this time.

Fiona's arms wrap around my neck

and I can feel whatever she's found digging into my skin. I have no wish to know what it is. Not when its discovery could have claimed her life.

Instead, I focus on her mouth. It's a drug kissing her, and I want more. I crave her wholly, and it's too damn dangerous given everything else going on, but I don't care.

Fiona moans under me, taken by the release of the fight. Her human body is overwhelmed and gives in to my ministrations, to the pull of the bond. It would be easy to take the physical, to use it as a starting point and show her everything we could be. It would be... That is, if she was in full control of her faculties and not pumped full of adrenaline.

"Fuck." That's what makes me stop and step away once more.

Fiona's glazed eyes open, and she stares at me. "What's wrong?"

"You... It's the adrenaline demanding this. You will regret it, after."

A flash of lightning goes through her eyes and she pulls me closer. "Let me be the judge of that."

Her mouth opens under mine, and this time, my zmeu fully controls me, not the other way around. Neither of us can deny the invitation, the sweet sounds of surrender she's making. And with her words still ringing in my ears, I let my hands roam freely.

Down her back, to her waist, to her rear end, revelling in each curve and dip of her womanly body. A groan escapes me and I deepen the kiss, even as my fingers trail up to her breast, hidden from my view by her shirt.

Not that it matters. The nipple is taut against my palm, even through the thin bra underneath. And when she arches against me, I let my other hand move lower, dipping into her skirt, and beneath the flimsy material of her underwear.

Fiona gasps against my mouth, and arches more for my touch, whimpering. My fingers seek entrance to her holiest place, and when she spreads her legs and allows me in, I no longer control the curses leaving me.

In contrast to my harsh words, Fiona is

all fire, vibrating under my ministrations, and still our mouths are clasped together, and our bodies generate unspeakable heat.

Fiona's whimpers grow more rapid. It's the sweetest sound I'll ever hear, and I press my fingers deeper, determined to hear her cry of ecstasy. She rocks more against me, biting her lip, and then throws her head back, moaning long and hard.

And hells be damned, but I want inside her so badly in that moment. And then something else hits my nostrils. Before I can grasp what it is, the smoke curls around me and chokes me. The last thing I see is Fiona's panicked expression before I lose all consciousness.

Fiona

With one last heave, I drag Tytus away from the noxious miasma that emerged. It smells bad, almost like sulfur, but I definitely don't have the same reaction to it as he does.

So I cover my mouth with a cloth and move forward, inspecting the hole, and its closeness to where I'd been almost crushed. Then I open my palm and stare at the fang

I'd found, wrapped in a small pouch. Whatever beast this belongs to… I shudder.

Should I go down, see what's there? Whatever is, could help Tytus.

And yet, something tells me Declan never intended us to find this. He might've teased me with the possibility of a cure that night, but this, he did not expect. Which means for once we have the drop on him. And if I stay awake long enough, I'll avoid falling under his spell.

Slowly, I back away towards Tytus. As I near him, though, my heart thuds wildly. Gone is the rogue who made me orgasm and burned my world with color. Tytus' cheeks are pale, sunken. Whatever the smoke did to him, it's bad. Bad enough that blood is seeping through his shirt, the wounds from Declan's fight back to the surface, no longer healed.

I heave him further from the miasma, to a spot that's a little more breathable. But what the hell can I do? Who could help?

"What happened?"

I turn at the female voice. A woman is standing in the hallway, looking anything but human with her sun-filled eyes and robe made of flowers. Long, flowing brown hair cascades down her back, and her accent is most definitely... other. I've seen her before, briefly, in Rockland Creek. "What are you doing here?"

"I'm a friend." She steps closer, her eyes never once leaving Tytus' unconscious form. "Is Tytus alive?"

"Yes," I say a bit too defensively.

"He doesn't look it." This comes from the man by her side. The shadows and his suit hid him, but now he steps out and I wonder how I missed his blond hair and icy blue eyes.

"He just fought off a bunch of fanatical maniacs, of course he's not okay!" I try to pull on Tytus again, but the woman moves closer.

"Let me help."

Before I can remark on her tiny frame, she lifts a hand and Tytus levitates into the air. I recall the same power on display when they'd imprisoned Declan, in the crater. "What... What exactly are you?"

"Immortals." She smiles my way. "The

good kind. I am Ileana Cosânzeana, and my consort here is Făt Frumos."

So they're the ones Tytus mentioned to me, way back in the caves. Talk about weird names. She says hers like *E-lya-nah,* and his like *Fuh-th Fruh-mohs.* Doesn't take a genius to figure out they're from around here.

My eyes narrow further, and I don't let go of Tytus' hand, even as we keep moving closer to his bedroom. Already, I'm running through possible runes to protect us, if it comes to it. "How did you get in here? And why would you want to help?"

"It is what we do," Ileana says in her soft voice. It only makes me more distrusting, since she's speaking to me as if I'm a child that needs placating.

"Sure, whatever. Like I'm going to believe you on your word? Just because I trust Tytus doesn't mean it extends to you."

Făt glowers and moves as if to do something, but Ileana holds up a finger. That's all it takes, and he stops mid-movement, clenching his jaw.

"Fair enough," she says. "Perhaps a bribe

might work better. Would it help if I tell you how to heal him?"

I glance at Tytus, now on his bed, then her. "It would be a good start."

"Very well. Did he explain about the legătură bond?"

"He did..."

Făt Frumos snorts, immediately drawing my ire. I'm too strung-up to keep my comments to myself. "What's so funny?"

"He evidently did not reveal all."

I cross my arms over my chest, even more annoyed now. "And how would you know?"

"Because you don't seem scared enough."

I gape at them, then the last shred of my control snaps. "All right, I think that's enough *help* from you two. I don't know what gives you the right to come barging in here, but I'll figure out Tytus' wounds myself. Now, leave."

When neither of them moves, I don't bother with further threats. Instead, I reach into the air and immediately draw two runes. One for defense, one for offense.

Smoke escapes them even as a window bursts open and a gust of wind enters.

Ileana and Făt share a look, and she steps closer. I lift my hand, raising my voice to be heard above the wind. "Last warning!"

"We mean you no harm."

When my stubbornness shows no move to stop, Ileana rolls her eyes and snaps her fingers. All I see is a spark of energy, then the runes go poof. Literally. One minute they're there, controlled by me, the next they're gone. And all I can do is stare.

Then, even more stupidly, I move backwards until my body is the only thing standing between them and the bed–and Tytus.

Făt snorts again, and I want to punch that smirk off his face. Ileana's tone becomes less amicable, and more firm. The kind that says I'm meant to listen.

"I meant it when I said we aren't the enemy here. And unless you let me come to your aid, Tytus will perish, meaning his brother Declan will get what he wants. Is that what you wish, Fiona?"

I grit my teeth so I don't tell her what I truly wish, and where she can stuff it. Instead, I take a deep breath. "Of course it's not what I wish! Tytus has been nothing but kind to me, and I want him unharmed."

"Very well. Then listen closely, as we have little time." Ileana steps closer, and motions for me to take Tytus' hand in mine. Once I do, she says, "You two have a bond, one he has evidently spoken to you about. What you must understand is that these bonds transcend all rationality and logic. It is why they make the two people involved act unlike themselves. And, much like with everything else in the world, there is a silver lining."

"Really?" I try to make my tone more enthusiastic, but it falls flat. Everything about this bond has gone wrong since the moment I found out about it.

"Da," Ileana says. "Tytus' weakness comes from Declan's venom."

"I know that."

Ileana's eyes flash at the interruption, and I gesture for her to go on. If she can be magnanimous, so can I. But I won't be silenced in a house that's not even hers.

"The bond allows you two closeness, but also sharing of many things. Much as you can share thoughts, you could use your vital energy to boost Tytus."

That gets my attention. "My what, now?"

"Vital energy," Făt says in a bored tone. "Your core energy, your life force."

I glance between them, hesitating a few times before finally speaking. "Isn't that dangerous? For the person who does it?"

"Of course it is." Făt scoffs. "And it won't even cure him, not really. Only Declan can remove that venom, and he'll never do it."

"Then what's the point of doing it?"

"The *point*," Ileana stresses with a glare to Făt, "is that you will have helped Tytus, bought him time, and he can continue with the quest. Find out what Declan hid underneath this castle. And while I would normally say take your time, the truth is time is running out. And if you do not wish Declan to succeed, we need this done. Soon."

I stare at Tytus, growing paler under the bedsheets. And it's not like there's any hesitation in my mind, not really. Between the bond, my growing feelings for him, and everything he's done for me... Even if I wanted to, I couldn't find a reason *not* to help him. "All right. How do I do it?"

Ileana points to the side table where an empty goblet sits. It levitates in the air towards me, lingering for a beat. "Blood is the first step," she says. "Add yours. And I will add a sprinkle of immortal magic."

I wonder if it's primordial magic she's wielding, and if that's why it's so powerful. Not that I can ask, I have a feeling neither of them would take kindly to the fact Tytus shared that bit of information with me.

So rather than satisfy my curiosity, I nod and grab the goblet. Făt tosses a dagger to me, which I use to bleed my index finger. As drops of blood trickle into the cup, I glance towards Ileana. "More?"

She tilts her head to the side. "It depends how much he is worth to you. A few drops will give him a few hours. A full goblet may win you a few days."

With a shake of the head, I move the dagger to my vein instead, and slice through the flesh. Blood pours and the room around me spins, but I hold tight onto the goblet, making sure nothing spills. Once it's full, I hand it to Ileana and focus enough to blast a healing spell. It fails–miserably–and blood keeps pouring down my forearm.

Swaying now, I force myself to sit on the bed next to Tytus. Mutters that sound like curses fill my ears, then Făt is there, kneeling in front of me. He grabs my wrist harshly, and I whimper at the pain. I want to smack him, but then he lifts his other hand and with one sweep, he heals my wound.

"T-thank you." As if he did nothing, he gets up and retreats to a corner of the room. Wow. Immortals.

I focus back on Ileana, more in possession of my faculties now. Her eyes are glinting a million shades as she focuses some kind of golden energy onto the goblet. It hurts to stare, yet I can't take my eyes away from it. Finally, she hands me the cup.

"What am I supposed to do with it?"

She points to Tytus. "Make him drink it. And, as you do so, focus on that bond of yours. And picture him healed."

With the cryptic instructions, she steps away until she's near Făt. I watch for a moment as he opens his arms, and she melts into his embrace, then force myself to look away. The moment seems intimate, and theirs, and I don't want to intrude.

I sigh, then tilt the goblet to Tytus' lips. "Please drink, Tytus," I whisper to him. "Be okay... Be whole, again."

As every drop of the blood meets his lips, and he swallows it, I focus on what Ileana said. Tytus whole. Tytus healthy. Tytus awake. With me. Kissing me. Holding me. My body warms, and at first I think I'm blushing. But it's more than that. Heat suffuses me, traveling up my arm, into the goblet, and into Tytus. I watch in fascination as the burgundy light continues to travel, on and on, and on....

Once the cup is empty, I place it on the bed-side table and sink into the mattress, barely able to stand. "Now what?" I mumble.

"Now, you wait," a whisper comes.

Vaguely, I notice Ileana and Făt walk out of the room. But I'm so tired, so lazy suddenly, all I can do is crawl into bed with Tytus and hug his chest. The slow rise and fall of his breath lulls my exhausted body to sleep.

¥

Somehow, I'm aware of him being awake. I glance up, finding the stormy gaze locked on mine. Stubble on his cheek. Heated eyes staring at me.

He licks his lips, then his hoarse voice rings. "What did you do, Fiona?"

Something in his tone warns me he's on the edge. I try to pull back, but Tytus tightens his arm around me, stopping my retreat. "Tell me."

"You… The miasma was full of Declan's venom. A trap. It made you worse. Ileana showed up and told me how the legătură bond puts me in a unique position to save your life. And explained how that could be done. I made a choice… Simple as that."

One moment, I'm in control, the next

Tytus has me on my back, hovering over me, his hard body pressed against mine. Heat blossoms in my chest, pools between my legs, and I arch against him. Tytus gazes at me for a long beat, his features unreadable.

Then his expression softens, and tenderness fills his eyes as he caresses my cheek. "Simple choice, da?"

His nose touches mine, then he nuzzles all the way down my neck, to my collarbone. Somewhere in between, I forget to breathe.

"Do you not realize what you did, my beautiful, selfless witch?" He lifts his head. "You linked us together, creating an even more unbreakable bond. It makes resisting you harder than it already was."

I stare at him, surprised at the tenderness in his expression. "It seems a small price to pay for having you back alive." The words are a mere whisper.

Lightning crosses his eyes then, and he lowers his mouth to mine. I'm too happy he's alive to even consider stopping him.

¥

Later that same evening, we stand in front of the rubble in the West Wing. Perhaps it was some stroke of luck that the Serafim mage tried to kill me, who knows? Either way, this is the best clue we have.

Tytus throws me a confused look. "And you're sure Ileana said that?"

I nod. "Yes. She was adamant we are running out of time, and since I found the fang here, I figured it was a good spot to start searching."

The last thing I wanted was to listen to the immortals, but Tytus seems recovered, and Ileana made it sound urgent. Plus, with Declan so easily in my head, I don't want to waste more time.

After a brief hesitation, I amend my answer to Tytus. "To be perfectly honest, Ileana also seemed nervous of Declan's reach. It wasn't so much in what she said, but the way she said it. And... I'm also afraid. If he can get in my mind so easily, I just..."

We stare in the dark hole, then Tytus nods and intertwines our fingers. "Nu, you are correct, sweetling. We knew his link to you was strong because of the zmeu magic you still use. But more and more I'm starting to believe our growing bond is allowing him to reach out. The sooner we get this done, the better."

He draws a rune in the air and soft puffs of wind surround us as we jump through. With Tytus' magic, we hit the ground floating, and I breathe easier. He squeezes my hand, and we go down what seems like a dark tunnel until we reach a dead end.

He scowls. "Damn Declan and his mind games!"

I bring up the pouch I'd found and take out the fang. "This isn't a normal artifact," I whisper, afraid to raise my tone. "But assuming Declan has some creature down here, through some secret passage, how would that threaten the entire world?"

Tytus exhales loudly. "I don't know."

He releases me and gets closer to the wall, inspecting every inch. Then, in complete contrast to his usual cool, he growls and punches it. Once, twice, three times. He smacks his fist against the wall, again and again. Frustration makes his back muscles rigid, and I move closer before he can hurt himself. When he reaches back to hit the immovable wall again, I grasp his arm with both my hands, digging my heels in to offset his force.

"Stop! Tytus, we'll figure it out." At my touch, he freezes, then drops his arm. I have a feeling he's doing it more to avoid hurting me, than because he's truly done beating the crap out of the wall, so I try to distract him. "At least we found this place. There must be a reason for it."

When he remains silent, I squeeze his shoulder. "We'll figure it out."

He shrugs. "Declan was always crafty, even as a young child. He drove the elders insane, and our parents even more so. After that stupid, idiotic prophecy of a Dark and Light zmeu... I didn't think it could hurt us. I had the foolish belief that our bond would last through anything, that we would always be there for each other. Protecting our land, together." He scowls more at the wall. "He left me a note, when I first arrived. It was a taunt, I realize that now. He wants me to talk to him, in person."

"Do you think that's wise?"

"The spell you did won't keep me awake forever. And I won't risk you using vital energy to save me again, not when I'm the one supposed to protect you. I must figure this out while my forces are at their strongest, that way I can fight whatever is beyond this."

"Let me come with you, then."

"I will not put you in front of Declan. He stays away from you now, probably knowing I'm around. Let us keep it that way."

"Tytus–"

"Please."

I sigh, knowing further pleading is useless. We head back up, but the entire time I'm trying to hide my worry. Tytus only now got better–and not even fully. What happens if Declan really gets into his head? What if I lose him before we've even had time to explore what this might become between us?

Back upstairs, Tytus holds out his hand. He must read some of my concern as he touches my cheek. "I'll be fine. Ileana and Făt have Declan handled."

I nod, but another worry nags at me. One I cannot name.

Chapter 9

Bunătate

"No act of kindness, however small, is ever wasted."

-Aesop-

Tytus

That night, I stare at the ceiling until I'm burning daggers in it. My restless energy won't allow for sleep. Perhaps I've had too much of it for three days, causing my body to be so alert.

Whichever the case, as I lie there, all I can think of is Fiona. Her courage to use the magic of her vital energy to save me, even if only temporarily. Her bravery, to trust Ileana and Făt when everything told her not to. And even earlier today, to stand in front of a place Declan had been, and be able to speak to me of what she thinks he would be doing.

The little witch may not realize it, but she is on her way to healing. Scars like what Declan, Thiago and Cade left behind will not heal easily. But Fiona has managed to move past them, to turn them into strengths. To take the darkness and make it light, same as I told her that one night in the cavern.

Which only makes me wonder what she would do if I revealed our bond is as impossible to avoid as the daylight. That eventually, my zmeu will demand I claim her as I see fit–as *he* sees fit. And that it will lead to a trial by fire, as literal as it is dangerous.

I wonder, will her bravery surprise me, then? Or only confirm what I have known since watching the last of my race die off... That I am condemned to a life alone, forever and always?

Thoughts of mating and Fiona only lead to other images in my head, which raise my temperature to levels unseen. When not even a cold shower helps, I leave my quarters and wander through the castle.

Everything is silent, as it should be.

Golden gleams light my path, radiating reflections of the moon. My feet lead me all the way to the chasm in the West Wing, and I peer down at the darkened depths. If only I could figure out what Declan meant here...

As before, echoes of the past come to haunt me.

Declan and I walked these walls together. What possessed him to go against me like this? He was always a mischievous spirit, and I know his hate for humans was cultivated by many screw-ups. But to turn our childhood home into a weapon of destruction...

Eventually, I head back to my room—and stop dead in my tracks. Fiona is standing at my window, the light of the moon making her gown almost transparent. I hiss loud enough that she jumps and turns around.

"What are you doing here, Fiona?"

The hand at her throat drops. "Finishing what we started."

"In what way, exactly?"

"I think you know." When I say

nothing, simply stare, daring her to finish, Fiona takes a deep breath. "We're both adults, and we've been dancing around this long enough. Let's stop, and act. If there's one thing I know, is life is too short. I have cravings, and evidently so do you."

"My zmeu alone rules my cravings," I practically growl.

"Sure." Fiona smiles. "But it's your human form that's suffering, no? Just like I am. I'm tired of living in fear, Tytus, in anticipation of bad things happening. I want to choose something good for me. Just once."

Fuck me. See what you started? My zmeu doesn't answer, lulled instead by the possibility of getting what he wants.

Despite my hesitation, already I'm moving closer, drawn by Fiona's ethereal appearance, by the way the moonlight shines off her hair. By the vulnerability in her tone, the confidence in her gaze. "You're playing with fire."

"Then let me get burned."

She removes the last space between us and kisses me, her tongue tracing my lips. I let her have control for a moment, perhaps two, until I can't stand it anymore. I pick her in my arms and turn to the bed, lying her down gently.

"I'm stronger than this," I whisper. "I should be able to resist you–this temptation. So why can't I?"

Fiona lifts a hand to my cheek. "I'm done trying to figure that out."

When she pulls me atop her, I allow it, the sweet torture of her body under mine. I kiss down her throat, then remove her nightgown and kiss every inch I can get my lips on. She writhes under me, panting and whimpering my name. It sounds so good on her lips, I could get drunk on it.

Taking my sweet time, I nibble up her thighs until I'm kneeling between her legs. I glance up once, and our eyes meet. Fiona's breathing is erratic, and I smile as I let one finger slowly enter her, watching as she throws her head back and groans. Her hips rise to meet my second thrust, and I'm tasting her until she explodes on my tongue.

As she's panting, returning from her ecstasy, I kiss back up her body until our mouths meet again in the softest of embraces. My body yearns for so much more, but I won't go that far. I want her to have this one moment to herself, to understand she is worth caring for. That this isn't just a quick fuck. This isn't lust. It goes deeper–bone deep.

Instead of taking the next step, I lie down by her sleepy self. The way she rolls into my arms, sinking into my embrace, is all the gratitude I need.

"Tytus… Let me…"

Questing fingers trail down my stomach, and lower, but I stop her wandering hand before it kills me. "That was all for you, sweetling. Sleep. Be at peace."

As I hold her, I wonder how to hide this new development from Declan. If he finds out, I won't put it past him to fuck us both over. And though there's the mission, I need Fiona to be safe. In fact, I want so much from her–and *for* her.

Fucking hell. I'm falling for her. The realization hits me like a ton of bricks, stealing my breath and the hope of any rest.

Fiona

I wake up first this time and spend the better part of the morning watching different shades of light play off Tytus' features. Even in sleep, he doesn't seem relaxed. If it wasn't for the heaviness of his arm around my waist, and the slow rise and fall of his chest, I would think he was getting ready for war.

Little by little, I edge out of my shyness and trace his collarbone. Tytus stirs in his sleep, mumbles something under his breath, then settles down again. I let out a breath I didn't even realize I was holding.

That's twice now he brought me ecstasy, without ever asking for anything in return. My experiences with men may be few and far between, but surely this isn't a regular occurrence for a man not to get his pleasure. I owe it to him... Don't I?

As I keep tracing his skin, my thoughts unravel further and further. How precious he made me feel–how worthy. Of attention, of desire, of... caring. I won't say the other word, I cannot even think it. But Tytus *made me* think of it.

"Where is your mind at?" His soft rumble startles me, and I jerk my head up. Those gray eyes gaze at me, filled with longing, and more.

Once more, I sense the pull. But the lust in my veins is for once overwhelmed by something more. A need for a connection, a deeper kind.

"I... just thinking of last night," I say, and blush furiously. With an effort, I hold his gaze and not look away.

His hand comes up to my cheek, and he shifts in a way that brings me up further against him, and higher so we're nose to nose. His thumb traces my lower lip, and he grins.

"I take it you enjoyed yourself?"

At a loss, I nod. Tytus seems satisfied with my response, as he pulls me closer and brushes his lips against mine. Just as I'm hoping for a repeat performance—one that will end with our mutual satisfaction—he lets go of me.

The moment after, he jumps out of bed, lazily tracing a rune to clothe himself.

"Where are you going?"

"To see Declan," he says.

"What, now!?"

Tytus sighs and turns to me. "I have to, Fiona. We're getting nowhere with these clues, and you've said yourself Ileana and Făt made it clear it's a priority."

"Screw them!" My shout surprises him as much as me. I try to even my tone, but fail at sounding neutral. Panicked is more like it. "You can't go. Not alone. Let me at least come with you!"

"Not an option," he says. "I've hurt you enough by putting you in direct contact with him. Now that we know how he has streamlined his link to your mind, there is no way I will allow this to go any further. I'll speak to my brother, alone. It is time for some one-on-one interaction."

"Tytus, please... I have a bad feeling about this."

He kneels on the mattress just enough to kiss me again, before pulling away. "Rest some more, please. I'll be back before you know it."

A moment later, he disappears through

the massive doors of his bedroom. But I cannot lie here while he puts himself in danger. If nothing else, I can continue my explorations. And if Tytus' plan fails with Declan, we will have mine as backup.

Tytus

Fiona's kiss still lingers on my lips when I cross the threshold of my palace. I should focus on the next step ahead, yet I am anything but. How did I go from lusting after the witch, to wanting her by my side–forever? I blame my zmeu for starting it, for getting us all wrapped up in the desire of it all. But I'm just as much at fault for continuing it.

Not that I can do anything at this point. The dice are cast, my zmeu has chosen, and I... have given in. Happily. Doesn't mean I can't spend the next few months trying to figure out exactly where I fell for Fiona.... Somehow, I doubt I'll get much of an answer from the fates.

Suppressing a groan, I look around and speak, "Ileana."

Instead of the immortal, it is her consort who shows up. "Changed your mind, I take it?" Is Făt's greeting.

"Where's Ileana?"

"Indisposed." I could say the same for him. I've seen him in a foul mood, but today it's even worse.

The moment after his proclamation, he lifts his hand and seems to pull on the air. It shimmers, glows, and a dark hole emerges, looking less appealing by the second.

"After you," Făt gestures.

I step in, feeling like a vortex has taken hold of me. Once I exit the portal, I'm in a different area of the Carpathian mountains. A growl tears from my throat. "Did you actually imprison my brother this close to me?"

Făt emerges from the portal behind me, but only stares. I fight back the impulse to rearrange his features.

"Have you spent perhaps *too* much time with humans?" His annoyed question is followed by a slight narrowing of the eyes. Then the landscape around us changes. "It's a mirage, zmeu. Designed to let you see what you wish."

As I peer around again, I'm no longer seeing the Carpathian Mountains. Instead, we are in a land devoid of any vegetation. The ground seems burned to ashes, and an acrid smell lingers in the air. Darkness coats every corner, rather than the light of the free sun I am used to.

This is definitely not home, but I refuse to rise to the bait. "Show me to my brother."

Făt rolls his eyes and turns on his heels, leaving me to trail after him. Each time, we pass through a portal, until I lose count of how many continents and realms we cross. Eventually, we emerge into a cave.

It doesn't feel like a cave, though. Rather, it's cold and manmade, similar to a monument. I follow in silence and cross one last barrier.

"Enjoy," Făt says. Is it me or is there a slight sheen of sweat on his forehead? "He is in a foul mood today."

Seems to be going around.

He leaves before I can say anything, so I head to the cell. The minute I enter, my eyes fall on Declan. He's picking at his teeth with a bone. In the corner is a lamb, or what's left of one.

"Took you long enough, frate."

He faces me, lips curled in a sneer, wearing nothing but a pair of jeans. His golden eyes reflect the flames on the walls, and his blond hair is cropped now, much shorter than when I saw him last. Two large cuffs are around his wrists, but still he moves around with his usual feline grace.

"Ileana has a funny sense of humor," he smirks, lifting his hands. "She's gone and turned me into a blasted genie."

"I don't see a lamp nearby."

Declan snorts. "That's because she holds it." He spits the bone he'd been toying with and grins my way. It doesn't warm his expression in the slightest. "Why are you here?"

"You know why. Your little games have run their course."

He pretends to look at his cuffs. "You never were very patient, hmm, Tytus?"

Rather than launch myself at him, I pace around. Ileana and Făt did a good job with his prison. I can sense the power emanating from the stone itself, muting my abilities. I couldn't conjure a storm if I tried and even trying to think of Fiona is hard. Which begs the question of how Declan got through to her, time and time again.

A shadow moves outside the metal door. It's only Făt, but his nervous pacing adds to my own restlessness. I focus my attention on Declan again.

"Interesting prison. It suits you."

A flash of anger in his eyes, gone just as quickly. I smirk. "You always were a tad claustrophobic, if I remember well."

"You should. You're the one who condemned me to a life of misery."

"For the last time, Declan. I didn't know they would keep you imprisoned. If it had been up to me, you would have been dead. Period."

Declan's expression shifts, for a second. Another noise outside distracts me. And in that same moment of inattention he's on me, slamming me against the nearest wall.

"Well then, let me give you your wish!" he snarls in my face.

There's a mad glint in his eyes, even as his nails sink into my throat, attempting to choke me. I sense an odd sharp bite coming from deep within me, but it's gone just as quick. Then Făt is there, pulling Declan off me, and unsheathing his sword.

Declan keeps his distance, almost flattening himself against the wall to avoid it.

"I warned you this was a waste," Făt mutters over his shoulder to me.

I glare at Declan. "You were right." As I turn to leave, Declan laughs. It's so cold, it makes the hairs at the back of my neck stand to attention.

"Frate, did you so easily forget our childhood games?"

I face him again, slowly. A victorious smirk curls his lips. "I always was the better master of snakes... Too bad your witch is about to run into my greatest achievement yet."

By the time I realize what he means, it's too late. And when Făt finally gets me out of there, I run like hell through the portals, hoping I can get there in time.

Declan

Rage makes my pacing harsh. After Tytus and Făt leave, I kick and pummel the door, roaring at the outside. To no avail, of course. I know I'm not getting out of here by sheer brute force, but one cannot fault me for a moment's madness.

Moments later, after they're gone, I go back to a corner and lean against it, then close my eyes. It won't be long, only a moment, but it'll be all I need to satisfy my curiosity.

I focus my thoughts on the little witch, picture her white hair streaked with violet, and see her clear in my head. She's heading to the library... *Perfect. Not much longer, now.*

With a huge effort, I shift away from her and straight to Tytus. I'm only allowed a moment's glance, but the sheer panic in his mind is enough to make me grin wildly. *About time you feel some of my pain, frate.*

Once I pull back, I'm calmer. At least for the time being.

And then the air fills with the scent of berries and the mountains of my home, and a true grin stretches my face as I lie back down, closing my eyes. "Back for more already, darling?"

All thoughts of my brother and his witch leave my mind, as my favorite visitor pops by my dreams for another taste.

Fiona

Recalling Tytus' words of warning, I try to fight the compulsion of going hunting for more information without him. Yet boredom hits within hours of Tytus' disappearance. My body is restless, craving him. And thinking. Always damn thinking, without an off button.

As I roam the halls of the castle, my feet lead me to the library. Books bound in beautiful leather, some with golden letters, high ceilings and shelves that reach them. I walk around, letting my hands trace the spines.

Did Tytus read all of these? He must have, he's been around for ages. I try to imagine what it would be like to live so long. Didn't he ever get lonely? Especially as his kind was killed?

Despite my attempt to compare the scholar to the ruthless zmeu, the patient mentor, and the skilled lover, it falls short. None of these facets are alike, yet they're all part of him. Could it be, then, that Declan has various masks, too?

My fingers freeze on a work called *Duality*. How odd, that thought. After everything he put me through... Yet, he never crossed certain lines. Perhaps that's where my confusion is stemming from. Declan had control of my mind, of my body at a time. It would have suited his needs to have me use said body to enchant even further the wolves he wanted on his side.

He never did.

And though Thiago and Cade beat me, starved me, kept me chained and used me for my powers, they also never used me sexually. Like an unspoken rule.

Would men in their places of power, with such low morals, have followed said rule, without a more powerful someone telling them to?

You're losing it, Fiona. I huff out a

breath, pushing the thoughts away. Just because one brother is good, does not mean the other is, too. I would be a fool to search for good in Declan. Surely there is none left, not if he is willing to play with his brother's life as he is.

After the tenth book or so, one particular tome draws my attention. The edges are a little too frayed, as if someone took it out and read it multiple times. I carefully flip to the table of contents.

The first thing that strikes me is that it's in English. The second is the writing–tight, neat, swooping strokes. Bold. Like Tytus.

Could this be a book he wrote?

I flip through more pages and land on a date.

January 2, 1092 B.C.

The Council is at it again. I write these records in English, knowing full well they will not bother with them. I am the only one who sees this language—my visions of the future still haunt me. They get worse every night.

But that is besides the point. What is the use of knowing these words, these things that may happen, if I cannot make head or tail of them?

And the Council speaks of moving again. Another kingdom. Another attempt to escape those renegade Templar knights. The Pope may have recognized the real ones as an Order intent to protect Christianity, but I alone have dealt with the fanatics, the ones calling themselves the Order of Serafim. They hate our kind, yet see no problem using necromancers to kill us. I fear this is only the beginning...

The reality of how old Tytus must be, all the events he lived through, hits me all over again. I flip through more entries and stop midway through the book.

August 7, 888 B.C.

After a brief period of rest, we are at war again with the dragon clans of the north. No amount of mediation from the Council will help.

It is getting dangerous, and I fear even our leadership has lost focus. The latest accident with the vasilisc has not helped, though they have imprisoned it deep where it belongs. It is a good choice, as killing the beast would have made more than one of us weak. We cannot afford that. Not now.

I glance up from the account. Vasilisc? I've seen that before. Distracted, I place the journal on the center table and go back to the other books. I find the account I had seen before in the book on myths and legends. A vasilisc–they describe it as a large serpent whose gaze can turn you to stone. Its venom, however, can be airborne and it renders even the strongest creatures weak, able to eat through their magic and practically anything. And at the end of the tome, hidden among other pages, is something else. A clue.

Eyes wide, I rip it out, drop the book on the table and rush out of the library. My feet pitter patter on the floor, my breathing loud in my ears. I know Tytus will be angry when he returns, but I have to test out my theory.

So I head down the rubble, into the darkness below the West Wing and use magic to light up a path. I'm reminded of the stories I read the other day. Zmei eating maidens. Maidens trying to escape. And with every hurried step, I'm hoping to hell I find nothing I cannot win against down here...

One peek. After I confirm I'm right, I'll wait for Tytus to return, and he'll be relieved we found another clue.

My throat dries and I force my hands into fists to hide their trembling. Finally, I'm back in front of the wall. The same one we couldn't get past. I pull out the piece of paper I'd found in the book, full of runes. This may be a stupid idea, but it's worth a shot.

Stepping closer, I draw each rune in the sequence the paper outlines, before moving backwards. Nothing happens for a moment, and then the runes shine bright red, bright blue, and the ground shakes. I fear it'll cause the entire tunnel to collapse, the way everything rattles. Surprisingly, it doesn't. The wall in front of me simply crumbles, like someone took a hammer and shattered it.

Rather than decide that I've done enough, I step through the damage and into the even darker pathway past it. My reasoning is, I want to make sure there's no other noxious miasma that could hurt Tytus. That's a legitimate worry, right?

Only, I didn't count on the tunnel suddenly giving way into some kind of arched room. And in its midst is... A massive, ugly as sin serpent. Easily half the size of Tytus' zmeu, its scaly body is a dark green color with streaks of mustard and muddy brown. The tail seems way too fat, and the body undulates side to side as it circles the room.

And then, culmination of all curses, the vasilisc stops moving. My first instinct is to close my eyes. But if I do that, I'm completely blind to its advances. Shit. A rumble echoes, and the giant snake slithers toward me. I don't even have time to move.

One moment it's drifting, the next it's lunging across the distance, its massive fangs extended. I try a rune–it only bounces off the scales.

I jump out of the way and the vasilisc misses me, but in my rush to escape I end up tripping over a piece of the wall, and fall to the floor. Something pierces my leg, and

I scream, drawing the beast towards me again.

Recalling the deadly power of its gaze, I try to avoid looking at it–and instead glance down.

My wound is bleeding profusely. And the creature is inching closer with uncanny precision. The damn beast is probably using my wound to track me. *Shit. Shit. Shit.*

I rip part of my shirt and use it to make a bandage, pulling it tighter around my leg, and forcing myself to look away. Out of my periphery, movement draws my attention and I risk a glance. A blur of something passes me... and my eyes land on Tytus.

Chapter 10

Orbire

"Forgive yourself for the blindness that lets others betray you. Sometimes a good heart doesn't see the bad."

-Unknown-

Fiona

Sweat pours over Tytus' body, and he's panting as if he ran all the way over here. How did he even find me? A stronger realization pushes at the forefront of all my questions. He's standing between me and the beast–facing it!

"Tytus, watch out! It's a vasilisc! Its gaze–"

"I know," he says calmly. "Get out of here." Not once does he turn to check on me. His entire focus is on the vasilisc, and the blasted snake isn't even moving.

It slithered backwards when Tytus walked in, and now it's swaying side to side. While Tytus is in human form, the huge serpent is almost three times his size. How the hell is he planning to defeat the thing? Especially when he's not even wielding magic—instead, he has a sword.

"Fiona, MOVE!" Tytus yells, turning his head to the side for a fraction of a second.

I have no choice. With a groan, I scramble to my feet and limp away, holding onto my bleeding leg. I evade the midst of the fight, ignoring the hisses of the beast. I'll be hearing those for the next months as I sleep.

Tucked behind a stone column, I slide back to the floor and unravel my leg. A quick glance around the corner shows Tytus and the vasilisc still facing off, as if they're sizing each other up.

I return my focus to my wound. The loss of blood is starting to make me woozy. I lift my hand in the air, ready to pull on the zmeu magic I've used in the past. The same one that kept me at bay from the snake.

And then I recall how easily the beast swatted it away, and gulp. Perhaps it's time to trust in my own brand of magic, and no one else's. If using the zmeu magic is truly what is still linking me to Declan, it's about damn time I cut the cord and stop giving in to something so addictive.

Easier said than done.

When I first try to reach my core, the pull of the magic won't come. Not even to heal me. When I used it on Tytus, it rose easily enough because I was emotional and knew I had no choice. His death was simply not an option. Now, for myself... it seems the same insecurities linger.

A scrap of metal has my ears perking– Tytus must be on the move, fighting.

I stare at my leg, gritting my teeth and trying not to faint at the sight of all the blood. I press my palms to the gushing stream and grit my teeth. This time, I keep my eyes wide open as I reach inside and pull on the magic within me. On the core of energy that is in me, that pushes everything I do, and so much more.

Finally, it gives in–for me. Not for someone else, not for a good deed, but for *me*. Magic streams out of my hands in white rivulets of healing energy, and wraps around the blood. Little by little, the flow ebbs away, until it completely heals my wound. The end result is as good as the immortals' healing, I must say.

I take a deep breath, center myself, and slowly get up. The wall is at my fingertips, ready to catch me if I fall, but to my surprise I'm… all right. Able to walk. Able to move.

I waste no time in turning the corner, then come to a standstill. I'd seen Tytus fight the knights in all his glorious swordsmanship. But, somehow, that doesn't prepare me for his attacks on the monster.

Despite the strain on his muscles, he holds the sword two-handed and is barefoot on the cool stone floor. Yet he moves without incumbents, as if he was born gripping a blade. As if this is where he belongs, parrying and slashing, ready to take on the bloody beast.

And as I watch him, I can't help admiring

his skill. The vasilisc feints right, and Tytus lunges after him. Left, right, he parries and the beast shoots a glob of dark venom he only barely avoids. The creature seems to register me sitting on the sidelines, and it angles its next glob towards me.

My attention is split, which is why I see the danger too late. But at the last minute Tytus yells something and a flash, like a barrier, lands in front of me. My shocked gaze collides with Tytus'. He protected me, at a risk to himself.

The vasilisc doesn't wait. It snaps towards Tytus, but I'm too far away and it moves too fast for me to realize whether he struck him or not. For a brief moment, Tytus wavers on his feet, then clenches the sword tighter and lashes out once more. The strain on his features makes me think he's been hurt, but his movements are even faster and angrier than before.

A moment later, Tytus drops. It's so sudden, the vasilisc hisses in victory. My turn to protect him has come, and same as he didn't, I don't bother debating. I run ahead, placing myself between the creature and

Tytus, my palms held up as if to fight him off.

"Fiona..." Tytus pants behind me, but he's unable to move.

"I got this." Focusing my entire energy on the advancing vasilisc, I pull once more in my core, only this time it's not healing I need. Instead, I toss the same protective barrier over us as I did many times in the caverns.

The vasilisc stares, a glint of menacing fire in its eyes, and hisses. It's probably thinking the barrier won't hold–and it wouldn't be wrong. So I jerk my free hand towards the side of the wall. Their fighting has caused a section of it to crumble, and it's those ruins I focus on.

With a jerk of my wrist, my magic leaves me and surrounds the stones, levitating them in the air. I'm panting at the exertion–this kind of thing used to be fun when I was young. How long, exactly, has it been since I've used my real magic?

Finally, just as the vasilisc advances, I toss the rocks towards it. They fly and dump on it, crushing its enormous slithering body underneath. More of the surrounding miasma fills the air, and I turn away, coughing.

So this is where Declan's venom had come from... But how would he have locked his venom in a room with a beast that's supposed to have been extinct?

My gaze lands on Tytus, unconscious on the ground. I kneel next to him, pushing away the hair on his forehead. He's feverish, like before, and a quick glance under his eyelids shows me dilated pupils. Declan's venom—it must be flowing through him again. Which means the reason for his sudden weakness had nothing to do with the damn vasilisc, but with his brother.

"What happened with Declan?" I ask Tytus.

He stirs against my hand, and his eyes open wide. "Watch out!"

I whirl on my knees, automatically placing myself to shield him. The vasilisc has been sneaking up on us, and its massive body throws itself on the barrier. The strength of it surprises me—especially when it bounces the damn beast backwards and makes the entire cavern rattle.

Behind me, Tytus pulls his sword, and it scrapes the ground as he uses it to stand. "Leave, Fiona."

"I won't."

He turns to me, pain etched on his every feature. "Leave."

For the first time, I feel the power of his persuasion seep in, coating my thoughts and rearranging them to fit his own demands. I don't know if it's because he's tired, or if he's doing it on purpose. But he's breaking a promise, and it pisses me off. More than that, it scares me.

"You swore you'd never use it on me."

Regret flashes in his eyes. "I'll do it if it means keeping you safe, Fiona. *Leave.*"

My feet move without my permission, and before I know it I'm away. He's inside my head, pushing me further and further from him, until I turn on my heels and reluctantly walk myself out.

The rest of my movements are a blur of me struggling and failing against his mental hold on me. Same as with Declan, it's useless. He has me fully at his mercy, doing his bidding, and with each step away from him, something breaks inside me.

I want to hate Tytus for breaking his promise, for leaving himself so weak in front of that creature. For forcing me to do something against my will, when he swore to me he never would. What was the point of it, to get me out safe and sound? What if he doesn't survive, weakened as he is?

By the time his hold releases me, I'm back up in the destroyed West Wing, at the mouth of the hole, and I drop to my knees. I'm a mess of tears and shaking sweats, beating my hands against the edge of the opening.

"Tytus! Tytus!" Nothing answers me, not that I expect it to.

Moments pass by. Seconds trickle into minutes that feel like they're turning into hours. I get ahold of myself, wipe the snot and tears off my face, and start pacing back and forth.

Tytus broke his promise. He used his power on me. He used it… despite swearing he never would.

I'm no fool, I know there were extenuating circumstances. But does that excuse what he did, if it's to save my life? And if I excuse him now, will this become a habit? The last thing I need is to be involved with a zmeu who can have me dancing at his whim.

Been there, done that. Only this time, it's worse. Because I'm emotionally involved with Tytus, and I trust him. Trust*ed* him, or trust him still?

Finally, I hear scrapes in the crater, drawing attention from my confusing thoughts. I freeze, not knowing whether it's the beast freed, or...

Tytus staggers through the hall, holding onto the wall for support. "Fiona..."

My heart stutters in relief. But even as I make my way towards him, his grip slackens, his eyes roll in the back of his head, and he drops at my feet.

¥

Unlike before, Ileana and Făt don't show up this time until I've gotten Tytus settled into his room. I'm putting a cold compress on his forehead, even when I know it's a futile attempt to bring down the fever.

That's when they walk in. Before either of them speaks, I'm first to jump from the bed and bar their way. Because another possibility occurred to me, something that would explain Tytus' behaviour, and his breaking the promise. And this particular possibility would also conveniently absolve him, if it's true.

Only way to find out. Hands on my hips, I scowl at the immortals. "What happened when Tytus went to see Declan?"

"I wasn't there," Ileana says and turns to Făt, an inquisitive expression on her features. "Well?"

He shrugs. The movement seems more tired than before, less insensitive. But I don't know them well enough to make such calls, so I focus on his words. "Brotherly rivalry."

"There's got to be more than that!"

"What makes you think it?" Ileana asks.

I glance between them and Tytus. "When he returned, it was to save me from what I found buried underground. A vasilisc."

Ileana frowns. "That is all?"

"What do you mean, *all*? Isn't it enough?" I gesture at Tytus' unconscious form. "He's not acting like himself. His visit with Declan weakened him, so something must have happened! The venom in him started acting up, burning him from the inside."

Făt says nothing for a long time, then snaps his fingers. "They fought. Declan put his hands on Tytus, and his touch, his rage, probably burned through all the protections you had given him."

I can practically feel the color drain out of my cheeks, and I hold on to the wall for stability. All my work, the vital energy I spent, the barrier I crossed within myself for Tytus. All gone in the span of a few seconds, just because Declan *touched* him. How did I ever think I could be useful when faced against him?

The uselessness, the hopelessness, quickly morphs into anger, directed at the only two people I can. Because then my thinking could be right, and Declan could have affected a hell of a lot more than just Tytus' wounds. He could have affected his *mind*.

"So why didn't you *do* anything!?" I shout at them.

Făt's features harden at my outburst. "It is not my duty to save a zmeu from another."

"You've got to be fucking kidding me!" I yell and toss my hands up in the air. "First you push Tytus when he still needed rest, then we find what's there and you say it's not enough, and now you tell me you don't even care if he lives or dies!"

"That is not true," Ileana intervenes. "Făt is on edge. We both are. But Tytus will not die."

"How can you know that?"

"I.... Because there must be a reason we had to save Declan. Fate is not this linear, tangible concept humans believe it is. Nor is right and wrong. We live, our actions affect others and not only ourselves. Our lives converging such, does not happen simply because. There is always a reason. We simply have to wait."

I shake my head at her rambling. "Wait for what, for Tytus to recover miraculously? For Declan to make another move?"

"Speaking of moves," Făt says. "It seems Declan already knew you would find the vasilisc. But then, that is no surprise, is it?"

I don't cower under their gazes, having no trouble to read the accusation in them. "Declan still has a link to me, yes."

"And why has Tytus not broken it?"

"Don't know. We haven't discussed it, but if I were to guess, he's afraid of what it will do to my mind if he goes ahead with it."

Făt shakes his head. "Sentimental fool."

I scowl and focus on his more reasonable partner. "Well, how do we fix him this time around?"

"Tytus' prior injuries have not fully healed," Ileana says, "and Declan's reignition of his venom has only added to the strain on his body. The problem is, we have no way of stopping that venom from doing what it is meant to."

"Declan could, though?" It's not the best of ideas, but do I really have another choice? If it means begging him for help, I am not beyond it. And I'm more than ready to give him a piece of my mind, rather than let him keep intervening in my life.

"Out of the question," Făt says. "Declan does not need more to hold over our heads."

"So what am I supposed to do? I cannot stand by here and do nothing!"

"Let Tytus fight it, on his own. He has lived millennia, surely something like this will not stop him." Ileana's words aren't as reassuring as I wish, especially as they sound more filled with hope than certainty.

I drop on the bed, holding Tytus' clammy hand in mine. I can deal with the betrayal, with my feelings, but after. If we don't stop Declan's venom, if it keeps attacking Tytus' immune system...

It's then that it hits me. "Venom!"

Like a crazy woman, I get back up and run out the door, ignoring their shouts. On my way down the hall, I pick up the sword Tytus had dropped and peer at it under the light. There is only blood on it, no venom.

Should've known it wouldn't be this easy. I fight back all my insecurities and feelings of not being able to do this on my own. Instead, I clench my hand on the hilt of the blade and go back down the path I'd been forced away from, back into the den of the wolf.

¥

On my way to the vasilisc, I have plenty of time to ponder my stupidity. What if the creature is still alive? Maybe Tytus only evaded it and didn't kill it. Still. I push further through, hoping that my crazy idea might work.

Eventually, I'm back in the creature's den. I tiptoe as quietly as I can, but I shouldn't have bothered. Soon as I turn a corner, I see its dead carcass lying in the middle. Whatever Tytus did, wherever he got his reserve of energy, it worked. Because there is no way this dead-eyed monster is getting back up.

I watch my step as I get closer, and focus on one of its fangs. My hand lifts and I think of all the venom in there and try to coax it out. It takes me one, two tries, and finally it oozes out of the fang. I thrust the sword forward to catch as much of it as I can until it's coating the blade.

As I back away just as slowly, I'm

reminded of what Ileana and Făt said above. What about this isn't "enough," I wonder? Which part of fighting the vasilisc didn't meet their expectations?

It's only as I'm climbing up that the pieces of the puzzle fall into place. Declan didn't mean for us to find it—he wanted it to be a trap, to catch us unawares. Probably meant for the miasma to trickle slowly in the castle, making Tytus sicker and sicker. Which means there is something more, something *worse* hiding past the vasilisc.

The only question is, will Tytus live long enough to fight it off?

With a sigh, I enter his room again. Ileana and Făt turn from the window, staring as I cross towards Tytus. Neither say anything, not even when I lift the sword to his face.

With my index finger, I swipe some venom and place it nearer his mouth, gently prodding him to open. It takes a second, two, but in his sleep, his tongue slowly peeks out and licks the venom from my fingers. Once it's all gone, I sit back on my haunches and sigh.

"What did you do?" Făt asks.

"The venom. Declan's venom is the reason for Tytus' weakness. Nothing else can stop it, especially as you won't let me see Declan."

"But?"

"I read something about the vasilisc earlier, it's what made me seek it out. If I'm to believe the books in the library, the creature can fight off most other supernaturals, including immortals." My gaze meets theirs. "I'm guessing it's why neither of you volunteered to go search the catacombs."

They don't answer, so I shrug and turn my focus back on Tytus. I replace the cooling cloth on his forehead, pressing gently. "It also says its scales have repelling powers of magic, which explains why Tytus had to use a sword to fight it. And, funny thing, the vasilisc also happens to be the only monster in the world whose venom, according to the legends here, can eat through anything, magical or otherwise." I lower my voice as I wipe Tytus' brow. "Well, my hope is its venom will also devour Declan's own brand of death."

Dead silence meets my words. "Is that where you went?" Făt almost sounds incredulous.

"Yes."

"But the creature could have been alive!"

My frown meets his surprised gaze. "Would you have hesitated, if it was for Ileana?"

"Of course not."

"Then don't have the gall to pretend like you don't understand why I did what I did."

Ileana speaks in the silence that follows, her voice soft, almost a whisper. "What happens if the venom doesn't work, Fiona? What if instead of one, Tytus ends up combating two deadly poisons in his system?"

"Then he won't survive."

And despite everything that transpired, I'm beginning to think neither will I.

Chapter 11

Salvare
"The knowledge of sin is the beginning of salvation."
-Epicurus-

Tytus

Once I lose consciousness, the fire inside me, the one that's been sapping my strength and eating at me little by little, takes over. It scorches through me, and though I have never been burned or in fear of it, this must be what humans feel.

Nothing compares to the agony, the burn, the ashy sensation in my throat. I open my mouth to scream, but nothing comes out. My jaw is locked tight, my eyes closed, and I cannot move. I'm paralyzed, captive in my body, prisoner of my thoughts, at the mercy of my memories...

"Tytus! Tytus, come on, you must see this!" I turn away from the mare I'm stroking, catching sight of blonde hair in the corner of a barn.

I try to ignore Declan, but it's no use. He comes back again, and again, until I finally give in and follow him down the mountain path. He bounces ahead, laughing, and I struggle to keep up with him.

Our human forms are in their teens, but our souls are already much older. Not that he acts anything like the wiser version he's supposed to be.

Suspicion creeps up my spine when I notice from afar he's dragging a sack after him. It looks full, and rather heavy.

"Dec, where are you taking me?"

He tosses a mischievous look over one shoulder, his golden eyes glinting. "You'll see."

I give in and continue following him. He takes me through the edge of the woods, past a stream and straight into a neck of the area that's filled with caverns. When I slow down, wary of where our adventure will take us, Declan tugs me forward.

"It'll be worth it, I promise!"

Eventually, Declan stops near a stream. We're far away from the castle now, in an area nestled between two medium-sized mountains. At first I don't get why we're here, but then I catch Declan staring at the mountain… and the cavern carved in its side. As I squint my eyes, a shadow moves inside, and I freeze. Rather than follow Declan, I hold back, watching from afar.

He moves closer, and noises—whispers—echo from within. Then a pale hand—a human hand!—comes into vision, trembling as it clenches a badly sharpened spike. "S-stai departe!"

The warning to stay away doesn't bother me. But the tone—I pull on Declan's arm, forcing him to face my anger. "You brought me to a human!"

Whimpers come from the cave, and Declan glares at me. "You've scared them! Idiot." Muttering under his breath, he moves closer to the cavern.

"Declan!"

He ignores me and kneels by the entrance. With careful movements, he pulls the sack off his back, and rummages inside. After a few tense moments, he tosses some bread and other things to the humans. Things he must've nicked from our kitchens. On the other side, past the darkness of the shelter, there's a shocked silence, then more whispers.

"Declan!" I hiss, louder this time. "Are you insane!"

"No." His jaw is set when he stands and faces me. "I'm not. See for yourself."

And then his eyes glitter, and he's in my head—as easily as ever. We've made a game of this, being in the other's head. We say it helps us from losing touch with our sanity. And it keeps us close when the elders take one of us on a hunt.

But today, Declan doesn't ask permission. And though I'm the eldest, and the best with runes, it doesn't matter. Declan means no harm. He's showing me the plight of the humans.

How he'd been flying and heard their cries of pain below. Some shifters attacked them. Declan protected them and has been feeding them in secret for days. Days! My *own brother, putting his life at risk by cavorting with humans.*

When he finally pulls away from my mind, I let out a loud exhale. "The elders will hate this."

"Please don't tell them," Declan begs, stepping closer to me. He doesn't seem determined any more, just young. So damn young. "Help me, help them, Ty. Please."

I glance between the darkness of the cavern, and my brother, and despite everything in me telling me to run, I nod. "Very well."

The memory leaves me shivering–both at Declan's ability to get in my head so fast, and his mercy towards humans. It has been so, so long since I've stopped to think of him–of the child he'd been back then. Of us, as young kids. To find out what happened. Perhaps this is my chance, my one and only chance.

Even as I think that, the scorching in my veins turns to cold fire, then pure ice. Agony fills me of a different kind, and my teeth start chattering–or is that my body shaking so hard? All I know is the darkness pulls me deeper and deeper...

Fiona

"You should rest a while."

I lift my head off the bed, meeting Ileana's gaze. My eyelids feel heavy, and my eyes are close to drooping. Am I not sleeping, already?

Shaking my head, I mutter, "No. I need to watch over him."

"I will continue standing guard," Ileana says.

"No offense, but I don't trust you or your husband."

Ileana snorts.

"Did I say something funny?"

She glances over at Făt, asleep by the window. "Făt is not my husband."

My mind is too tired to grasp the meaning behind her words. "I don't... Then what is he?"

"He is my consort."

When all I do is arch an eyebrow in confusion, Ileana chuckles. "Marriage is a human contraption that humans devised to ensnare each other. Immortals, and shifters, do not play by such rules."

I think back to my parents, happily married. "I don't agree with that. Marriage can be good. Like anything else, it depends in whose hands it grows. Same with magic. Same with religion."

Ileana tilts her head, as if considering my words. "Perhaps. And yet... If marriage can be so good, what is it that keeps you from tying the knot with Tytus?"

"The *what*?" Făt grunts in his sleep at my shout, and I lower my voice. A day ago, her assumption would have enchanted me, maybe. Now, it fills me with dread. "First off, Tytus and I are nowhere near that point. And, um, we weren't even talking about us. You were explaining about your...consort."

Ileana smiles. "Făt and I are two sides of the same coin. While shifters have mates, and zmei have a *pereche*—a pair—we have consorts. It is a union of the soul, that passes through time, space, everything. Neither one of us could live without the other."

"Isn't that... I don't know, harsh?"

"No," Ileana chuckles. "It is our life, and a good one. Eternity is nothing without the person you love at your side. And, Făt has always been that for me."

"Really? There was never anyone else?"

Her eyes twinkle. "One, or two... Perhaps even one with whom I had a strong connection, strong enough to pursue something. But Făt was meant for me and..." She glances at him, and her smile grows brighter. "He is everything to me."

I stare at Tytus, feeling my heart swell. "Yeah, I can understand that." Despite my mind fighting against it, despite my wariness after his betrayal, it is a reaction I cannot fight against.

"Then why the hesitation?"

I feel her attention on me, scrutinizing and uncomfortable. Like a coward, I take Tytus' hand in mine and squeeze it, then trace his fingers. They feel hot to my touch, and even as I trace them, they burn hotter still.

"Tytus told me about the... legătură." I struggle to say the word–*leh-guh-tuh-rah*– but somehow stumble it past my lips. "But I... I have trust issues. Things I've seen, lived through, don't make it easy to let someone in. Not to the extent Tytus expects it."

"Does he?"

I look at her with a frown. "Does he what?"

"Expect it."

"I... Maybe, maybe not. Either way, the connection he speaks of, it's not something that can be taken slow and rationally. To meet each other, see if we're a good fit. It's a lot more complicated than that."

"It is raw, primal," Ileana says. "It can burn as hot as the hottest flame and be as cool as a summer's breeze."

"I guess, yeah."

"And which part of that does not meet your expectations?"

"All of it! I don't... I don't want to be tied to a man. At his mercy. Not ever again."

Without realizing it, I've been squeezing Tytus' hand too hard. His broken promise has tainted our time together, and I'm unable to even remember that fondly. I want to give him the benefit of the doubt. Maybe Declan did screw with his head, like he screwed with mine.

But if he didn't, if Tytus did what he did because he could, then where does that leave us? How am I to trust he won't do it again? Perhaps my fear is not so unfounded, after all.

"Especially not when he's a liar," I whisper.

Ileana is quiet for a long time. Yet still not long enough to avoid having the last word. "You may think Tytus wants one thing, but the way I see it, it is only your well-being he is after. Da, the pairing is not ideal–not when you were hurt and battered. I have seen it, I know you did not have ideal conditions."

She looks at Tytus, then back at me. "But regardless of what he has done to deserve your ire, he is not his brother. And you would do well to remember that."

Before I can think of a reply, Tytus' hand jerks in mine. Then his entire body shakes, trembling from head to toe like he's under the harshest winter conditions.

"What's going on? Tytus!"

Tytus

Even through the darkness, I feel Fiona's

hand on mine. The cadence of her voice carries through, though I cannot make out the words. She's mad–at me. For using my powers on her, for forcing her to leave me. It is my deepest regret, but I could not risk her life.

I try to squeeze her hand back–but the damn shivers rake me over again, and I lose control of my body as it gives in to the cold, until I know nothing but darkness and turmoil all over again....

"Where is your brother?"

It is years since the last memory, and I'm in the castle's armory, replacing a sword and shield. Both have the marks of a recent fight, and I am weary—beyond tired.

I don't bother turning to the zmeu. All I wish is for my bed, and a hot bath. Over my shoulder, I say, "I do not know where Declan is."

It is only the truth. I have not seen my brother for over a century, not since I joined the blasted wars against the humans. The order of fanatic knights intent on killing us has only grown in power. They're now hunting us, using the bones of our fallen to track more of us down, and ambush us.

The Council sent me at the head of a group to wipe out a few of the Serafim, but it was a long fight. Too long. Long enough that I lost my Solomonar in it and watched more than a few others fall. Suffice to say, the last thing I need is to be interrogated in my own castle.

Rather than pick up on this and let it go, the elder zmeu follows me. "How do you not know?"

I whirl on him, grasping him by the throat. "I am not Declan's keeper! How about you search for him in one of those human brothels he loves so much?"

"We did." He gulps and whimpers, "He's gone."

I let go of him and step backwards, already regretting my bath. "For how long?"

The man won't meet my eyes. "Close to a year."

¥

What the hell is my brother doing in a cottage in the middle of nowhere? It took me the better part of a week to find him. Unlike *him, I don't invade people's minds without their approval. Still, in the end, I had to peek, if only to give myself a clue. Or two.*

Imagine my surprise at what I saw... Worse, at what I felt.

There was no choice left. I flew as fast as I could until I landed in his neck of the woods, so to speak. Now in my human form, I'm hiding at the edge of the forest and watching the cottage.

It has all the makings of a human abode. Dainty roof, circular shape, smells of baked goods and meats wafting through the open window. When Declan comes out, he's followed shortly by a woman. A redhead with high cheekbones, brown eyes and a slight figure. Pretty enough—but still a human.

Shaking my head in the darkness, I wait until he kisses her and moves away. I follow him from afar, listening to his happy whistling, before finally crossing into his path.

"What are you up to, Dec?"

"Tytus?" Rather than be shocked or afraid or whatever I'd expected, his features morph into pure, unadulterated joy. He

runs towards me and pulls me into a hug. "Finally, frate!"

"What do you mean, finally? I've been looking for you for over a week! The zmei at the castle said you up and left, that you were going on some quest."

Declan smirks. "I did. And I found the greatest treasure."

"Is that why you couldn't be bothered to help me fight the Serafim?"

A little of the joy falls off his expression. "I told you I didn't want to."

"Not even to save your own kind, Declan?"

He frowns, then looks away as if unable to hold my gaze. "I no longer condone the killing of masses of humans. I understand that has been our way for too long, but... There has to be more to it. To life." He tries another tentative smile. "And I might have found it, Tytus. Will you not let go of your anger for long enough to witness it, to try to understand me?"

Bemused, I follow him as he retraces his steps back to the cottage. He pulls open the door, and the woman inside is even more stunning than from afar. Her eyes land on me with interest, but when they meet Declan's, her face fills with warmth.

"Brother, meet Alina. Alina, meet my brother, Tytus."

He switches to old Romanian, so I do the same, kissing the back of her hand and making small talk. Declan always had an odd fascination with humans, from the time we were young and he kept helping them out despite our Council's warnings.

It seems none of that fascination has ebbed away with time. Worse, with me away more and more on official business, Declan has found himself a new toy.

Or so I think at first.

But as the day goes on, and Alina sets about cooking a stew to celebrate my homecoming, I watch them both. How Declan can't stop touching her, little caresses here and there. A kiss on her nape, a touch of the fingers on her waist, a lingering glance even as we're chatting.

I can no longer dispute it. My brother truly has fallen in love. With a human.

Later that night, once Alina is asleep, I

jerk my head to the outside and Declan follows. "Does she know? About you being a zmeu?"

Declan nods. "Da. And she accepts it."

I wipe a hand over my face. "Dear gods and pantheons above, Declan... Did you imprint on her?"

He frowns. "Is that any of your business?"

Perhaps it's a fancy. Nothing more. I let it go and focus on Declan... but that was not the last time I saw Alina.

Why am I recalling all these things with such clarity, now of all times? I have gone centuries and an entire millenium without thinking of that time. Buried it at the back of my mind, once Declan's betrayal became known. And now, these memories are at the forefront, more vivid than ever.

I do not know why, what the purpose here is. But as the flames and ice mix in my body, and I go deeper down the vortex of recalling, I know there's a reason for this... something I'm not seeing. Not yet.

So I jump headfirst into the next memory.

"Declan."

The brother I see now is the darkest compared to the one from the previous memory. He looks up from his goblet—filled with țuica, our local drink, judging by the stench.

"What do you want?"

I take a seat opposite him in our dining room. "Don't you think it's time you let it go? Let her go?"

"No."

I tap my fingers on the table. "I don't understand. It's not like you imprinted on Alina. Losing her–"

"It's not losing her! It's the betrayal!" He shouts, getting up in my face.

I step back, stunned at the rage and hate in his eyes. Yet just as soon as the outburst came, it's gone.

Declan drops back on the chair and drains his cup. Twirls his index finger in a rune, and it refills again. He drains it once more. And repeats. And repeats some more.

I watch him, not knowing how to help, and feeling that same despair pulling me under.

I snap out of the memory with a jolt,

panting. This one hurt–perhaps because of Declan's own despair I was feeling mixed with mine. Even now, as I try to cast my thoughts to that time, I realize I never truly found out what happened. Alina hurt him, betrayed him somehow, and Declan took it to heart. Badly.

Worse still, he started pulling further and further away from me, and went from loving humans to hating them. In the end, it was the beginning of a downward spiral, but I was too caught up in the politics at the time to lend out the helping hand I should have.

Before I can think on it further, another memory pulls me under.

"Declan is out of control." One elder, Iris, stops me as I exit the castle a few months later. *"You have to watch out. We all must. He will attract the ire of the Serafim upon us."*

I shrug him off. "I'll take care of my brother."

Despite walking into the woods, I cannot find him, not at first. Then my steps take me back to the cavern, the same one where long ago, hundreds of years earlier, Declan had saved a family of humans.

He is there, now. Only, he is not alone. His whispered words carry to me. "I will make them pay. All humans. They do not deserve to live."

He could be talking to himself. But he is not. The air itself is filled with something... else. Something... other.

"Their duplicitous nature is their downfall," a voice finally says from the shadows.

"Yes," Declan looks up and into the sky. Even from afar, I see the dead glint in his eyes. The malice overpowering the good. "Duplicitous. They must pay."

Flames consume his human form, and the zmeu taking his place flies away.

And just as easily, I'm back. Back to the flames, the ice, and the never-ending pain.

Fiona

It's been three days of waiting for Tytus to recover. Three days of surviving on basic food, very little sleep, and less and less patience. Three days of going back and forth between condemning him, forgiving him, and lingering in between both states.

"He's not dead, that's already something," was Făt's sage advice. Ileana alternated between impatience and worry before disappearing yesterday. She still hasn't come back.

The one immortal still in the room with me drops a goblet of water on the bedside table and nods to it. "Drink. Before you pass out."

His gaze sweeps over me before turning to Tytus. "Last thing he needs when he comes back from the land of the dead is you, *dead.*"

"That's not funny," I mutter. Still, I drink. The water feels good going down my parched throat.

Then something Făt said registers, and I narrow my eyes on him. "Why did you say he's in the land of the dead?"

"Slip of the tongue, witch. Relax. If he was with Hades, we would not be getting him back. As it is..." He gestures towards Tytus. "He is returning. Taking his sweet time, but returning."

I try to see what he does. Tytus is still pale–much too pale. His lips are dry and cracked, and there are dark circles under his eyes. But his breathing has evened out since last night, that part is true. Perhaps Făt is right... Perhaps...

I squeeze his hand, whispering under my breath. "Come back to me. Please."

The betrayal, him using his powers on me and breaking that promise, I don't want to forget it. I cannot, not after what I've been through with Declan. Does it really matter, when he did it to save me? Yes, it does. Should that be an excuse, or is it simply that I'm ready to forgive him anything, so long as he comes back? Perhaps a little of both.

But to have him die on me, with so much unsaid between us, would be just cruel. So I hold on to him, fighting my tears, and whisper again. "Come back to me."

Ileana chooses that moment to storm in, hair disheveled, eyes blazing with anger. "That blasted zmeu!"

She goes straight into a corner and Făt

follows. More furious whispering ensues, until she finally drops into his arms, exhausted.

I watch them, frowning. Whatever Declan did now, is not good news. And with every passing day, as Tytus doesn't recover, Declan probably gains strength. And gets that much closer to surviving, to escaping his prison again.

The thought alone should bring me fear. And on some level, it does. But perhaps being here, with Tytus, and seeing where they grew up has taken away some of the mysticism around Declan. I see his brother, so different and kind, and his human side. And I cannot help but sense Declan, too, has those same weaknesses.

Either way, he is no longer the untouchable zmeu in my mind. His motivations, his reasoning–I may not know them. But I, too, have had time on my hands during these long days and nights. And if Declan escapes, I will be damned if I let him control me again. I would rather be dead than allow that... ever again.

As if my strength and determination have seeped through to Tytus, he groans.

Ileana and Făt stop their whispering and step closer to the bed, eagerness and hope clear in their expressions.

Tytus coughs, groans again, and finally, *finally,* he opens his eyes.

Chapter 12

Iertare
"The weak can never forgive. Forgiveness is the
attribute of the strong."
-Mahatma Gandhi-

Tytus

Being back is like coming out of a deep, deep fog. Declan's words fade out of my head, the memory of that last time before everything went to shit disappears, and I blink a few times. The soft murmur of voices breaks the last of the fog away, and I finally jolt awake.

The first sight my eyes land on is Fiona. She's by my bedside, dark circles under her eyes, underlined by a faint glimmer of hope. I want to speak, but my throat is dry, like I've been in a desert with no water. Instead, I squeeze the hand she has in mine, trying to communicate my apology.

For breaking my promise. For taking away her free will. I wasn't thinking–I needed her safe.

But before I can focus on getting the words out, something moves in my periphery, and I catch sight of Ileana and Făt.

"You're awake!" Fiona distracts me, grasping my hand in hers as if she never wants to let go.

I squeeze it back, surprised at the strength in my veins. The hold of the venom, the pull of weakness in my blood, it's... gone.

"You'll be okay, now."

The words escape me in a horse whisper, none as gentle as I want them to be. "What did you do this time?"

Fiona bites her lip, glancing towards the immortals and bringing my focus back to them. Though they hold themselves at a distance, it's clear in their body language that they need to be closer, and they have questions. Irritation seeps through me. I need to talk to Fiona, not them!

Agreed, my zmeu rumbles.

"What…" I clear my throat. "What brings immortals in my quarters again, uninvited to boot?"

Ileana rolls her eyes. "Worry for your soul, zmeu. You were unconscious for many days."

"Funny that a vasilisc is what finally puts you under," Făt says.

I glare at him and hiss, "It was not the vasilisc, fool, but Declan's venom. How…" I lick my dry lips, then glance towards the bedside table and move my index finger, conjuring water for the goblet there. I drink greedily until it's empty, then try speaking again. "How did you heal me?"

"Fiona figured it out."

I look back at my little witch. "Figured what out?"

She shrugs, pretending like it's a small thing. If I'm to judge by her nervous finger tapping and avoiding my eyes, it's a pretty damn big deal. "Declan's venom, the one making you weak… It's canceled by the vasilisc's."

"Please tell me you did not use zmeu

magic... You know how dangerous it is, and the toll it takes on you."

Fiona shakes her head. "No, I only collected the vasilic's venom, is all."

"You went back down there?"

I search her expression, torn between anger at her putting herself in danger, and an odd warmth filling my chest knowing she did it for me—to save *me*. Despite my screw up. Despite my broken promise. Could it be she's coming around to the idea of the bond, and willing to take it further? Or is she only doing this out of the kindness of her heart, and in another attempt at redemption?

"I had to," Fiona says. "Once I realized it was the only way to keep you alive."

I hold out my hand, grasping her frail one. "Thank you." Lower still, and for her ears only, I add, "Thank you for doing it, even after I broke my promise. I needed you safe, please understand."

I will thank her properly—later—but my gut says these immortals aren't here just to watch me recover. So I turn my attention to them. "What's really going on, Ileana?"

"What you fought down there, is only the beginning."

I say nothing, having figured out as much. The vasilisc was a pain, especially in my weakened condition, but it was no real threat. More a massive inconvenience, something Declan is great at creating.

"Your brother…" Ileana regroups and starts again. "Declan seems convinced that whatever is here, will get him out of our prison. Have you found what that might be?"

"I've been a bit busy fighting a vasilisc, Ileana. Not much time for roaming around."

Făt scowls. "Should have been an easy feat. Would have been, if you had continued to ignore humans rather than fall–"

"Enough." My growl tears through his words, thankfully. When Fiona finds out how I feel, it'll be from my own lips and in a much better setting than this. My blazing glare lands on Făt, even as my knuckles grow white around the goblet I'm gripping. "To answer your question, no, I have not figured out what that is, but I plan to as soon as I get up from here. Anything else?"

Ileana looks like she wants to say more. It is also just as evident she won't, not around Fiona. So I turn to the witch that stole my heart, yearning for some alone time to properly apologize. Instead, I ask, "Do you mind heading to the library?"

She seems dazed, and I frown at her expression–it's almost pained. But then she clears her throat, and her tone gives none of her inner emotions away. "What for?"

"When I was down with the vasilisc, I noticed a change in the place's structure. Declan may have rearranged the underground of the castle, but some areas were moved way before he ever got here. Which means whatever is hidden down there is older than both of us." A meaningful glance to the immortals, then I squeeze her hand again. "The library should contain a binder with maps of this place. I want to see if any have been touched recently, as Declan will have left his scent on them."

"I…" She looks around, then nods,

something akin to relief filling her. "Of course." Without another glance, she shuffles out, leaving me staring after her in confusion.

What just happened?

No sooner is she gone, that Ileana turns to her consort and nods at him. "Keep her company. Best we don't take any chances. Who knows what else Declan hid around here?"

Rolling his eyes, Făt steps outside to follow Fiona, leaving Ileana and I in the bedroom.

Once we're alone, she drops the mask. Her shoulders slouch inwards, the shine goes out of her hair, as if pressed by an exhaustion she cannot control. The transformation is shocking enough that I end up sitting straighter, taking in her new appearance.

Was the rest an illusion? It had to be. Rather than the vibrant immortal I'm used to, before me is a tarnished apparition. Ileana is weak–something is sapping her energy.

"What's going on?"

"Declan." Her voice shakes on my

brother's name. "Whatever this escape plan of his is, he is winning at it. And keeping him imprisoned is taking its toll. On both of us, me and Făt."

"This makes no sense. How is his prison...?" Something that's been nagging since I went to visit Declan dawns on me. "I am giving you the benefit of the doubt here, and hoping to all the pantheons and beyond that you did not do something so stupid."

Ileana sighs, avoiding my gaze and confirming my fears. "The prison, the cuffs–they are made from our essence, mine and Făt's."

"What the hell were you two thinking! To bind yourselves to him, to his prison? Neither of our kinds has done this in centuries!"

She keeps looking away, picking at her dress instead. "We have done it before, without any issues."

"But this is Declan! *Declan,* whom you knew had already started affecting the balance in this part of the world you are responsible for."

Ileana shakes her head, running a hand through her matted hair. "We did. It is why we thought our essence would be the only way to imprison him. But these last days–weeks!–something has been eating at our control. It is attacking the frame around Declan, and the strongholds we have established throughout this region. Slowly eroding them."

"How could something be stronger than you two, the protectors assigned by pantheons? It was not just a case of favoritism when you were allowed your whim, to protect Transylvania. It is because you are both as strong as gods, through your Light magic alone."

Ileana meets my eyes then, and the fear and panic in her gaze rattles me. I don't get rattled, period. Her words are even worse. "So the gods believed. So we believed, too. But whatever this is, it is Dark. Powerful. Enough to counter my Light."

"That is worrying." For an immortal's magic to be contested... It used to be only the divine were above either of our kinds. But if these two are being subjected to something else, that's more than a little problematic. *What the hell did Declan do?*

Ileana remains quiet, dejected and hunched over. At a loss, I give in to her demand.

"I will find out what it is. The vasilisc was a clue. I just need to get into Declan's head."

"You may have need of your little witch for that."

My fist automatically clenches in the sheets. "No."

"Tytus… You know it is the only way."

"I refuse to put her in more danger."

Her eyes shine. "Făt was right, then. You have fallen for her."

"And if I have?"

"Do not get defensive with me, zmeu. Your life is your own. But have you been truthful with her about everything, including the price she may pay if you continue with the legătură?"

I shake my head. "No, but that is no business of yours, Ileana."

She sighs. "It is when your distraction allows your brother's plan to come to fruition.

It is time to let it go, or go all the way, Tytus. We both know the closer you get to danger, the more you will fear for her safety."

I don't answer, lost in my own thoughts. Enough so that memories of me and Declan arise again... Could any of what I focused on while sick be useful to me? Could I talk him out of this insane plan?

When I meet Ileana's gaze, she reads my intention. "You want to see Declan again."

I nod.

"No," she says. "It is taking our every strength to keep him as is. If we open the prison again, it would be foolish, dangerous even. Unless you can neutralize that threat, I cannot open the portals again."

"What if I can talk him out of it?"

"You tried once and failed."

"But I have more ammunition now." More understanding, too, but I don't say that piece out loud.

"I doubt that," Ileana says. "Especially since you are cavorting with a human."

I wince. "Declan doesn't hate humans."

"Could have fooled me."

"He hates *a* human and has been projecting that onto others." Ileana frowns, and I explain further. "It was a *human* maiden who entered our lives, and who broke our brotherly connection. Long story, too long to get into it now, but I swear I can get through to him. Let me talk to him."

"No."

I watch her closely then, catching unto the underlying emotions. The determined set of her mouth, the tightness of her fists as they're clenched in her lap. "I see. You'll hold on to my brother as collateral, then, until I fix this mess?"

She says nothing, only holding my gaze. At one time, deities trusted us both to keep them safe. When the gods demoted the zmei and immortals took their spot as guardians, my kind hated theirs. It led to much in-fighting, and too many deaths to count. Some of that animosity has remained, but it has lessened given we are both among the last of our kind.

Still, at that moment, I am ever more aware of our history. As frail as she is, power still emanates from Ileana. But though it should, it's not enough to keep me cowering.

"Watch yourself, immortal. You do not want to make an enemy out of me."

"Nor you, of me."

It's a standstill as we glare at each other until Ileana gets up from the bed and turns her back to me. "Hate me if you will, but I will do what is right. I have to for our sake, and the world's."

Fiona

As usual, the library completely overwhelms my senses. And I need it, after Tytus' admission. My hopes were dashed when he practically confirmed it had been his choice, and his alone, to break the promise. To control me. In order to get me to safety, yes. But it is still control.

I had hoped to get a moment of peace, even felt relieved when Tytus asked me to come search for the maps. But Făt's presence at my back doesn't help my frayed thoughts, instead it feels intrusive.

"Are you here to help, or stare?" I toss

over my shoulder.

His eyes narrow on me. "Watch your tone with me, witch."

O-kay. No pissing off the immortal, then. Even as I keep walking, I think back to the room I just left, to Tytus recovering, and something nags at me. The atmosphere itself has changed, I sense it even with Făt drilling his glare into my skull.

I stop in my tracks, whirling on him.

"What is it?" His tone is as bored and annoying as ever.

"Seriously. Are you and Ileana here to help, or to monitor us?"

His aloof expression doesn't change. "Does it matter?"

"Yes! Tytus just recovered, and it'll be some time before we can restart the search of the castle grounds."

His expression darkens, then. "We do not have time. Now find the blasted maps. Hurry."

I turn away, hiding a scowl. It's only as I rifle through with shaking hands that I realize—I was able to stand up for myself, and to an immortal, no less. A man ever more powerful than Declan.

That sweet victory fills me with pride, and I smile to myself. I guess the Carpathian air is good for me, after all.

I step by the bookshelves, looking around for anything resembling a red binder. My attention falls on a table with the journal I'd left, the one with the diary entries. I go to pick it up and flip through the pages once more.

September 13, 132 A.D.

I write again in haste. The Serafim hunted and killed two Council members last night. We wrapped up a meeting only a few hours ago, and most of my brethren are preparing for an all-out war. They say someone has incensed the knights, made them truly hunt us down, but they don't know whom.

I'm worried for my brother, as I know he'll be on the front lines. And while I'm in the majority, I also want to warn the zmei against eradicating the Cavaleri, as it will only make those who survive even more likely to come after us.

No one will listen. Fear is a powerful

thing, and though we are clearly the apex predator between the Serafim and the shifters, it is also clear none of the elders are willing to stomach any more defeats. They say losing the gods' backup was worse enough. Perhaps they are right. I cannot know, as I never served them.

These are dangerous times indeed...

Făt's restless pacing behind me pulls me out of my perusal of the journal, and I place it gently back on the table before resuming my search. My mind is going haywire, thinking of the Serafim. I'm reminded we are not rid of them, and Tytus has fought them for so long. So has Declan, apparently. Is that why he hates humans so?

My ruminations are interrupted when I knock into a small writing desk and papers scatter all over. "Shit!"

I kneel on the floor and start picking them up. A flash of red grabs my attention.

As I sort through the papers, I see a portrait of a younger Tytus, barely in his twenties. His arm is wrapped casually around a redhead with expressive brown eyes. I may be mistaken, but her features have nothing otherworldly. If I didn't know better, I'd say she was human.

A few papers later, other faded portraits arise. Tytus with a younger, blond man. I stare in shock at a Declan I never would have pictured. Smiling eyes, lips curled in a grin, his entire being is alight with mischievousness. There is nothing of the cold, bitter zmeu I met in this guy.

"How is this possible?"

"Hmm?"

Făt moves closer, and I hastily hide both portraits. "Nothing, I thought I found something."

"I'm sure Tytus said to find a collection of maps. Not leaflets."

"Right." I place the papers back in the desk drawer, my hand lingering a tad longer. I'll come back and have a closer look, later.

Even as I search for the binder, my mind keeps going back to those portraits. Tytus, Declan, and a human girl. One Tytus seemed very fond of. A redhead, like Lucrezia from the wolf pack...

I try to rein in my emotions, but

jealousy rears its ugly head. And with it, the inexplicable sting of betrayal. Again. I trusted Tytus. Told him everything, yet he evidently kept massive parts of his story away from me. I shouldn't be overreacting, after all, it's not like we planned for forever. But between his broken promise, and this new development I wasn't aware of... He made me feel like the only one in the world for him. Like he'd never had this, a deep connection, before. Least of all with another human.

Yet, that's evidently not true. And with the betrayal, something else slithers its way into my mind... Distrust. What else has he kept from me? What other secrets that might affect my existence as much as his? And how much longer will it be before he tries to control my mind again, like Declan?

"Could you move any slower?"

I glare at Făt, then finally grab the binder we'd been looking for. Encased in dark leather, bound by one massive strap, it contains blueprints of the castle. Pages upon pages.

As we leave the library, my eyes linger

on the smaller desk. My feet feel heavy all the way to Tytus' room. And when we enter, the atmosphere is charged.

Ileana is by the window, arms crossed. Tytus is clenching his jaw, his eyes drilling flames at the back of her skull. Făt immediately navigates to Ileana, leaving me by Tytus' bed.

"What happened?"

"They won't allow me to speak with Declan. Whatever he did is causing them to wither away and making his prison less secure."

Panic seizes me, my earlier victory against Făt evaporating like dew in sunlight. "How bad is it?"

Tytus looks at me then, and his expression softens. He reaches for my hand. "I won't let him hurt you again."

I slide it out of his reach, ignoring his frown. "Here's the binder you asked for. Do you think it's enough?"

"Fiona… I'm sorry, for before. For breaking my promise."

I grit my teeth, and glance at the immortals. They're still deep in conversation, unaware of our own drama.

So Tytus thinks that's what this is about—I might as well let him keep thinking it. It's true finding out about the redhead has messed up, but the last thing I want is to give him ammunition against me. If he knows how much the discovery affects me, he'll know I've grown to care about him. More than just physical. And I cannot—will no—allow that piece of information to fall in his hands.

Instead, I do what I do best, and deflect. "It's fine."

"It's not," Tytus says. "I hurt you. You gave me your trust, and I hurt you when I made that choice. I only did it for your protection, because I was so out of my mind with worry. I know it's no excuse, but I need you to hear it."

Meeting his gaze finally, I arch an eyebrow. "And the next time you do it, will it be the same excuse? That it was for my own good?"

Tytus' jaw clenches, and his eyes glitter. "There will not be a next time."

"Sure there won't."

He reaches for my hand, tugging me so I sit on the bed next to him, and set the binder aside. Uncaring for the immortals, he cups my cheek and forces our gazes to collide.

"There *will not* be a next time, Fiona. I swear it on my life, on my honor, on my legacy if you'd like. Give me one more chance, and I won't screw it up again."

There is sincerity in his gaze, I'll give him that. And while I'll be afraid for a long time to be vulnerable with him, like before, I cannot help the bond. The way my body softens around his, the way I crave his caress more than my next breath.

Frustration makes its way in his expression, and Tytus growls softly. "Don't let the zmeu affect your reasoning, not now. Forgive me because *you* wish it, not because the zmeu is forcing it, or the bond."

I stare at him for longer than I want to. The gray eyes stare back, intense and vulnerable and–remorseful. Yes. More than I ever got from Declan. I could use this chance to ask about the redhead, to put it all to rest, but I won't. I will keep that card close to my chest, and not show him how I feel about him. Not yet.

Instead, there is something else I will demand. Something I need more.

"The immortals said there is a way for you to break the link between me and Declan."

Tytus nods, searching my gaze. "Da, there is. It is dangerous, and it will take time. I have thought about it, but I was afraid of the burden it would take on you, on your mind."

So I'd been right, when I said much the same to Ileana and Făt.

"I appreciate it, but I think I'd like to take the chance, regardless of the consequences. Will you do it?"

"Da, I will." His thumb caresses my cheek again. "Anything for you, sweetling. As soon as we get a moment, I will teach you."

"Thank you." I close my eyes, so I don't see his face when I ask the next question. "Will this, whatever it is, also stop you from ever controlling my mind again?"

My sense of sight may be gone, but I still hear the pain in his voice when he answers. Pain at my rejection, at my distrust.

"Da, it will."

I nod, and get up from the bed, blinking away tears as I do so. Tytus hesitates, trying to catch my eye, but I stubbornly keep my gaze focused away.

Eventually, he gives in and takes the binder I'd set on the bed, rifling through it. He removes a few sheets away and tosses the rest on the bed. His movements are jerky, annoyed. When he finally finds what he's looking for, he scowls.

"Here's what you want. There's a set of tunnels built under the castle. Where we found the vasilisc was just the beginning."

"And why not mention that before?" Făt questions.

"Because the tunnels were sealed long ago, and I haven't been here in centuries. Obviously Declan figured out a way to unseal them and reseal them without leaving a trace. His scent is all over these papers."

"And how would he have done that?"

I step in then. Frustration may still be ruling me, anger at Tytus for the broken promise, but in complete contradiction the bond underneath the surface rouses my protective side.

"I get you two have an agenda, but Tytus only just woke up. He needs rest, time to recover, before being assailed by all your questions." *And apparently his zmeu is demanding I ensure these happen. Shit.*

"We don't *have* time," Ileana snaps. It's the first time I've seen her lose her cool. And, judging by Tytus' expression, ditto.

"It's fine," he mutters after a beat and goes to stand.

His bare chest glistens in the faint glow of candles, and my mouth dries up. I want to hate this bond, this connection that makes my hormones go haywire. I try to focus my thoughts on being strong, not giving in, but it's getting harder. That annoying pull is there again, begging for completion, and I know it won't be long, now.

Our joining was practically written in

the stars, if I'm to believe the stories Tytus told me of the pairing. I can attest to the pull, the attraction between us, by simply recalling those nights spent in caverns. With his lips on mine, his hands on me, nothing has ever felt so complete. And even back then, I did not fully trust him.

Evidently, I'm back to square one. And still unable to resist him.

Am I all right with giving him my body, with satisfying our mutual need, when I still fear he might control me? I don't know. All I know is the fire burning in my veins is getting harder to staunch, and for the first time in my life, I may have to jump off that cliff into the unknown, if I'm to find out.

I have to stop letting fear rule me. If I can keep my heart out of it, keep him from knowing how truly invested I am emotionally, then I will be all right.

With a big effort on my part, I push the desire thoughts away and focus on what's at hand.

Tytus is a bit wobbly on his feet, but otherwise fine. His glower speaks to his annoyance at being ordered around his own home. "To answer your question, Declan wouldn't have been able to unseal the tunnel. Not alone. It takes powerful mages, more than one, and zmeu bloo–"

He stops, and for a second I think he's about to faint. But he's only gathering his thoughts, trying to get over his shock. He runs a hand over his face and the determined set of his shoulders slouches a little as he sways. "Elisandra," he whispers. "That's why he took her."

"Who?" Făt frowns.

"Tytus' descendant." Thanks to our earlier conversations, it doesn't take me long to catch on to Tytus' meaning. "She'd been repressing her zmeu side and ended up causing a split personality effect. The bad part of her took Declan's side, fought against us all. Declan stole her away from the wolves for a while… A few days."

"More than enough time," Tytus mutters. "Her blood was mine, and she fulfilled the role of the second zmeu."

"Why didn't you protect her, if she's so precious to you?"

Tytus only glares at Făt, refusing to

answer. But if I were to guess, guilt is filling him even more than it already has. And if Elisandra was the key to this whole thing, and he'd protected me, but let her go... Then that means the guilt extends to me.

I take a step backwards. Nothing in Tytus' expression changes, but I see a new rigidity to his back that advises he noticed my movement. He says nothing though, instead clenching his fists.

"I played right into his hands."

"How so?" Ileana asks.

"Declan wanted me to let Elisandra go, so he could better manipulate her. He'd intended to reach her. Probably even called out to her way before I got involved. He must have sensed her nearby, same as I did. And when I started spending time around her, it only caught his attention more, and more. He would have started planning then."

"But why so far in advance? And what is hidden here, that Declan would reseal? Is it something he cannot control, another creature?"

"Perhaps something that eats immortal

energy?" Făt adds, his expression grim.

Tytus shakes his head, as if to avoid all their questions. Despite the distance I want, nothing can stop my feet from moving towards him, pulled by the bond as much as my irrational need to comfort him. I place a hand on his shoulder, squeezing it.

Tytus meets my gaze then, and the fire in there returns tenfold. My throat dries. Before he can say anything, *do* anything, Făt speaks.

"A better question than all the above is, why in hell would Declan delay an attack, when he could have done this weeks ago? Months, perhaps?"

His question breaks the spell, and Tytus looks up, frowning. I'm close enough to count his lashes, meaning I have front-row seats to the surprise that rocks him to his core. And that same surprise shakes the rest of us when he says, "Because he must have foreseen he'd be imprisoned again."

Declan

I only get snippets, now. After my rather badly timed loss of control with Tytus, the two immortals increased the prison wards. It's rather annoying, when before I could connect to the blasted witch without an issue. But, through her bond to Tytus at least, I'm able to garner little snippets.

They've found the vasilisc, then. I didn't expect them to, in fact I rather had hoped they wouldn't until the last possible moment. It would have weakened Tytus more if he'd had to fight the snake beast and then landed on Igor, my little surprise.

Still, all is not lost. If Tytus continues this way, he will soon be following in the exact footsteps I wish him to.

I glance at the restraints around my wrists. *And soon, I will be freed of this.* The skies, the world, will be mine again. And I won't have to rely on dreams and dream goddesses to get my satisfaction.

Chapter 13

Dragoste
"Better to have loved and lost, than to have never loved at all."

-Augustine of Hippo-

Tytus

With the realization, my gaze lowers to the maps of the castle. The underground, where Declan and I played as children. Am I following exactly where he wants me to? Or did he inadvertently mess up, and this is the break we've been looking for?

I must stare at the papers in my hands for too long, as Făt loses his patience and snatches them away. "Get back to your senses, zmeu! Or has all the sleep dwindled your mind?"

I glare at him. The animosity between us ratchets up a notch, as does the tension in the room.

"You can glare all you want," he says. "I fought your kind longer than you've lived."

"And I have *eaten* yours for just as long."

Făt loses some of his arrogance, anger seeping through it instead. Good. His fury at our joint, bloody history is something I can deal with, something I can fight. Unlike Fiona's distrust, caused by my own callousness.

"Enough," Ileana says, pulling on Făt's arm to create a physical distance between us. "It is good you are well now, Tytus. Time is running out, and the sooner you can figure out Declan's ploy, the better. As for us... We have extended our welcome here, dragul meu."

Reluctantly, with one more incensed glare my way, Făt heads out of the room like a storm ready to blow. Ileana follows behind, but turns one more time with her hand on the door. "It is needless to emphasize how important this quest of yours is. If we lose against Declan, it is not only us who will suffer."

With a meaningful glance at Fiona, she leaves, following Făt. I run a hand through my hair, wincing at the dried sweat.

"I need a shower," I mutter to Fiona and head out of the room into the en-suite bathroom. I crave silence–a moment to collect my thoughts. Whatever Declan did, he did so with a purpose. If I could figure out what that is, then following his bread crumbs should be easier.

Only it's not. The brother I knew is gone. No matter what memories and hallucinations my sickness brought upon me, Declan is master of his own fate. It was his decisions that brought him where he is. Despite the deeper part of me warning I could have done more, could have been more, I have to keep that in mind.

The scalding hot water beats against my back, and my tense muscles. I wash the grime of the sickness away, and with it, recall the immortals' words. It was Fiona who figured out how to save me. Without her, I could have died from Declan's poison. And he wouldn't have done a single thing to help me.

Bastard probably would have danced on my grave, if given half a chance.

The memories from my dreams contradict that. Remind me that Declan is a complicated man, with emotional baggage as equally complicated as mine. And when I saw him, face to face in his prison, I'm reminded of his lashing out. He didn't, at first. He was only mocking me. But when I mentioned I would have seen him dead, rather than imprisoned, that was when he lost his grip.

Was that real anger I'd seen, or was it masked by hurt?

Could it be there's more to this, more to what he did, and why he has changed so much? And what was that creature he was speaking to, in the last recollection...

I shake my head under the water and step out, towel drying my hair and my damp body. Then I go by the sink, brushing my teeth and tossing more cold water onto my face.

"If he's so master of his fate, what was

he after? Why bring Elisandra here, then back? Why latch onto a witch?"

Frustration builds in me and I clench the edge of the sink too tight. It groans in protest, and I let go with a sigh. A soft fragrance from behind draws my attention.

"Can I help?" Fiona asks.

I turn to her, recalling the beaten expression in her eyes from before. The agony in her voice, when she asked me to teach her to protect her mind. Against Declan, and against me.

"I am so sorry, sweetling," I say again. Her wide-eyed gaze stays on mine, even as I hold myself back, giving her distance. "We had made progress, before all this. You and I. And with my actions, I have broken it. Will you trust me ever again?"

She bites her lip, then shrugs. "In all honesty, it's too early to tell, Tytus."

"Fair enough. Can I hold you, at least? If nothing else." I need her in my arms, if only to reassure myself she's all right, that *we* are all right.

I open my arms to her and after a slight hesitation, Fiona walks in my embrace, her body frailer than before. It's a reminder of her human mortality. If I let the legătură take place, move to the next level, she could be mine forever. *If* she survives...

I'm loath to offer her the option, fearing it will only scare her away after everything else that happened. After what I did to cause her mistrust. And yet, whatever Declan planned will not get easier. Fiona will be in more danger than before. And Ileana was right, I will worry about her.

My arms tighten around her. Enough that she realizes something is wrong and pulls back.

"You were talking to yourself."

I nod, unable to escape her bewitching eyes.

"About Declan?"

"Da." I pinch the bridge of my nose, trying to find a focus I desperately need right now. Fiona's still keeping her distance, but I am as aware of her presence as ever. Too much. My zmeu *wants*.

"Ileana and Făt will have to wait," she says after a beat. "You need rest."

I glance up, narrowing my eyes. "I am better. There is no need to treat me like a child."

"Tytus, you were in a coma for three days."

"Zmei don't do comas."

Her eyes flash. "Whatever the heck you call it, then. Point is, you're supposed to be recovering."

I can't resist it and step closer to her until she's backed against the wall. Her lips part, and my thumb traces them. I'd seen the desire, earlier, in her eyes. It confused the hell out of me, given the hard conversation we'd just had. But then I realized regardless of what our minds fight over, our bodies will still be primarily ruled by the bond.

And is that such a bad thing, after all?

"I assure you, I am quite recovered. In fact..." I hold my mouth an inch away from hers as I breathe, "I feel more alive than ever before. Shall I prove it?"

Fiona meets my gaze then, and I see clear as day the conflict in her gaze, sense it in her mind. This bond is the only thing keeping us together, keeping her from completely distrusting me. And I will stop fighting it, if it means it will help me gain her forgiveness.

"You need rest, Tytus."

My fingers move down her neck, lightly touching her collarbone, then tracing her jaw. Fiona shivers under my touch, and I smile. "I think you want me to prove it. And you want me, as badly as I want you right now. And I also think we have a quiet moment and it would be a darned shame not to take advantage of it."

My hand drops by my side, and disappointment creeps in her expression. It's enough to convince me I'm not alone in this, and that I still have a chance at victory for her heart.

"You–"

I cut off the rest of her sentence with a searing kiss. Fiona latches onto my shoulders, pulling me closer. Everything fades away at her touch, her kisses. When her hand moves lower, sneaking under the towel and touching my hardness, I nearly lose it.

I let her have her fun, focused instead

on plundering her mouth until she forgets to breathe. Until her grip on me slackens, and all she can do is give in to the power of the kiss. And then I scoop her up in my arms and carry her back to my bedroom. Lay her down on the covers, watching her flushed face. "If at any point you change your mind–"

"I won't."

I remove her clothes one by one, kissing every inch of her I can get my hands on. Her skin is burning to the touch, and soft–so damn *soft*. I monitor her every expression, soaking in every moan and breathy whisper that escapes her, figuring out what she likes, and what drives her truly insane.

When she's finally naked under me, I take a long moment to look her up and down. Fiona's eyes open, and she sees me staring. A blush covers her cheeks, and she looks away. I force my body to cool, to slow down, and lie down next to her, parallel but not quite touching.

"What's wrong, sweetling?"

She reaches for the covers, as if to hide

her body from me, and I grab her wrist in my hand. Finger by finger, I undo her grip and bring her hand to my mouth, kissing every knuckle.

"Talk to me, Fiona."

She finally turns to me, a question in her eyes. "You were staring for so long..."

"Da, I was. In adoration, in awe of your body." Continuing to kiss her knuckles, I reach with my other hand and trail my fingertips around her collarbone, then around one breast, and the other, never quite touching her nipples.

Fiona shifts under me, and lust replaces some of that wariness in her expression. "I... There's no need to flatter me," she whispers. "I know you've lived for ages."

Ah. Now I understand where her shyness is coming from, and her wariness. Relief spreads through me that it has nothing to do with her distrust, simply her self-consciousness.

I kiss her shoulder next, then her neck, until my mouth is by hers. "Zmei don't carry any human diseases, you can rest easy on that." A gentle butterfly kiss follows. "And I assure you, no woman has ever brought me to my knees. This is as new to me, as it is to you, sweetling."

Fiona searches my expression, and I can't understand the emotion in hers. So I kiss her again. Without pressure, simply wanting her to know I cherish her, that I am hers if she wants me. Whenever that is.

Her free hand reaches for my neck and pulls me in for a deeper kiss. Our mouths clash, tongues battling for dominance, but this is a game I am very good at. When Fiona arches against me, I read her cue and move my hand to her breast, finally touching her as I've yearned to. My fingers graze her nipples, tugging and playing with them until she breaks my kiss to draw in gulps of air.

I shift her free hand, the one I've been holding on to, and draw one of her fingers in my mouth. When I suckle on it gently, Fiona's eyes widen and something akin to a whimper escapes her. I do it again, and again, the entire time not lessening my torture of her nipples.

Fiona's whimpers become louder,

mixed with words she's not even aware of saying. Pleas, begging me for more, for so much more.

I finally let go of her hand to move my fingers down her body, to the apex of her thighs. When I touch her, driving through her slickness, Fiona clamps her thighs on my hand and rocks against it. Once, twice, and then she's screaming my name and crashing in my arms.

I gentle my touches, bowing my head to kiss her perky nipples softly. She spreads her legs in invitation, catching my gaze with hers. And through the glazed daze of pleasure, she says, "I need you."

Three tiny words. And they impact me like nothing ever has.

I'd intended to take it slower. To keep savoring her through the night. But I can only hold out so long. And with those violet eyes latched onto me, her mouth reddened from my kisses, I cannot resist. I toss away my towel, then place myself between her legs and drive home inside her.

Fiona arches beneath me, holding me like I'm her anchor in the middle of a tornado. Nothing could be further from the truth. *She* is *mine.*

She breaks me with every sigh, every moan, every shift of her hips. And I know it'll be impossible to let her go. One way, some way, I have to convince her to stay. But in that moment, all I can focus on is the feel of her tightening around me, the pitch of her voice that grows hoarse, the scrape of uneven nails on my back.

When she reaches paradise, her muscles clenching me, I grit my teeth and wait for her eyes to open. "May I?" I need this last assurance that she's in the moment as much as I am. That nothing else is ruining this utterly perfect moment.

My zmeu chooses that second to manifest, pushing inside me with a force that jerks me. He wants Fiona–wants to wrap this up. The urge rises within me to bite her, mark her, be one with her and the fire.

My hand clenched in the sheet sizzles, and I pull it back, drawing deep breaths instead. I focus on Fiona, on the glow of her skin, the satisfied expression on her face.

The way she's undulating underneath me, waiting for more.

She chuckles at the strain in my voice and angles her hips to take me deeper, at the same time clenching her internal muscles. "Yes... *Now,* Tytus."

A feral groan escapes me, then I lose myself and race to a sweet oblivion. And when that pinnacle hits, stronger than I've ever felt it, I know I'm completely and utterly lost to the witch beneath me.

Fiona

"You definitely proved you're better now."

Tytus laughs, a deep rumble that shakes me, since I'm resting my head on his chest.

A moment later, I try again. "It's almost dawn." My whisper carries oddly in the mostly dark room. Despite the exhaustion pulling me under, I'm energized by the night's activities. Freed.

For the first time in the longest time, perhaps even in my entire life, I am also at peace. His bed skills are part of it–I never knew sex could be like that. Like a unison between bodies and souls, a constant joint movement towards mutual pleasure. It was... eye opening, to say the least. Even now, satiated, my body craves more.

But it's more than that. I was able to stay true to myself, to allow my body this pleasure, this moment we've both been straining towards, and not fall apart emotionally. I didn't think I could do it. After our earlier conversation, and my muddled thoughts, I thought for sure this would be the nail in my coffin.

Instead, it ended up being what set me free. I chose this step, chose to be with him, to take strength in my ability to take what I want, what I need, and still keep myself safe. By giving in to the pull between us, I have removed the shackles holding me back. I am my own woman, because I can be with him, and learn from him, and not allow myself to be hurt again. And if I love him in silence, without his knowledge, that will be my little secret. My small treasure.

And through this choice, I have learned to see the difference, to believe in the future, and to stop second guessing myself. If that is not power, if that is not peace of mind... I don't know what is.

It will not last, a part of me warns. And I know it won't. It cannot. Despite what Tytus believes, there is no way my human life, the isolation I need and crave, match anything he wishes for us. And... I'm okay with that. I'll take what I can, in the now. And keep myself safe, so that when the time comes to leave, I will be able to do so without looking back and knowing I have the tools to keep my mind safe.

I push the thoughts away, stretching slightly against Tytus. My lower back is sore, and a few other parts I never knew could get sore.

"Mm," Tytus says, tracing lazy circles around a nipple. I shift just out of his reach, getting up on one elbow to grin at him.

"We have to get up. Save the world, and all that."

Tytus throws an arm over his face. He looks so relaxed, so young, that I hesitate to voice the idea that's been playing in my head for the last hour. Eventually, I risk it.

"If Declan brought Elisandra here... Do you think talking to her might help?"

The arm drops to his side, and he stares at me, blinking slowly. "It wouldn't hurt, I suppose. But I cannot portal back there, though. I refuse to bring the Serafim to her door. Nor do I have one of those contraptions humans call cell phones."

I bite my lip. "Is there not a village nearby, where we could go buy one for cheap? We could ask the operator for the phone number to the bakery and try her there."

Tytus thinks on it for a moment, then nods. "Let's do that. There is a village, but I'll come with you. For now, though, I have other ideas for spending our time."

And then he's on me, pushing me to my back, nuzzling my neck, and whispering in my ear. "May I, sweetling?"

That question alone leaves all the power of the choice in my hands. And as I meet the blaze in his eyes, my own needs overwhelm me. My answer gets lost in a long moan of pleasure as his fingers slide down my skin, playing my body like a maestro.

¥

Hours later, I get off his zmeu back, shaking my head. "Was there no other way to get here?" We've landed in a valley, semi-hidden by spare trees. But if the village is within walking distance, that's nowhere as safe as it should be.

Tytus shifts back to human and shrugs. "These mountains are full of lore. One zmeu or another won't gather much attention."

"In this day and century?"

Tytus only grins and briefly kisses me, then releases me just as quick.

I roll my eyes and wait for him to take the lead. Which he does–after grabbing my hand in his. It feels odd to be strolling around in the woods, fingers intertwined like teenagers on a date. Unbidden, the image of the redhead comes to my mind again. I force it out, refusing to let it ruin this moment.

We emerge from the woods into a small town. Red brick houses decorate each side of the street, and a worn cobblestone path runs straight through to the main square. Everyone seems to know everyone. Old and young people alike greet each other, yell over the distance to grab the others' attention.

The cars are old, some practically abandoned on the side of the road. The buildings even more so. The bustle of the place and presence of so many people in one spot should have me running for the hills. But I find myself... intrigued. By the words, the colors, the noises, the scents. And through it all floats a sense of peace, of hard work. I can feel myself softening, wanting this, especially when Tytus leads us into the heart of the village to a market.

Tents are spread a few feet apart in a semicircle, with various goods displayed. Jewelry, postcards, key chains, portraits, traditional clothing. On one side of the market is an area dedicated to sampling goods–the smells alone wafting from there make my stomach grumble.

Tytus heads towards the food area and speaks to an old guy as if they're best friends. Within moments, he walks away from him with a warm, steaming loaf of bread, which he hands me.

"Try it. It's a smaller version of a colac."

Coh-lak. At my blank stare, he chuckles and adds, "Local baked good."

I reach for the round item that's still hot to the touch. The dough is a golden hue, wrapped around itself almost like a croissant. For all intents and purposes, it looks like bread. Pretty bread, though.

"No conjuring food this time around?" I can't help but tease.

Tytus only grins, watching as I tear off a piece and stuff it in my mouth. The warmth, the buttery yet sweet flavor melts on my tongue and I moan in appreciation. *This isn't just bread.*

He presses closer to me, bowing his head to my ear. "Watch those sounds, sweetling. They make me want to do things." I nearly choke on my next bite, and heat suffuses my cheeks.

With a wink, Tytus steps away and lets me enjoy the colac. Within moments, it's all gone in my stomach, and I'm wandering around again, following him from afar. The surrounding Romanian conversations should alienate me. They don't. On the contrary, I feel like I'm part of something. A confusing thought, given how hard I'm working to not get more invested in Tytus' world.

After a few moments of aimless wandering, we find a cell phone booth and Tytus bargains with a younger man. Curious, I look around, taking in the variations of tents and faces glancing at us. We must make an odd couple, him with his dark hair, me with my white one streaked with purple. In some eyes, I see curiosity, others hold almost... fear? Could it be they know, or guess, what he is? Like Tytus said, lore lives around here...

My inspection comes to an abrupt stop when my eyes land on *him*. Perhaps it's his black clothes on this sunny day. Or the rigid posture. The pale face. Or, more than likely, his fixed stare–on us.

A shiver runs through me, and I nearly trip over my own feet while trying to get to Tytus. He's pocketing his new acquisition– a flip cell phone–when he notices my panicked expression. "What is it?"

"The man."

He looks over my shoulder. "What man?"

I hesitate. The stranger didn't have a mask, like the rest of them... What if I'm wrong? *But I can't be.* Lowering my voice, I add, "I think the Serafim are here."

Tytus stuns me with the rapidity of his movement. In less time than I can think, he grabs my hand and pulls me through the crowd, moving at a swift pace. I see no more of the guy, but something tells me he's not much further behind us.

"How did they know we'd be here?" I gasp while running.

"I have an idea," Tytus mutters and takes off even faster. As soon as we're away from the crowd, and just barely out of the village, he's shifting to zmeu and carrying me with him.

As we fly out, I hear the roar of an engine over the wind and notice a monster truck following us. People in it are pointing up at us.

"Tytus!"

He glances below, and his speed increases. There's desperation in his movements, like he's afraid. And then I realize why–the fear is for me, not for himself. The only place I'm safe is the castle. And that castle is far away now.

Tytus growls and shifts to the left. Something explodes to our right. These warriors got new weapons, and deadly ones by the look of it. Finally, we fly over the barrier of his home.

There's no way they didn't see us cross here. And they will follow, this time with enough arsenal to take us down. After switching back to human form, Tytus ushers me in, straight to the library.

"I need you to do something for me."

"What?"

"Not hate me." He kisses me fiercely, then pulls back and heads to one of the shelves. He picks up one tome, then heads to the opposite side and grabs another. His hand searches the now empty shelf and comes back with a vial.

I stare, recognizing it from weeks ago. The vial holds Declan's blood. I'd found it, led to it by Declan himself, years and years ago. It's how the connection between us was formed, and then it simply built upon itself the longer he was in my mind. That vial went to the wolves that served him first, then ended up back in Tytus' hands shortly before he left Rockland Creek.

It's odd and scary all at once, seeing it in his hand. Odd, because I'd forgotten about it. Scary, because this is a piece of Declan, hidden in this castle, and I hadn't even known about it. Just like I didn't know about the redhead.

Perhaps it's a good thing you chose to keep your feelings to yourself.

Instead of dwelling on it, I push that thought aside and focus on Tytus' words.

"I think Declan figured out a way to see the future while he was here. And he knew you and I, that we'd... That I would come to care for you." He tosses the vial on the ground, crushing it with the heel of his boot. "This is what the Serafim are following. Through the link Declan still has, with you. Somehow, they must have gotten his blood, too. Perhaps from long ago. From a time I didn't protect him. Either way, consciously or unconsciously, Declan has led the Cavaleri to us."

"That's insane. Why would he want the last of you gone?"

Tytus shrugs. "Revenge. Perhaps more." He hesitates, then admits, "For a brief moment, I thought you were working with him. Willingly. I apologize for that. You deserve my trust, not just now, but from way before."

The honesty in his expression makes it even harder not to bring up the redhead, to talk to him about my doubts. But this is not the time, and I shove the thoughts further away.

"I promised I would teach you how to protect your mind. From both of us." He takes a step closer to me then stops, as if thinking better of it. "The night we just spent is yet another proof of your kind soul, Fiona, but I know you're still hurting. There is no way you cannot be, what with your history and what my stupid, thoughtless action triggered in your mind. No matter how well intended it was, I was wrong. And I will spend forever and beyond making it up to you."

I don't know what to say, how to

respond to the pain in his words, the emotion in his expression. He's holding nothing back, and this would be the time for me to return these sentiments. But I cannot, frozen by indecision.

Undaunted, Tytus goes on, "I cannot pretend to know Declan's mind anymore. But the bottom line is, I need to protect *yours*. He cannot reach out to you and backstab me, I won't allow it. Especially if I'm to fight these knights, I don't want you in danger while away from me. So we have a little time until they get through. Then I'm going back out there to wipe out those fools. And I'm not asking you to help. But at least I know you'll be here, safe, both physically and mentally."

"And what you'll teach me, it'll get Declan out of my mind? For good?"

"Yes," Tytus says. "It will be hard. It will exhaust you. But you can do it, I know you're strong enough."

I gulp, more aware of the duality of our relationship. While he's been honest, and the way he is approaching this is through transparency–minus the redhead–I am not. Will that hurt my chances down the line? Probably. Will I change my mind, and tell him everything I want to? Absolutely not.

Despite what happened between us, I made a promise to myself, and I intend to stick with it. And no amount of fairy tales Tytus spews is going to change my mind.

For a chance at getting rid of Declan, barring him from my head, I will do anything. "Okay, let's do it."

Chapter 14

Viață
"You get in life what you have the courage to ask for."
~Oprah Winfrey~

Fiona

When Tytus said he wanted to teach me, I thought he meant then and there. Instead, he jerks his head towards the door and holds out his hand. "Not so fast. Come with me upstairs, for a second. Then we'll finish this."

"But, the Serafim?"

"They can wait." There's an odd glint in his eyes, almost like mischief, but not quite. "The more, the merrier. Come."

My mind stuck on his future lessons, I don't pay attention until we're all the way back up to his room. The door closes behind us, and Tytus smiles at me. "Before we do any teachings, I have to apologize in advance for the hell I'll be putting you through."

"Okay…"

I'm still blissfully unaware, until he comes closer to me, and drops to his knees in front of me. When his hands move under my skirt, my body recalls his earlier touch and my thoughts melt. "Ah, Tytus…"

"Yes, sweetling?" he asks, even as his fingers trail higher up my thighs, past my underwear, and dip inside me.

His mouth follows the trail, kissing my skin, until my skirt is gone and so are my undergarments, and nothing stops him from kissing me where I need him most.

A gasp escapes me… And then I'm lost to his touch and the pleasure he brings me. The door behind me is the only thing keeping me standing. Tytus plays my body like he's always known it, touching places I didn't know could be pleasurable, until all I see is stars and stars and stars. And when waves of ecstasy descend on me, my legs wobble, and I fall into him.

He rolls us over on the plush carpet so he's on top, and keeps kissing up my body, removing clothes as he goes. By the time his mouth latches onto a sensitive nipple, I'm arching against him, losing the last fragments of my mind.

"Fiona…" He groans in my neck then, a low, guttural sound that rocks me to my core.

I shift under him, tugging off his pants and spreading my legs. When he goes to take off his clothes, I wrap my limbs around him, holding him tight against me. His throbbing length pulsates against me, and I meet his gaze.

With my arms around his neck, I angle my hips upwards and slowly take him inside me. My eyelids flutter close, and I enjoy the sensation of being stretched, of being claimed. When I next look at him, Tytus' every feature is tense, determined as he holds himself back.

"I'm ready for more." There's a whine I hate in my tone, almost as much as I resent the neediness of this bond, of the physical connection. Yet nothing could stop me from rocking against him, silently pleading for more. "Unless you're determined to torture us both?"

Tytus exhales, and it's like all the tension goes out of him. The gray eyes I love darken with passion, and then he thrusts deeper inside me, groaning as I clench around him.

"You're going to kill me, sweetling," he murmurs, then lowers himself to claim my lips. "But I will enjoy every second of it." As he lengthens the kiss, his thrusts lose their control, until all I can do is hang on and relish each and every one.

His hands drop to my hips, holding me still, and on one last thrust he shouts my name, as we hit that ever-elusive pinnacle together.

¥

I jerk awake in the middle of the night, from some kind of nightmare. Unable to go back to sleep, I escape Tytus' hold and head on to take a shower, then put on a robe. I hesitate between joining him back in bed, or taking a walk…. And finally settle for the latter.

Down the hall, I sneak a glance out the windows. I don't understand Tytus' ability to relax at a time like this. Granted, the loving was distracting and well worth it, but the Serafim have grown in numbers. It seems their entire forces are at the castle doors. And even so, the necromancer among them is attacking the barrier, and they could get through at any point.

Why Tytus isn't doing anything is beyond me. Then again, he has been around for millennia, and perhaps that strategic thinking comes from experience.

As I continue to walk down the stairs, I try to push aside my warring emotions. With each moment spent together, I can sense the legătură, the bond, cementing between us. More and more often, Tytus' zmeu flashes in his eyes, showing his satisfaction, and I don't think he's even aware of it.

Instead, he's talking about making it up to me, about doing everything in his power so I forgive him for his misstep.

When in truth, I cannot allow myself to forgive him. If I do, it'll only mean nothing else stands between me and my feelings. And it's easier to cling to the idea he could still hurt me, still try to control me, and do everything possible to protect myself. Much easier than admitting the truth.

After all, how am I worthy of such a man, when my own redemption has fallen recklessly to the wayside? I came here to do good. In a way, I have, by saving Tytus and helping him on his quest. But I've also gotten distracted. Fallen for the fairy tale.

I step through the doors of the library, biting back a sigh. A fire is burning in the fireplace, and I pick up the journal I'd left earlier once more. I wish I could read it from beginning to end, and maybe one day, I will. For the moment, I flip a few more pages and start reading again.

December 7, 444 A.D.

I never thought this would happen, not to me. But it has, and in the short time I've been with her, I have fallen head over heels. I long for full honesty, to tell her everything, but instead as I sleep at night next to her, I whisper everything I cannot while I'm away.

I can't get you out of my head... The softness of your skin, your hair on my pillows... I live for the next day I see you...

One day, I'll be strong enough to walk away from it all. For her, I'll do anything, even if it means standing up to my clan.

The book falls to the ground from my trembling fingers, and I lift a hand to my throat to control my breathing. Tytus loved someone... Immediately, my mind flashes to the redhead. All my resistance of asking about her, of respecting his privacy and focusing on the present, flies out the window. Who else could it be, but her?

I move to the writing desk and shuffle through the drawers for her picture. She is everything I'm not–laughing, unburdened, youthful. And as I stare at the picture for much too long, some little shred of hope inside me shrivels and dies. Everything I'd hoped to keep in the past resurfaces, reminding me how I don't measure up.

¥

"Where have you been?" Tytus nuzzles my neck when I join him in bed again.

The moment I'm under the blankets, he wraps an arm around my waist and pulls me closer. I fight away the tears, the questions, determined not to have a meltdown at such a crucial time. My wayward emotions will simply have to wait. There's no point starting a massive fight, when I can't even figure out how to put my anger in words. Starting anything, at this moment, would only lead to showing all my cards, and him aware of how much he truly affects me.

"Couldn't sleep," I whisper instead, hoping my low voice will hide the trembling of my tone. When he says nothing, I try again. "Shouldn't we move?" His arm on me tightens. "What about the Serafim outside, Tytus?"

"They can wait. I don't want to leave you, not yet. Besides, I need more of them to arrive."

My mind and heart war silently, each wanting two completely different things. My mind wants distance, space between us, so I can gather my thoughts and bring up my defenses. My heart, however, wants nothing more than to give in to him, to the heat of his body.

It's the heart that wins, at least for the time being, and I let him pull me even deeper against him. This part, it's easy. We fit together like pieces of a puzzle, and I cannot deny the joy and pleasure he gives me. If it was just physical, I could keep at it. But every time he looks at me, and the way he touches me.... I see Tytus wanting more, needing more.

And I'm afraid I'll never be able to give it to him. How can I, when I'm still putting myself together? How can I, when the mere thought of all the power he can turn against me sends me running for the hills? Worse still, how can I, when it's clear there would be someone to compete with, at least in his head, in his memories?

Tytus chooses that moment, when my thoughts are already haywire, to speak. "Do you believe Declan is inherently evil?"

My pulse starts racing even as I try to think of a proper answer. An honest one. As if Tytus senses my hesitation, he speaks again.

"I don't want a fake response, Fiona. I need honesty."

"I… think it's complicated. He has made evil choices, yes. Hurt many people, including me. It's clear he loves control, perhaps because he lacked it at some point in his long life. I can't tell, as I only knew the tyrant. But is he inherently evil?" I pause, before finally voicing what I've been struggling with for days. "I don't think so, no."

Tytus is silent for a long, long time. It's probably not the answer he expected. It's not even the one I thought I would give. But as I assess my feelings, I cannot deny it is the most honest answer I can provide.

"Why not?" he asks.

"Because he had plenty of chances to make his control of me worse. And he didn't. He didn't force me to humiliate myself, or to use my body, or anything of the like. I was his conduit, his messenger to the wolves. And, to some extent, I think he even instilled in them a command that I was off limits."

"You were still hurt, though," Tytus says. There is a dark anger in his tone that scares me, and I intertwine our fingers.

"I was. By Thiago, by Cade. They didn't see me as useful. They were greedy. Ultimately, they got what was coming to them." I clear my throat, then add, "*They* were inherently evil. To the bone. Declan... I still don't think he is. But that doesn't mean I'm not afraid of him.'

Tytus' hold on me tightens even more, and he kisses me behind the ear. "He will not harm you, ever again. My zmeu..."

He trails off, and when he next speaks, his words freeze me.

"Sweetling, I wasn't entirely truthful. Nu, that's not right. I omitted part of the information, because I didn't want to scare you. But I think it's time you know it all." A soft sigh, and he continues. "When a zmeu chooses his pair, and they eventually join to complete the împerechere, the zmeu... burns his soulmate. They come out of the fire stronger, immortal almost. Only able to die if the zmeu does. It is where our bond is headed, eventually, and it will make you safe. Forever."

I gulp, my eyes wide in the room's darkness. Tytus turns me around, cupping my cheek. "I know how scary what I just said is, but I cannot lie to you anymore, Fiona. I don't want you to leave for your island, your isolation, after you're done here. After we fix all this, I want you here, with me."

He presses his lips against my temple for the softest of kisses, then pulls back. "But I will wait. As long as you need me to. You've only just escaped captivity, and I know you must see this as something even worse, perhaps. I swear to you, I would treat you right. You would be safe with me."

Forever.

The unspoken word lingers in the air, and I move away from him in an effort to hide my shaking. "I... I need to shower, before we do the lessons."

Tytus lets me go, his concerned gaze following me all the way into the bathroom. I wait until the shower beats down on me to burst out crying, trying and failing to stifle most of my sobs.

He's right, in a way. His words didn't

bring me any comfort. Instead, they sound like the doors of a prison closing around me. Even worse than his prior betrayal, even worse than hiding he'd been in love before, this… this, I cannot get past.

Why does he have to pretend like this bond would actually mean we'd be equals? That I would be his to protect, his to treasure, when the truth is I'd only be his plaything? He has proven it once, albeit not on purpose. But it happened. And regardless of his reassurances, who's to say it won't happen again?

The truth is, no matter how nice Ileana makes eternity sound, Tytus' idea of the future scares me shitless.

¥

Before long, I'm regretting trusting Tytus. When he said this would hurt, he meant it.

The basics of what he's doing are teaching me to protect my thoughts, my consciousness. A shield is no use—since I have to be actively conscious to cast it. Or, Declan more often than not catches me unaware while I sleep.

So, basically, Tytus is strengthening my mind. It's not meant to be a fix just for Declan, but for all times. According to him, the time Declan spent in my head, easily accessing it, has made the barriers usually around a person's thoughts weaker. And, for me to resist Declan or anyone else who might try–like Tytus himself–I have to work on strengthening my susceptibility to subconscious commands.

Like Tytus using his persuasion abilities on me. Yeah, fun. And he's aiming to teach me all this in a few hours by repeatedly trying to breach my mind, commanding me to do things, and keeping me distracted with magic all at the same time.

Needless to say, less than two hours after we started, I drop to my knees, close to tears. "I need a break."

My head is pounding, throbbing on both sides. Everything is numb, and I'm even starting to lose my ability to speak, slurring my words.

Tytus steps towards me, hand extended, then stops himself. When I glance up, pleading, his expression hardens. "Take a minute, but we're going back to it."

"I need more than a minute."

"You don't have more."

My glare doesn't seem to affect him. Nor does it amuse him.

"Tytus," I gasp, and force myself to stand. Failing, I wobble on my feet and nearly topple back on the floor, but he reaches out a hand to steady me. Tears of frustration fill my eyes. "Why are you being so hard on me?"

"You would hate it if I wasn't."

I stare at him, realizing he's right. If he tried to go easy on me, I'd loathe it equally. And, realistically, the reason for my weakness isn't just because of the constant barrage of mental assaults. Rather, I find my mind constantly drifting. Thinking of what he told me about the zmeu, as well as the words he'd written, trying to see him as the guy who could fall for a human like that. Trying to figure out if his silver-tongued words are more than empty promises.

I can't get you out of my head… The softness of your skin, your hair on my pillows…

With a push away from him, I try to stop

thinking about the redhead, and Tytus, and the two of them together.

Tytus doesn't give me any time before turning me back around, staring into my eyes. "Kiss me."

I glare at him even harder, sensing the pull of his powers on me. Not that he has to use them for a kiss... I've been wanting to. Badly. Damn the bond, the connection, and that damned journal I came across!

"Kiss. Me."

My focus narrows on what he taught me. Strengthen my mind. Concentrate on my own desire, my own will. Let that be the shining light at the end of the tunnel, not whatever his voice is telling me to do.

"*Kiss me*, Fiona."

With a jerk, I manage to step away. I'm still panting, and he's staring at me. Then a slow smile spreads on his face. "You did it."

"That wasn't fair."

He runs to me, ignoring my sulking, and picks me in his arms. "I don't care. You did it!" Then he's kissing me all over, leaving me breathless and panting for a completely different reason.

And then... the ground shakes. And with it, the entire castle.

Tytus

"I have to give it to the Serafim, they have impeccable timing."

Fiona sighs in my arms, dreading this moment probably as much as I have. Now that at least her mind is clear, I need her help with something. The problem is, I dread even more asking her. But there's no way I can be in two places at once, and having Fiona go ahead, especially since she has the tools to protect herself...

I clear my throat. "Fiona, do you remember the map I showed you? With the tunnels, past where the vasilisc was?"

She nods.

And now, for the hard part. "Would you go into those tunnels, as far as possible? See if you can open them. Don't go past them, as I'll be there as soon as I take care of the Serafim. But if you find the entry point, it will save us time down the line."

To my surprise, she nods again. "All

right, that's doable."

"And be careful of the zmeu magic. Remember what I said about the price–"

"I know," she says before I can continue. "You've made it clear before, so repeating it is useless."

I frown at her, unsure of her mood. She's been all over the place since I told her about the next step, or more to the point, since I broke her trust. I need to fix things between us, to see what she's thinking, but it's hard when she won't look at me. Despite the fire in the bedroom, I'm getting the feeling I need to try another approach, and soon.

"I'm not trying to isolate you from me, sweetling. But having you there with me, within striking distance of the Serafim and their dark mage, will be a distraction I cannot afford."

"You're just saying that."

Her accusing tone jolts me, and my zmeu grumbles in disapproval. "Which part, exactly?"

"I know how these things work, Tytus. It's unnecessary to baby me or pretend like

I'm the center of your world."

"Where the hell is this coming from?" I try to move closer, but she steps away, holding up her hand. "No, you don't get to just toss something like that at me, and then walk away."

"I'm only going where you need me. For the mission."

"Forget the damn mission!" I stomp to her, grasping her arm. "What is this really about, Fiona? I've been nothing but honest with you about the bond, the connection–you know everything there is to know. And my feelings are clear, are they not?"

Tears fill her violet eyes when she finally looks at me. "There are no *feelings*, Tytus! Not really. What's a zmeu like you doing, caring for a human like me?" A bitter laugh escapes her. "As if! Your castle may be straight out of a fairy tale, but we don't live in one. And I'm trying to tell you, that you don't have to go through all this trouble to make me feel like I'm worth something to you, other than a plaything for the time being."

My shock at her words is physical,

enough that I stumble back and release her. *What in the world...?*

"A *plaything*?" I shake my head. "A play... Fiona, what in hell!? You're always finding a reason for my feelings. First magic. Now this shit. Why can't you just accept what I'm saying, that I'm falling in love with you? I didn't plan it. I definitely didn't plan to ask you to be my mate just as an ancient order assails my castle." Frustration seeps through me. "But, it's happening. And I don't expect an answer now, but I needed you to know."

Is this because of Declan, has he gotten in her head again? I can't figure it out, and she's not giving me enough clues. What, of what I've done so far, could have made her draw these conclusions, rather than see herself as I do?

The castle shakes again, reminding me that outside, fanatical knights are attacking my barrier in order to storm through here–to kill me.

I try one more time, softening my tone. "Why can't you just accept I love you, for you?"

Fiona looks away, unwilling to believe

me. Unwilling to give this thing between us a chance. How do I fight against this, get her to see things my way without breaking the fragile trust she placed in me? How do I convince her we're worth it, when she is so determined to ignore her own worth?

I cannot lose her. My zmeu rebels against the mere idea, almost close to panic. I've never had this gut-wrenching sensation, and I don't particularly like it.

Another shake of the castle jolts me.

Fiona looks around. "You should go. I'll find the tunnels."

She goes to leave, but I can't let her. In two steps, I'm blocking her exit, opening my mouth and hoping the right words will come out. And then a sound, like a bell, rings in the library. I frown in confusion, even more so when she points at my pocket.

"It's the cell phone. Must be Elisandra, calling you back."

Right. I'd forgotten all about it. I tried calling her earlier, but with no answer, I ended up leaving her the phone number to return my call. So I pull out the contraption and answer. "Elisandra?"

"Yeah, who is this?"

A beat of silence as I meet Fiona's eyes again. "It's me, Tytus."

"Tytus! Are you nearby?"

"No, why?" My sharp hearing picks up some noise in the background, sounding like a fight. "What's going on?"

She doesn't answer for a while, and I think the connection might have cut. With the Serafim at my doors, I fear they have found her, too. Fiona moves closer to me and takes the phone out of my hand, then presses a button. Elisandra's voice comes back on, only now it's coming out through the speakers.

"Nothing, never mind. What's up?"

"You're lying."

She sighs, a sound of frustration. "Lucas ran into a bit of trouble, is all."

"What kind of trouble?"

"The kind we can handle, don't worry. Tell me, what's happening? How's Romania? Did you get there safely?"

I chuckle at her barrage of questions. "I arrived back home, Romania is beautiful as always, but there have been developments."

"Like what?"

"Let's just say Declan seems to have hidden something in here. I was wondering if you'd had any weird dreams lately, or if any memories of your time with him came back."

Elisandra is quiet again, and I wish I could see her face. Brown wavy hair piled atop her head, hazel eyes that glint with the gold of a zmeu's power, and a soft face permanently streaked with flour from the bakery she runs. Blood of my blood, but across an ocean. What a life.

I'd watched over her for months before the wolves interfered, before one of them fell in love with her, and they mated. That connection was the closest I've come to caring for someone, and it unfortunately led to me caring about way more humans than I intended.

When Elle is back on, her voice is softer. "I've dreamed of something, lately. It's like a tunnel, and I'm surrounded by these walls with weird carvings. It's dark. And at some point I get through it, and I come out the other way… And there's a creature."

"What kind of creature?"

"I… I don't know, exactly. I just remember a big head, a roar, and flaps like wings." She's silent for a bit more. "And… there's noises. A woman crying. Does any of this help?"

"It does. Thank you." I meet Fiona's eyes, reading the consternation in her expression. "One last question. From your time here, did Declan keep to a particular area of the house?"

"Not that I remember, sorry. My alter had taken over my body, and she kept pushing me in the background, unable to see or witness everything."

"Thank you, Elisandra." I want to say much more, to ask about Finn, to make plans for the future… But there is no point, not when things here are so uncertain. "Take care," I say by way of goodbye instead.

"Wait! Will you… You'll keep your promise and return, right?"

"I will. I would never break it."

"Okay. Be safe, yeah?" The line goes dead a moment after.

I look back at Fiona, realizing how

close we are. Perhaps it's a cowardly move, but I take advantage of her nearness and brush my lips against hers. She may deny this, she may fight against it, but the raw, primal bond between us will not be denied.

When she doesn't push me away, I grip the back of her neck and angle her head, taking the kiss deeper. It's her sweet surrender that does me in, confirming there's something here.

Then the ground shakes and she takes it as an excuse to move. I cannot reconcile her evasive nature with the woman who's been so responsive in my arms.

"You have to go," she says.

"I'm going, but this, you and me... It's not done, Fiona."

She shakes her head. "You don't owe me explanations, Tytus. We are adults, and we had a tryst. Now the sun is up, it's a new day, and I think it's time we both wake up to reality. We're not compatible, not even close."

My jaw hurts from the force I'm clenching it with. Something tells me she's being defensive, but over what? What the hell changed between when I had her in my bed, and now? "You are the stubbornest witch I've ever come across."

Her eyes glint steely in the light. "But not the most stubborn woman, evidently."

"What?"

She purses her lips. "Never mind. Go."

"No. Explain what you mean."

This time, the shaking of the ground brings a crack across the surface, and I have to step backwards. Fiona does the same, then waves me onwards. "Go! Protect your land before they get through the barriers."

I scowl at her. "This isn't over."

Fiona says nothing, instead turning away and walking towards the opposite door. I force my feet to move, to head outside. But with each step away from her, I'm starting to feel like it's the wrong choice.

Chapter 15

Liberà
"Man is free at the moment he wishes to be."
-Voltaire-

Tytus

I have an odd sense of déjà vu as I storm through the halls of my castle, ready to take on the Serafim once more. I know they've come here to finish what their previous party couldn't–and I fully intend to wipe them out.

Yet whereas before I had focused on the knights, on the fight at hand, and left Fiona behind on purpose, now I cannot shake it off. Even as the walls shake around me–they must be attacking the barrier repeatedly for such an impact–all my focus is on Fiona.

So much so that once I get to the white

oak doors of the entrance, I hesitate. My gaze lingers on the stairs I've just descended, with half a mind to go back and shake some sense into her. How can she think all we had was one night, that we're not compatible? Is it because I'm immortal? Because of what I am? Because the împerechere would take care of that, ensuring she has nothing to worry about.

Or does her fear run deeper, entrenched into the belief I'm somehow like Declan? Have I not done everything to prove her wrong?

This destabilizing sensation is not one I am accustomed to. It is not one I particularly enjoy, either. For eons I have lived through life unperturbed. Even as Declan fell in love and got hurt, I avoided it.

For so long, I thought I was invincible until she got through to me. And now I must once more go out there and pretend I am the feared zmeu, lest the Serafim catch onto my distraction and it'll be the death of both of us.

With a sigh, I turn away from the stairs and move through the doors. By the time I make it to the gates of my castle, the line of Serafim has grown. They have come with human cars, trucks, and weapons of all shapes and sizes.

When I see them lined up, sense their energy, it's a reminder of other fights in the past where my kind was fiercely defensive of their own. Perhaps because of those, perhaps because of the realization I have someone to protect now, I try the negotiating route first.

On the other side of the barrier, I open my palms and keep my expression as non-threatening as I can. "Cine e şeful?" When I'm met with blank stares, I switch to English and repeat my question. "Who is your leader?"

Swords, spears and guns continue to be pointed my way. Even as I inspect every masked face, a cluster of the knights from the back line shifts. I tense, expecting an attack, but they're only letting someone through.

The emerging man has no mask. A navy ribbon holds back his white hair, and cold, black eyes stare at me. He is not the necromancer, I can tell just by looking at him. In his forties, he has an air of rightness about him, but still very human. Perhaps I could negotiate, indeed.

"Thank you for showing yourself," I say.

"What do you want?"

"I was hoping you could explain why the Serafim have tracked me across oceans and continents, when I have done nothing to deserve it."

His gaze narrows on me. "Nothing? *Nothing?* What about the town of Rockland Creek you incinerated? The lives you cost?"

Elisandra. A muscle ticks in my jaw, and I try to rein in my zmeu from going all protective. Perhaps there is still a chance to reason with them—I must try, at least. "That was not me. It was my brother."

"And where is he now?"

"Taken care of. Imprisoned."

The man narrows his eyes. "Your prisons do not fool me. You will rise again, *he* will rise again, and more cities will pay the price. We cannot trust your kind."

"I beg to differ, kind sir. You are speaking with me now, and I am willing to give you my word. Leave my land, and I will make it my life's mission to ensure my brother never escapes his prison and harms any other human."

He laughs. "Your words are sweet honey, but this bee has grown wiser. You have murdered in cold blood enough of my men. There is nothing that will save you now." He nods to one of the Serafim. "Prepare the weapons. Bring forth the necromancer."

"You don't want to do that." I know I'm playing right into his hands, but the callousness and inability to rationalize is too much. When did humans get this petty, this unwilling to reason?

I warn you, they will turn against you. Declan's words ring in my head with more clarity than I wish. Da, my brother had been right on that end, but it's not like we aided the matter further. Especially him.

"And why not?" the man asks. "My men have clear orders. You will be eradicated, and your home, too. I will make sure no living soul is left here before I leave it all burned to the ground. Only ashes will remain of it." The hate dripping from his words leaves me baffled.

"I am telling you, I was not responsible for what befell that town! I tried to save it."

The man smirks. "Yes, because you had something to protect there. A descendant of yours. Do not worry, she is next on our list."

My blood runs cold at his warning, and all thoughts of negotiation leave me. I lower my head to the ground, clenching my fists. The air changes along with my rising rage, becoming full of static–like before lightning strikes.

All I'm aware of is the steady thump, thump, thump of the blood in my temples, blocking every other noise. My nails dig into my palms, drawing blood, but not even that pain can ground me enough.

Let me eat them, my zmeu begs. There is no reining him in, not anymore. Not when a clear threat has been made against what is ours. *Defend.*

When I next look up, the leader of the Serafim takes a step backwards, even as I cross the barrier.

My eyes survey the army. "If you are so intent on killing me, this better be your entire forces you brought."

He laughs. "Only the best for you, zmeu."

"Good." A cold smile escapes me. "You threaten me, I can live with that. You threaten my kind, those I care for? You'll get what you wish."

I toss my head back, and in the same movement, the change ripples through me. My zmeu extends his wings, panting from the change. Everything becomes background noise. The human is yelling orders to his people. The necromancer is preparing spells.

I hit back with one of my own, ensuring they cannot escape this place through a portal or anything else. And then I jump to the skies, taking cover in the clouds as I prepare my attack.

Fiona

Why can't you just accept I love you, for you? Tytus' words run on a loop in my head as I head down to the vasilisc, and the tunnels beyond it.

He's faking it. As irrational as it sounds, despite everything we shared, it was still only one night. With a couple extra romps in bed. He gave me the speech of the legătură, the împerechere, sure, but I'd bet anything it was also said to the redhead. Maybe it is all a lie. Maybe there's not just one mate. Maybe it's just something zmei tell unsuspecting human females to get them in bed, and at their mercy.

Either Tytus feels like he owes me something, or he probably sees me as the best thing to come along in a while. A witch, with a weak mind to control? It's only human nature that he'd want to keep me around.

Except Tytus isn't human.

My footsteps falter. I've gone and gotten involved with a zmeu shifter who now says he cares for me. If that's not a sign of his human nature, then what is it?

And what is so fearful–aside from the part where his zmeu would burn me–is that I almost want his words to be true. I want his love, his devotion, his protection. I want the equal relationship he promises.

The fairy tale, with all the bells and whistles.

If it wasn't for the deceit, for the fear that he's so completely out of my league and I'd end up his plaything, at his mercy... If he wasn't intricately tied to the man who enslaved me...

I have given Tytus everything I possibly can—my body, my trust, even my reluctant love. Not that he knows that last part, not that he ever will. If learning he has lied to me about one past relationship can affect me so, can make me even more insecure, what would I achieve if I were to truthfully admit I have fallen for him? Nothing. Except expose more weakness.

I realize now I should have asked my questions way before this, while I'd had the chance. Before we fell into bed. Before he admitted what he did. Before the Serafim attacked us.... And now it's too late.

I'm distracted from my thoughts by a groan. It sounds like it's coming from around me, but once I stop moving, the sound is more a vibration through the ground. I kneel, pressing my ear to the cold stone, and hold my breath.

It happens again. And again. Like something being torn, or refusing to give way. I have a sudden image of a creature trying to escape its binds, and those binds emitting the noises.

Gulping, I get back to my feet. Regardless of what's going on with me and Tytus, we split up for a reason. And while he's out there figuring things out, I need to, as well. So I move further into the pathway, straightening my back and refusing to let fear get to me.

¥

An hour or so later, I'm still walking through the tunnels. Only this time, I'm not alone anymore. For the last hour now, Declan's prodding has become more and more insistent at the back of my mind. Like Tytus taught me, now that I know what to expect, I can sense it coming.

With nothing else to do but think, my thoughts have returned to Tytus. I wonder how he's doing above ground, fighting against the Serafim. Is he injured again? Or has he already demolished them, and he's on his way to join me and demand answers for my cryptic behavior earlier?

Or maybe he's not, the same voice says.

I try to ignore it, I really do. Focus on my intentions—but he's strong. Persistent. Eager to get himself heard.

Come on, witch. Talk to me. Has my brother taught you new tricks. is that why you now block me? It's not nice.

The prodding gets even more insistent. I'm reminded of those commercials I used to see on TV for pain relievers, showing little drills into someone's mind. It's exactly what it feels like. And perhaps because of an unconscious need to not be alone, or perhaps because Declan really is that strong, the voice finally gets through.

A satisfied sigh, then he says, *About time. I grow weary on my own.*

Is that why you bother me, Declan? Because you're bored in your gilded cage of a prison?

He's quiet for a moment, absorbing my words and the implication Tytus told me about their encounter. *My brother should learn to keep his mouth shut.*

He hides nothing from me. The moment I say the words, I realize they are the wrong ones.

Really? Declan laughs. *Nothing, not a thing, from his entire millennia of existence?*

I try to ignore him, but it's too late. Now that he got through, it's like he's dug himself into my mind and refuses to leave. *What about the redhead, has he told you about her?*

I jerk to a stop, completely giving away my eagerness to learn more. No matter how painful it will be.

Ah, he has not. Another chuckle. *I suppose you'd like to find out, yes?*

No.

Nice try, Fiona. But I know you better than you know yourself.

Screw you, Declan. You don't—you never did. To know someone, you have to stop using them long enough to care about them. Let's not pretend you ever did.

He's silent for a while. A long while. And for once, I don't dread what his reaction will be. In fact, I almost hope he's gone... Almost. And then he speaks again.

Her name was Alina. And, funniest of all things, she was mine—she was my wife.

I try to coat my surprise, but it's no use. Declan must feel it. If he does, he says nothing. Instead, he keeps talking. *And Tytus, my dear brother, seduced her from me. Warped her mind. Turned her against me—enough so that she would betray me.* A bitter laugh escapes him, making me wince. *Enough so that she came after me.*

I remember the portraits–Alina's brilliant smile. The two zmei by her side. Tytus' written words, his self-proclaimed love for her. Jealousy is hot and heavy in my gut, as is dread. This was a mistake, but it's too late to stop. If I can't have the answers I need from Tytus, then perhaps his brother will give them to me.

When Declan grows quiet again, I hazard a question. I'm surprised I even want to ask one, but I've recognized in his deluge of words something I'm very familiar with–hurt, betrayal. *How is that even possible, you having a wife? Don't zmei not marry?*

You've been speaking to immortals, then?
Maybe.

If it's Ileana and Făt, watch yourself.
They'll sooner backstab you than save you.

This time, I'm prepared for the surprise and mask it well enough that he doesn't even catch a whiff of it. Declan, my captor and tormentor, offering... a warning? What the hell?

They seem decent enough. If pushy. And annoying. But you didn't answer my question.

And you seem to have grown a back-bone, little witch.

Don't call me that.

Why, is it a pet name claimed by my brother? A derisive laugh. *He was always good at that. Micuță, he called Elisandra. Little one. All it took was a little coaxing, and she told me everything he'd revealed and everything she had put together. Too bad I couldn't keep her by my side. Hmm...*

He trails off, and I force myself to bring him back on topic. Whether he's drunk or something else, now's the time for me to get my answers. *The marriage?*

Alina asked for it. Insisted on it before

she even knew what I was. I was too enamored to give a shit and agreed. Even stayed away from our clan of zmei for a time.

And then Tytus found out?

Da, as he always does. He came over, and I introduced them. I should have known with the way he kept coming around, something was wrong. But it wasn't until I was shown the truth that it really clued in how far they had deceived me.

Shown? By whom?

It doesn't matter. I've prattled on long enough, little witch. You should take one warning out of it, though—I may have been bad, but my brother is a thousand times worse.

Why did I ever bother listening to him, when I knew it would end with him bashing Tytus? Still, rather than keep my silence, I fight back. *I don't believe that. He is good.*

Good? Sure. If by good, you mean he will make you feel like the center of his universe, then break you into pieces. You will never be able to put yourself back together after he's done with you.

I hate the voice in my head, a reminder of everything I already believe deep in my core. I force myself to block it, but all of Tytus' teachings are wiped clean. Because Declan is saying a lot of the shit I've been telling myself, for longer than he has.

He is sending you to your death, Declan laughs, back to his normal self. *And I will enjoy this.*

You lie.

What makes you think that?

Tytus cares for me. I realize how stupid it sounds even as I say it. Wasn't this specifically what I was arguing with him about? Right before he went into battle?

My brother cares for no one but himself.

That's not true. He's selfless. A hell of a lot more than you are, that's for sure!

My, my. Now you have fire, witch. Had I known, I would have had other uses for you.

I stop walking, scowling at nothing in particular. Part of me wishes he was here, so I could confront him face to face. Another part fears that I could not stand up to him on my own.

And then, deeper than that, is the part fearing he is right and I'm nothing but an impostor, a weak witch. Someone completely undeserving of anything. Even love. Especially Tytus' love. If I ever wanted it, that is.

I inhale deeply. Recall Tytus' words, his kindness. His passion. The way he looks at me. No, that's not true. It can't be.

But Tytus... To take his own brother's wife? That is the worst kind of betrayal, and he did it callously. Ruthlessly. Same as he took control of my mind when I was weak, to get me to listen. Yes, it was to get me safe, or so he says. But if he's so good at deceit, is there not a chance I've gotten in bed with the wrong person?

Regardless, one thing remains. Tytus aside, I am not an impostor. And I am not weak, nor am I worthless. I never was, but I let myself think it, let myself find excuses and allow someone else to rule me simply because I thought he was more powerful.

Or, the power to say no, to change my destiny, was always in my hands. Still is. And this time, I'll make the right choice.

Drawing in a deep breath, I let it all out. *You know what, Declan? You've had control of me for too many years. And I allowed you to. But I have a choice, we all do. And I refuse to be a victim any longer.*

So, what, you'll cry for help back to my brother?

No. I'm going to do what he gave me the tools for—stand up for myself and believe that I am done being a pawn in someone else's game. Goodbye, Declan.

Then I close my eyes and focus, just as Tytus taught me. On myself, *my* thoughts, *my* wishes. Above all, on *my* free will. When I open them again, my mind is clear. There is no Declan, no more taunting. No more fear.

I did it.

A sense of freedom engulfs me, and my heart soars. The last shackles have been broken, and I am utterly, completely free. It doesn't get better than that. I was able to take the tools given to me, find my inner strength, and be my own savior.

That, I think, is even more empowering than anything else. To be my own heroine, my own knight in shining armor. When I grew up in a world where man alone can do so. And if I was able to do this, then I sure as hell can face Tytus–my supposed mate– when I see him next, and ask him to explain himself.

Feeling braver, stronger, I head further. I pass by the dead carcass of the vasilisc and move into the hole in the wall. Tytus said to check it out, and surely I can go and just take a peak.

For a moment, once I'm past the rubble and the stench of the deadbeat, everything is fine. The ground appears smoother, as if this particular area was carved out by a crafty hand.

And then my foot slips on something, and I'm falling, unable to find a grip anywhere. When I hit the bottom, long moments of tumbling later, I groan at the noxious fumes billowing around me.

Then I blink through the dust and peer around. *Where the hell did I end up?*

Declan

The little witch.... She figured out how to push me out. But not before standing up to me and saying her piece. How incredibly human of her.

Annoyance creeps through me, more at the fact I got outdone. Still, it doesn't come as a surprise. The moment I foresaw she and Tytus would hook up, I knew it would lead to losing her. Besides, it's not the first woman I've lost because of my brother, albeit in a different sense.

I chose Fiona for her fire, knowing full well it would help withstand the powers I bestowed upon her. And yet now I find myself... alone. The plan made sense when it hatched, way back when. Now, not so much. Not when my mind has become occupied with memories of Alina again, and of Fiona, and of what in hell my brother did to deserve her loyalty.

And meanwhile I'm still in this damn prison, away from the fire, the action. And through it all, my brother has the nerve to imprint on my toy and enjoy his freedom.

That bothers me more than anything else.

Chapter 16

Mizerabil
"The truth will set you free, but first it will make you miserable."
-James A. Garfield-

Tytus

Enough toying. I peer down at what's left of the Serafim's forces. They have pushed me enough, and I will give them what they most fear. The irony is I don't enjoy killing them, nor hearing their cries of agony as I tear them limb from limb. But when negotiations fail....

I go for another sweep, ducking when they least expect me. My tail clobbers their cars, the screech of metal being torn apart filling the air. Haphazardly, I grab a few of the men and fly off with them. My claws dig into their bodies, destroying vital organs, then I dump them. Their bodies drop, gravity taking hold, and nothing and no one could save them now.

No, I take no joy in killing them.

My zmeu, on the other hand... The haze of the hunt is upon us both. I have held him too much at bay, like a leashed dog, and now he wants blood. There is a reason they sent me in the wars. There is a reason the Council trusted me. And it had nothing to do with diplomacy, rather with the knowledge that when push came to shove, I would do the right thing. For the clan, for the zmei, for our future together.

And many times before, I did. Now, I do the same. Once the zmeu merges with me, I am as much animal as I am human. Though I maintain my consciousness, I am also more. Enhanced.

My zmeu and I, we need their full submission, *now*. To protect the land. To protect Fiona. And we *will* burn the world to the ground, if it comes to it.

Everything blurs as I move faster, zigzagging in the air and avoiding the

Serafim's poorly aimed blows. They think me mortal, or what? Finally, the necromancer steps into the play. Unlike the rookie I killed a while ago. I sense his power reverberating below. He sets up a shield to protect the Serafim, and they believe themselves safe.

Imbecili. Bunch of idiots.

With a roar of rage, I fly into the skies, pulling onto the magic of lightning and clouds to shield me. When I next come down, lightning surrounds me in a barrier of its own, crackling and sizzling everywhere. The necromancer's dead magic tries to strike me—and fails.

My shot of pure lightning, however, bursts through his barrier and burns the remainder of the Serafim. No cries of agony this time, only the sizzle of charred flesh and pure, dead silence.

With a snort, I fly away again, re-assessing and targeting.

The necromancer and the leader alone are left. At least the warlock is smart enough to back away, attempting to create a portal. My defenses, set before I flew off, stop him. I snort out laughter, and puffs of angry smoke escape my nostrils as I land.

Without care for their mental fragility, I toss my thoughts, forcing my way through their feeble minds. *You thought you actually had a chance against me?*

The necromancer holds onto his head, like my voice is too loud and will split his poor brain. *Good.* Uncaring of his plight, I add, *ANSWER ME!* As I push forward, he falls to his knees, looking more than a little pale.

"S-sorry," he whispers, lifting pleading eyes to me. His change of heart does not surprise me. In my full zmeu form, this close by and with none of their army left, he would have to be a fool to contest me. "M-mercy, p-please..."

I give him a minute. Sixty seconds in which he can pretend I will listen. Sixty seconds in which he can almost taste his freedom. Sixty seconds where he can dream of a future. And then I open my jaws wide and let loose the fire I had prepared for him.

As his charred flesh smell fills the air, I

turn to the leader. He stands straight, knowing death is coming and willing to look it in the face. I could admire that... If it weren't for the fact his actions threatened my mate, my home, and my very being. They threatened innocents whose only fault was to live near me.

So, no, I cannot admire such a man. I can only detest him. And with my rage comes a thirst for vengeance I need to quench. For the first time, I understand some of what Declan felt, the rage and desire to wipe out humanity. To make them pay. To show them we are better— more. That dark desire takes root inside me, churning and pushing.

And for once, I do not control it. I do not talk myself out of it. I give in and let it all loose.

The leader's head falls at my feet, wiped clean by my claws. I look at it, then toss more fire onto his carcass, and those around us. One rune spell will turn the bodies into bonfires for anyone who looks too close.

Yet even as I waste time with the

illusion, my zmeu tugs at me. *Fiona.* Something is happening below my castle. And judging by his panic, it's nothing good.

With a beat of my wings, I fly up high, then dive inside the barrier once more.

Fiona

The smell of sulfur and rot hits me first. I get up from the ground and dust myself off, feeling an odd twinge in my back. *Probably hurt something.* Hesitation courses through me for all of two seconds, before I completely ignore Tytus' warning and head deeper into the new tunnel.

To my surprise, after barely a few moments, I reach a metal door. It looks more like the door of a prison, with bars as thick as my wrist. Torches light up the entrance, and deeper past it.

It seems odd to have something lighted this deep inside the castle… Unless I'm not alone.

Perhaps it's the victory against Declan, or my own reckless mind. Either way, I draw a rune and watch as the sizzle of fire pops the lock holding the door closed. It creaks open, as if inviting me in.

A deep breath later, I cross the threshold and have to duck as the passage narrows. Eventually, it expands into a massive library, three times as large as Tytus', with a massive archway. And hidden within its depths, past many shelves, I notice an odd shape.

When I stare, it moves, prompting me to follow it. Though I try to tiptoe, my footsteps still feel loud. Or perhaps that's just my extra-fast heartbeat. Either way, as I turn the corner of the ancient library, the columns on every side, I find... a zmeu.

Only he looks all wrong. He is as large as Tytus, but rather than a majestic arch to his back, he is bent over, almost deformed. One of his wings is torn at the bottom, and his scales are a dirty brown, almost slimy. The sulfur smell–it's coming from him.

He glances up from the wall he'd been staring at, sniffing the air. Then his gaze turns to me. Two white orbs take me in– only, they don't. He's blind, judging by the way he's getting up and clambering about.

"Who goes there?"

My jaw drops when he speaks in... words. Actually formed, not just thought. I could deny my presence here, but something tells me not to do that. So I step further, holding my head high. "I'm Fiona. Tytus' guest."

He freezes, then his dulcet tone comes out kinder. "Tytus? Then you are my guest, too. Come, enter. Come closer so I can get a good whiff."

I hesitate, and he drops back to his hind legs, then to the ground. "Is this better?"

"Yes, thank you." He lowered himself to make me comfortable, guessing my fear. I'm not sure if I should be wary around such a creature, but I get closer still. "Are you a zmeu?"

He shakes his head. "My name is Igor, and I am what they call a balaur. We are cousins of the zmei."

"Oh. Tytus didn't mention your existence."

This new world I've landed in seems to always be expanding. I recall seeing the mention of a balaur in the stories I read, but I cannot for the life of me remember what it said.

"Tytus doesn't know I'm down here," Igor says.

"How come?"

"The Council of zmei, long ago, imprisoned me here. They did not agree with my views that they should encourage interactions with humans, not forbid them. And then Declan found me, more recently. He…" A hesitation. "He plans to use my body for a sacrifice, to bring forth another creature. Though I do not know which."

Maybe it's stupid, but that bit of information alone, so forthcoming, makes me automatically trust him. Igor may stink, but they always say not to judge a book by its cover…

"Shit." I pace around, restless. This is the information we'd been searching for, the culmination of our mission. "Is there a way to find out?"

"That is what I have struggled with. These old books may hold some information, but I have gone blind from my time down here. And while the stars might tell me something, I have not seen them in ages."

"The stars?" I frown, glancing up. Only an ivory dome surrounds us. How could Igor have lived here for so long?

"Da, I used to read the stars," he says, distracting me again. "A rather unique ability of mine."

"That must have come in handy."

His jaws open wide, as if he is smiling. "You have no idea."

Tytus

Hurry.

Unlike in the skies, I cannot move fast enough. I crash through the doors of my castle, run up the stairs to the second floor and towards the West Wing crater. One jump through, and the moment my feet hit the ground, I take off running again.

Faster.

Something's got my zmeu in a frenzy, and I have to trust that age-old instinct. If anyone would know our mate is in danger, it would be him. And he does. Obviously.

If something happens to her because I was stupid enough to send her here... I speed up even further.

Past the vasilic, through the broken wall, and then I slip on something. Slide and fall on my ass, hitting yet another level I didn't know existed in my castle.

Up ahead.

My zmeu is adamant we're getting closer to Fiona, so I get up and prepare to run again–only to slam straight into a barrier that sends me flying back onto my ass.

I sit up, shaking my head and standing once more. "What the *fuck*!?" My voice echoes in the darkness.

Two runes escape my fingertips, but they have no impact on the barrier other than dissolving like fireworks. After a few steps closer, I pass my hands on it. Static crackles across–it's powerful. But who the hell left it here?

At a loss, and with my zmeu even more intent on getting to Fiona, I reach into the depths of my mind and talk to the one person I want to avoid at all costs.

DECLAN!

After our disastrous face to face, I probably won't get much out of him. And I have no time to reach out to the immortals, but I sure as hell won't believe he's not implicated in this.

So I push my mental shout through the barrier of my mind, seeking the brotherly connection that helped us out many times in the past. This once, I hope it will get me what I need, and nothing more.

It takes Declan way too long to my taste, but he answers in a bored tone. *Yes?*

How the hell are you able to toss a barrier into this realm?

Don't know what you're talking about.

Yes, you do! You've lured Fiona into a trap. And now you've made sure I cannot follow.

Lured her? Perhaps. Last I recall, she came of her own volition. It was you who sent her to her death.

The words are enough to strike fear in my heart, and my knees buckle. *Is she...?*

Not yet, no.

The bastard. He sounds too damn indifferent. *So you can talk to her?* Did my teachings not work? I thought she had grasped it… That I had managed to protect her from this much, at least.

Oh, enough with the sappy foolish shit, Tytus. She kicked me out of her mind before I could do much harm. Which is why I am glad she landed where she did.

And where is that?

No answer comes.

Declan!

Still nothing.

DECLAN, ANSWER ME!

When it comes, his tone is seething, and a little too satisfied. *I owe you nothing, darling frate. Other than suffering and despair. For you to hurt as I did. And for once, you will. Even if it will not be at my own hands.*

What the hell does he mean? It's useless trying to get more out of him, so I don't even bother. Instead, I bang my fists against the portal.

"Fiona? Fiona! Can you hear me? FIONA!"

Fiona

Something strikes me, as I'm talking to Igor. "You've been down here for a while... Can you answer me something?"

"Perhaps."

I watch as Igor moves side to side, wondering if I should try. But if he knew both brothers, perhaps I can learn the truth once and for all. "Was Declan ever married?"

Igor freezes, then his massive head tilts to the side. "Da, to a beautiful human named Alina."

"What happened to her?"

"She died." Igor sighs, and I try not to wrinkle my nose at the extra sulfuric smell emanating from him.

"How?"

"She was killed, for betraying Declan."

I gulp, recalling Tytus' written words. "How did she betray...?"

"Through her tryst with Tytus."

So it is true. For once, Declan wasn't lying, nor trying to manipulate me. Tytus had a romantic liaison with Alina, and broke up his brother's marriage. Betrayal runs through me anew. I hate that he did that–but

I cannot change it. Nor can I change my feelings about it, at least not now.

A problem for another time.

Even as I'm talking to the balaur, a shout echoes in the distance. When I focus on it, I recognize my name—and Tytus' voice.

"Is that Tytus?"

"I hear nothing."

I give Igor a weird look—how could he not? When I move closer, as if to head towards the exit, he places one paw in such a way it blocks me from nearing the entrance. For a blind creature, he sure moves with accuracy.

"I'm pretty sure that's Tytus," I say.

"He can wait a little longer."

Why did he lie about hearing him? My gaze sharpens on him, and something nags at me. I'd been so ruled by my desire to prove myself, and then to find out more about this world I've stumbled into, that I ignored the obvious. Which is, if the door was locked and it was keeping something inside, what was it? So far, I've only seen Igor here.

"I want to see him."

"Not yet."

I narrow my eyes on him. "Why not?"

"Because I am not yet done filling your head with information, my dear."

The glint in his eye doesn't look wise, not anymore. It looks downright mean. Like he's enjoying this too much.

I try to move out of his reach, but I'm too slow. Igor reaches for me and grasps me by the arm, nearly yanking it out of its socket as he pulls me towards him. Off balance, I stumble and fall to the ground, where he pins me.

I stare at him in shock and anger–at myself, at my naïveté. I completely fell for his act! "You lied to me!"

His paw on me clenches, the claws retracting much too close to my neck. One wrong move, and he'll decapitate me. I need to play this smart.

Igor laughs, shaking the surrounding cavern with it. "Do not play games with me, witch. Where is it?"

"Where is what?"

He sighs, and the rotting breath makes me gag.

"Declan's blood. I require the blood of a powerful zmeu, one from the original lineage, to get out of here."

"Original... The Council, you mean?"

Igor inclines his massive head. "The Council thought they were smart, imprisoning me here. Protecting their precious princes. But they could not control the darkness that turned me. I was far beyond their reach and still am. But my words were not. And thanks to my rumors, the lineage of the last zmei, the last royals, was doomed."

I'm too focused on his muzzle near me to grasp the words at first. And then I realize what he means. "Rumors about... what, exactly?"

"The two brothers, of course."

I recall Tytus' words, about the prophecy that changed everything. *One Light, one Dark.* "You were the one who set them at odds."

"Of course. Someone strong had to take the throne, the leadership of our clan. Neither zmeu had it in them to do so, to do what had to be done."

"How could you? You pitted them against each other, forever ensuring they would hate the other! And for what, power?"

Igor snorts, and this time a bit of the fire falls on my shoulder, burning through the cloth and making me cry out.

"Fiona!"

The sound is both a relief and makes me panic. If Tytus is here... The balaur cannot know I don't have the link with Declan anymore, or the blood that tied us. But Tytus...

I gather all my strength and scream, "RUN AWAY! Tytus, run, it's a–"

Igor smacks me, tossing me into the nearest wall and I lose consciousness for a second, maybe two. When I blink awake, Tytus enters the cave, and Igor awaits him, blocking access to me.

Chapter 17

Durere
"Numbing the pain for a while will make it worse
when you finally feel it."
-J.K.Rowling-

Tytus

After millennia of existence, it takes a
moment to gather my thoughts. I sort
through all the memories, trying to place this
creature among them. And once I put the
pieces together, the unyielding realization
hits me that Declan has completely fucked
me over.

My own brother... My blood. And still he
saw fit to cross the line to a place I cannot
follow. My mind sticks on the memory of
him in the woods, the echoing voice.

"How is this possible?" I ask Igor, if only to buy time while I attempt to get nearer Fiona.

From what I can see, her shoulder is hurt, and she's trying to put some distance between her and Igor. I need to be closer to her, to protect her, whether or not she wants me to. This isn't something she can fight alone. And if I had known what we would run into, I never would have sent her down here.

"A little of this, a little of that," Igor laughs. "Mainly, though, your brother."

My jaw clenches at the confirmation. "He found you?"

"He sought me, more like. And yes, found me. Just as easily as your witch did." Igor snorts and puffs of a noxious miasma escape in the air. It won't hurt me again, not like last time. But Fiona...

I can't hold back. My gaze seeks hers across the distance. Pain twists her features as she holds onto her shoulder. "He said he was a balaur, a cousin of the zmei... That he could help."

Poor Fiona. She never could have known.

"He is no such thing," I hiss and draw Igor's attention on me again. I don't want him focused on her, not when he's so close, and could so easily crush her. "A balaur is what a zmeu turns into when he embraces dark magic. Isn't that right, Igor? It's why you can speak. You no longer have the ability to return to your human form. You are stuck forever in the monster—the creature you have become."

His laugh starts low, then increases over and over until it's all I hear. The sound reverberates in my ears, loudly—too loudly. "Enough!" I roar, clenching my fists.

Igor settles, but only just. His head moves from me to Fiona, then back to me. "How did you pick a human so gullible? You are a disgrace to your kind."

Fiona recoils, and I'm even more pissed at the new pain etched on her features. As if I needed this, on top of all the reasons she already has to fight *us*.

"Don't speak about disgraces," I hurl at the balaur. "I know of you, Igor cel Nebun—Igor the Mad. You used to be on our Council. But they kicked you out when you crazy delusions brought upon us the wrath of the Serafim." More things start making sense, things I did not piece together in the past– things I did not have time for. I take a step closer. "It was you behind the human genocides, wasn't it? *You* are the reason the Serafim hate us so."

"Those human bastards…"

"Only because you made them so. Declan only finished what you had already started."

Igor glares at me, or in my direction. His blind stare is more proof he got what was coming to him, after all.

"And in the woods, all those centuries ago… You were with Declan. You manipulated him, led him to turn against us, to kill his own lover."

Igor's tail twitches, as if in annoyance. "I only showed him the true path."

"And what path is that?"

"That of the strong."

"What you did was isolate him, feed upon his mind in a vulnerable moment." My jaw clenches, even as shame runs through me. I could have done more–*should* have done more for Declan. Instead, this entire time I thought him the bigger evil, when really there was something much, much worse. And it was right under my nose the entire time.

"And you did it again, didn't you?" I can barely hold on to my rage, when all I want is to morph and kill him, the way he should have been executed eons ago. "When Declan came to visit here. He must have realized they captured you, still alive. How?"

Igor shrugs, his massive wings lifting and falling. The rush of air sends Fiona even further in the distance, and a whimper escapes her. I chance a glance to make sure she's fine, but she's not looking my way.

When I angle my next step towards her, Igor shifts. He must do it on purpose, because his wing falls just so, blocking my view of Fiona. His glazed eyes shine with malice. Even blind, he moves with uncanny accuracy, probably due to his other senses being enhanced.

"Declan heard my call. Saw my power. Wanted the same."

"To become a balaur?" Outrage fills me.

"Liar! My brother is many things, but he still has a moral compass." Something deep down, I always knew. It was only easier to ignore it.

Igor snorts. "Is that why he kept your witch captive for so long?"

Some of my surprise must show on my face as he laughs again. "Da, Declan and I had long, long talks."

"And then you screwed him over."

"*Nu.* I gave Declan everything he would have ever wanted."

I force myself to move closer, despite the stench. "Which is what, exactly? Declan was already free. What did he want so badly?"

Igor shuffles a paw, as if to shrug. "My, you really don't see past what is in front of you. Declan knew he would get captured again, thanks to you and your allies. And, he made sure there would be an escape plan."

"Draining Ileana and Făt, you mean?" And then it dawns on me. He's been in here for centuries, millennia, yet his form is still fine, and he looks almost... healthy, minus the grime. "*You*! You're the one draining the immortals. But how?"

Igor swipes his tail, and it only narrowly misses Fiona. She cringes and moves away further, trying to find an escape, no doubt.

"Your descendant made it all too easy. She had knowledge of the immortal, and your brother did the rest. Zmeu magic may be potent, but add a little dark magic.... And it was perfect."

"If it worked so well, why is Declan still imprisoned? He could have been free. He was here, away from everything. He could have run away, never to return to Rockland Creek. Or stayed here. Why would he tie himself to some convoluted scheme? What does he gain from draining the immortals?"

"The Underworld," Igor rumbles. "He didn't see it, at first. But I showed him. We were the original protectors, masters of the skies as per the gods themselves. Then they demoted us, and immortals took over. Our life was never the same, relegated to the land of humans, living in hiding, being hunted down like animals."

He snarls, and his tail twitches a little too close to Fiona. Thankfully, she moves away, her eyes never leaving him. I can only imagine what this is doing to her acceptance of our bond, but Igor is still ranting.

"Well, the final laugh will be ours. There is one spot where we can still amass an army, one that will allow us to get what we rightly deserve—our place as rulers of the skies."

"You are delusional. The gods demoted us because we got arrogant, and greedy. We were unstable. Immortals were much cooler-headed."

Igor snorts. "I do not expect you to understand. But your brother does, and he will help me. Ileana has something very precious hidden in the Underworld. And *we* have our fallen comrades. If we open that gate, we can return our kind to life."

"To do *what*?" I toss my hands up in the air, getting closer still to him. "To rule over humans?"

"How little imagination you have, little zmeu," Igor says. "It is not this world I wish."

It takes me a moment, but the last pieces fall into place, forming an insane picture.

"You want Olympus. The pantheons…"

"Da. And the Underworld so happens to have the one god who can get me through the door."

My voice is a mere whisper. "Hades."

Fiona's eyes are wide and filled with fear, and even I feel all color drain from my face.

"Come now, enough of the surprise!" Igor is volatile now. "Zmei were not created to hide, to submit to humans. You've proven that. And now that you have eradicated the Serafim for us, no one will be skilled enough to stop us. Do not look so surprised, when it was you who killed them, no?"

Shame fills me at the thought of the charred bodies on the surface. "Yes, but I had to. It was self-defense."

"And was it self-defense when you enjoyed their screams, toyed with them? Once this tunnel was open, sound travels, you know. You cannot lie to me."

I say nothing, because every word will only condemn me further. Already, Fiona is looking at me differently, and it burns.

Igor must sense some of my inner conflict.

"What a pity. Falling for a human, of all creatures. And one as broken as this one. Do not worry, I will rid you of the burden."

"No!" I cry, but it's too late.

He whirls on her with a roar, pinning Fiona to the wall. Her face twists in pain, and the rest of my control snaps as I throw myself at him.

Fiona

I thought for sure Igor meant to kill me. After all, he made it clear he thinks nothing of me. But when he pins me, it's to have his claws dig into my flesh, and something else.

My mind.

A cry of pain escapes me at the unwelcome intrusion. Unlike Declan's determined connections, or Tytus' subtle pushing through, Igor tears at my thoughts, shredding them and pushing forward, deeper into my psyche. Single-minded, he tosses images my way.

The girl I'd seen in the picture. Alina.

Tytus and her, walking hand in hand. Kissing her. Pining for her. Making love to her in this same castle.

Tytus lied. Lied. Lied. Lied.

The proof is incontestable, and I can't even berate myself for being a fool. For so long, he hid this from me. He had ample time to reveal the truth, that he'd fallen for a human before, that he'd had a relationship, ages and ages ago. Yet he didn't.

It's not hiding it from me, that's the problem. Nor the jealousy I feel. Those, I can get over, given time. But it's what this says about his character, when put side to side with my own experiences with Tytus.

His ruthlessness with the Serafim. His inability to be merciful. His silver-tongued demeanor, and that immovable bond between us. His ease of breaking a promise, when it's most important. And now, finding out he was able to inflict such pain on his brother. His *brother*. Declan may be evil now, but surely back then that was not the case. So what explains Tytus' betrayal?

Can anything explain it, even? And

should I even give him a chance?

Through all these thoughts, another pushes more. How can I fault Tytus for defending himself, for defending me? And is he really as cold-hearted as Igor makes him? He was only ever careful with me, making sure at every step I approved. That I was with him, one hundred percent.

How can I turn against such a man, even if he did lie to me? Even if he loves someone else. Even if I have stupidly fallen for him, believing in the idiotic happily ever after he hinted at.

There is a reason he is alive, and she is not. Tytus is beyond anything a human girl can grasp, and I have to accept that. In a way, I always knew it at the back of my mind. I only wanted what I could get, to prove to myself I had the power, and the choice.

And I did.

And it was great while it lasted.

But the dream he hinted at, it cannot be.

The images tear at me more than Igor's intrusion, and even as he pulls away, he leaves them there.

Roars echo, and I'm dimly aware of a fight. But then darkness pulls me under, and with it, the most unwelcome of dreams.

Laughter catches my attention first, followed by a low rumble. A female and a male. I'm in a dark corridor and it seems oddly familiar, but I cannot... I cannot place it. Still, my bare feet tiptoe further down.

The laughter dies away, but the light of flames flickers underneath a door. I move closer, pushing it open slowly. At first, all I see is his back as he thrusts inside her. Then her moans of pleasure. The way he's touching her body, like he wants to get lost in it.

His mop of dark hair.... And then Tytus looks up in the mirror directly across from them. "See how beautiful you are?"

And with her red hair, his dark one, the picture they make is striking. And my heart tears and tears and tears...

Declan

The air around me shifts, and the Romanian

witch steps out from the shadows. I take some delight in seeing her pallor.

"You look a bit at odds. Not getting sick?"

Ileana scowls, and that alone tells me more than she ever would. "I am not here for games, zmeu. Whatever you did, whatever illness you have bestowed upon me and my consort, is ending. Now."

"And why would that be?"

"Despite your machinations, Tytus will triumph. He has figured it out, and he will defeat the creature you have under that castle."

I shrug, pretending to look at my nails. "Be it so. He cannot stop what has already been put into motion."

"Tell me," Ileana comes closer, her tone nearly pleading. "What are you planning, Declan?"

"Now where would be the fun in revealing it all?"

She scowls again. "You will not escape. We will die if it means keeping you captive."

"Then perhaps that is how it has to be."

She shakes her head and goes to leave, but at the last moment turns to me. "Do you not realize, even now, that you and Tytus must both exist? You are two sides of the same coin, the only ones still alive of your kind. How can you live with yourself, sending him to his execution?"

"Because he had no problem doing the same to me."

"Is that what you think? Tytus was never involved in the Council that decided your fate. But another was. One whose stench you have laid over this entire thing."

Her admission shakes me. "How would you even know that?"

"I am immortal not only because of how I was born but also because of what I can do, Declan. Never forget that."

Then she's gone, but her words ring in my head in a pattern. *Dammit to hell!*

Chapter 18

Neîncredere

"Mistrust carries one such further than trust."

-German proverb-

Fiona

"Fiona, open your eyes, sweetling. I need to see you're all right."

I'm being rocked back and forth, cushioned by something equally soft and hard. The motion is soothing, but it's only adding to the fierce headache pounding between my temples.

"Why...?"

"Shh," a voice whispers in my ear, and the arms around me tighten.

Panic settles in–that I can't move, that I'm a captive again. It's idiotic, I know these arms. I slept in them. But why...

And then it hits me. Tytus. The redhead. Igor in my head, prying my mind open, showing me what I didn't want to. And a roar of pain so loud, it left my bones shaking....

Surely that couldn't have been him?

I blink awake, and Tytus' face appears above me. It's definitely his arms. And when he sees me awake, he pulls me tighter, ignoring my groan.

"Thank the gods!"

I allow the embrace for a minute, maybe more. He smells of smoke and fire, his body hard against mine. There's nothing I want more in that moment than melt into him and forget any of this ever happened. Turn back time and go back to that night of pure happiness. And stop second-guessing every moment of it.

Instead, I sigh and push away from him, crawling out of his lap and allowing some distance as I sit cross-legged on the cold floor. A sparse look around confirms Igor is gone, though where, I have no clue.

"He escaped," Tytus says.

"How?"

"He was invading your mind, and I swore to protect you. So I fought him off. These tunnels weren't built to hold two zmei. The force of our attacks knocked the pillars loose."

He jerks a thumb over his shoulder and I lean to the side. My eyes widen when I see the huge gaping hole where there used to be a wall, and half the ceiling caved in.

"How is the castle still standing?"

"Good construction," he says wryly.

"Right." I resume my position, meeting his gaze again.

"May I come closer? Please?" He asks.

He's always given me a choice. And that choice has always been in his favor. Not this time, though.

I shake my head. "No. I need you to stay where you are."

"But why, Fiona?"

I hold up a palm. "Just... do. For now. Igor. Everything he said to me, then. It was a lie?"

His tight expression softens. "I don't know what lies he told you before I got here, but probably. He's no zmeu. He's as far from one as one can get."

I recall bits and pieces of their conversation. I'd been so focused on escaping that I hadn't given it my full focus. Still, it seems I caught more than I intended. "What happened to him, can it happen to you?"

"It could. If I ever decided to delve into the Dark Arts. Which I never would."

"What about Declan?"

"What about him?"

"Did he not... How come he's not...?"

Tytus shakes his head. "Declan didn't fuck with dark magic. Only Igor did. And hell knows what kind of havoc he's wrecking out there right now."

"So why aren't you stopping him? And don't give me some bullshit about how you had to stick around for me."

He frowns then. "What do you mean?"

I look at my torn jeans instead of holding his gaze. "Igor showed me your past. With that girl."

"What girl?"

I glare at him then. "The human girl you had a relationship with! Are we really so forgettable to you?"

"When you live millennia, da." He shakes his head, running a hand over his face. "Ignore that. I speak out of anger. Could you please give me more context?"

"Fine." I get to my feet, crossing my arms and tapping my foot. "She was about yea high, red hair, features similar to Lucrezia's. And you were in love with her."

His features only get more and more confused. He must be a great actor, this one. "You mean Alina?"

I grit my teeth. *Ah-leh-nah.* Even her name has to be pretty coming from his lips. "Yes, *Alina.*"

Tytus gets up slowly, standing way too close. His scent envelops me again. But despite the bond, I'm only more confused. How stupid was I for deluding myself into thinking we had something?

I close my eyes, refusing to let his mojo get to me. "Stop it!" I hold out my hand. "And *don't* use your abilities on me."

"I'm not, and I wouldn't. Besides, I taught you how to keep me out of your head, remember?" This time, I risk a true glance at his expression. He looks hurt, like

I've really wounded him. Then his gaze shifts to my still bleeding wounds. "Will you let me heal you, at least?"

I hesitate, wondering at the smartness of it. But if I keep bleeding, I'll soon weaken and it's not like I have it in me to use my own magic right now. After another moment of internal debating, I finally nod.

Slowly, as if not to scare me, Tytus moves closer. First, he pulls the sleeve of my shirt apart, then goes about calling forth magic to heal me. A rune shimmers in the air, then breaks apart in little fireflies that fall on my skin. There is a sting, like a burning, and then the skin heals in front of my eyes.

With each passing second, each moment of silence, I'm even more confused. If he wanted me at his mercy, he could use his powers on me. I'm no match for him in my current state. But, he doesn't. He's only focused on healing me. My mind and my heart are at complete odds, and I don't know which to believe more.

Finally, Tytus steps back, giving me the space I asked for. "Alina was not my lover.

I cannot fathom what Igor was playing at, though it probably has to do with messing with your head, in order to mess with mine." He pauses. "I said nothing because it wasn't my secret to tell. Declan was the one who fell for a human. And then, from one moment to the next, he started hating their kind. I don't know the full story of what went wrong with him and Alina, or whatever else happened. All I know is he became reckless, and that's when all the stuff with the Council happened."

Moments pass without me saying anything. One of them is lying, and we've already established Igor isn't truthful. But Tytus....

Eventually, he breaks the silence. "Please say something."

"I saw pictures, though. In your study. And Igor's images, or memories, whatever they were... They matched."

"What exactly did you see?"

"You, Declan, Alina, in a portrait."

"And Igor's vision?"

I look away. "It doesn't matter."

"Yes, it does."

Something in his tone has me look up, and this time there's no denying it. "You know what he showed me! Why ask me to relive it, then?"

"Because I wanted to see if you would trust me. Evidently, Igor has managed what he wanted." Tytus opens his palms and shrugs, his eyes dark with internal agony. "How could you believe I would touch my brother's wife? You think so little of me, after everything we've been through together?"

My thoughts are too muddled, too raw, to answer.

Tytus runs a hand through his hair, clenching his jaw. "I cannot deny it forever. I *won't*. Humans are good at that, at destroying something pure, and I will not bend myself over backwards to prove you wrong. Not when you should know better, and we don't have time. Each moment we're in here, he's out there wrecking more and more damage."

I glare at him, tossing my hand to the side. "Then go after him! The last thing I'd want to be is an *inconvenience*."

"I can't!" Tytus takes a deep breath and

speaks softer. "You're the key to getting out of here. Igor said it himself, before sealing us in."

"Sealing us in?"

Tytus throws open his arms. "Look around. Do you really not see the circle?"

Well, now that he mentions it.... A second in depth glance reveals what I didn't catch at first, because it was belding in with the light from above. But we're definitely surrounded by a silver dome.

I'm reminded of that day in the forest, when Tytus used fire to keep me warm from the rain. And the rest of our journey... When my eyes land on him, on his pleading expression, I revert to anger.

"What do you expect of me?"

"Nothing. Absolutely nothing. I only thought you might trust me, after everything... But I guess I was wrong."

He goes as far as he can from me before silver lightning warns he's gone far enough.

Tytus

If I ever get out of here in time, I will wring

Igor's neck with my bare hands—or claws. That old bastard. He took images from our youth and used them against me. And if he did this... What are the chances he did more?

Like Declan's fall from grace. Alina's betrayal was bad, but I never knew the full history. Now, the more I think on it, the more I want to kick myself. It's highly possible that Igor was there at the right time, that he took advantage of Declan, already knowing she betrayed him.

And if Igor himself showed Declan the "truth", exactly as he did to Fiona, then it's no wonder my own brother hates my guts. Is that what he thinks, that I seduced his wife? That burst of shame hits me again, for having let him down. For not having tried harder.

When he returned to the castle, all those centuries ago, I did nothing to help him. I saw his pain, lived it as my own. But I was so annoyed over his moping around for a human, that I simply dismissed it. So focused on the politics at the time, and believing what I was being told.

Declan... Fuck, brother.

Fiona clears her throat behind me, snapping me out of my thoughts. "I have to tell you something."

I turn, slowly. I can't stand the way she looks at me now, like I'm the enemy, when all I've ever wanted was to protect her. I need to get through to her. But how?

"Tell me what?"

"Igor. He said something else, while I was here. He implied the whole deal, the prophecy about the Light and Dark one, about you and Declan, was his own doing. He set you up on purpose to be against the other."

Shock runs through me. "Does Declan know?"

She knows why I'm asking her, she who's been the closest to him. "I don't think so. I... I managed to block him from my mind. Like you taught me." A pause. "Thank you for that."

I nod. "Good. Keep him out."

I walk away, but Fiona follows this time. It seems she has gotten over her need to keep me at bay. "Wait! What will you do?"

"Try to get out of here."

She slinks back to her side of the prison, and that hurts more. The fact she's not even willing to argue, to fight this out.

And once more, I'm torn between two demands. To do everything I can to escape and go after Igor. Or get to Fiona and make her see the truth. That she was played—we all were.

Even Declan? That's the question of the hour. One I've already asked myself. One that will have to wait until we defeat Igor.

And that in itself will be hard. There's a reason I'm his prisoner. A balaur's physical force doesn't surpass a zmeu's, but their magical abilities do. Only Solomonari could help zmei defeat them, way back when the world was a simpler place.

And given the only Solomonar alive is on the other side of the ocean....

I grit my teeth and speak over my shoulder. "You may want to create a barrier for your own protection. At least temporarily."

Once I sense Fiona's swift magic click into place, I focus all my attention on the barrier. Draw a rune in the air and let fire blow through–nothing.

Draw four of them, each with an element–nothing.

I get more creative. Each burst of magic does nothing other than make the dome tremble. And tremble some more. But it doesn't break. And still, I try. If I don't get free, if Igor gets to carry out his plan, not only are we truly screwed, but the consequences will be much graver than anyone realizes.

It's not just the zmei Igor will disturb–it's the immortals, and the gods themselves. And though I never served the divine, having been born way after the split, I do expect they won't take kindly to having their retirement, so to speak, interrupted.

Especially not by a bunch of angry zmei that are supposed to be dead.

When another rune fails, I throw my head back and bellow, "ILEANA!" As I expected, nothing happens. If Declan told Igor about me and Fiona, he must have foreseen much more, too. Like the fact the immortals would help us.

Which means Igor prepared fully for

this, and ensured our cries for help would not be heard.

Through all my failed attempts, Fiona watches me. Her gaze is burning on my back, but she says nothing. Her silence continues the accusation, the idea that I did something wrong. When I did nothing. Other than not be there for my brother, who then turned into a maniac intent on inflicting pain.

Frustration at the situation rankles through me. So much to fix, so little time. And, worse still, I haven't told Fiona what Igor did before he left. How he ensured there's only one way out of here. One she won't allow me.

A cry of anger escapes me and I give up with the magic, instead thrusting my hands into the barrier. The electricity crackles against my skin, and I howl, agony racing up my arms. Still, I don't let go, hoping for that break–

"Tytus, STOP!"

Fiona's there, pulling me away until she's between me and the dome. I'm panting, even as she goes about healing my burns. Not even my innate protection against fire was of help here. *Damn it all to hell.*

I watch her surreptitiously, cursing the bond between us and my body's immediate response to her. My head drops, and I inhale her scent deeply. I want to kiss her so damn much that it hurts. I yearn to hold her, keep her safe from this craziness.

But she won't allow me, and the worst thing is... I may not have been dishonest with her before, but I sure am being it now. One option remains, one I haven't yet tried. Give her the facts and allow the choice to be in her hands.

"There really is only one way out. Fuck."

Fiona

It takes a moment for his words to penetrate, and even longer for me to realize what he means.

"You know how to get out of here?" I wrap up the healing on his arm, then chance a glance at Tytus. His brow is furrowed, and conflict is etched on every plane of his expression. "I don't get it. If you knew all along, why not tell me?"

He only clenches his jaw, looking at a fixed point above my shoulder. "Because it's pointless, and will make you trust me even less."

"No, it won't."

"Yes, it will."

It's a stupid denial on my part, but the stubbornness is impossible to ignore, and seemingly my specialty. Plus, I don't want to be kept in the dark. I've had quite enough of that.

"Tytus, let me decide. You're not doing yourself any favors right now."

"Aren't I?" He gets up in my face, eyes searching mine with desperation. "Perhaps it's time to remind you just how good we can be together, then." And before I can do anything, he crushes his mouth to mine.

So far, he's kissed me gently, passionately, ravenously... but this is savage. Like he craves a taste of me even more than life itself, yet at the same time knows it'll be his last. His tongue plunders my mouth until

I surrender, my body remembering the pleasure he can bring. Just as suddenly he stops and pulls away, dropping his hand and not meeting my eyes.

"The only way out is to let me into your mind. And for me to allow you into mine."

I balk at the thought. "Like Igor?"

His expression softens. "No. I would be gentle."

"Like Declan, then."

Tytus grits his teeth. "And this is why I didn't want to tell you. You're already comparing me with him, based on what you heard, and my earlier mistake." He turns away from me, muttering under his breath. "There has to be another way."

I think through the implications. Since Declan, my mind never truly felt mine. Tytus' well-intentioned control with the vasilisc situation triggered old fears. Igor's invasion just now only brought back the trauma. The inability to control myself, to protect my mind. What is it with zmei and their need to be in someone's head? And yet...

This is Tytus.

Kind, generous, passionate Tytus.

He's always respected me.

Not once have I thought he would harm me, even when he controlled me. And he has protected me more times than I can count. The hurt he caused was through fault of his own and mine. We've both made mistakes. Said things we wished we could take back. Took some of them back, even.

Realistically, this comes down to one question only–do I trust him enough to let him into the recesses of my mind? Of my own volition this time, completely willing, and regardless of how our relationship will turn out?

I stare at his slouched back, at the burden I feel weighing heavily on his shoulders as if it were mine. Despite his faults, despite what I still believe he hid from me, he has tried, time and time again. He has shown me love, taught me how to protect my mind, and turned this castle upside down to save me more times than I can count.

Even when I rejected him, he returned.

So, do I trust him? At least, enough to take this next step?

Yes, I do.

"What do I have to do, to make it happen?"

Tytus freezes, turning around. There is hope in his expression, but also doubt. Like he's afraid I'm deciding this for the wrong reasons.

"I'm choosing this of my own free will, because you trust me to get you out of here."

Still, he hesitates. "But do you trust *me*?"

I gulp. "I guess we'll find out."

Inch by inch, he gets closer to me again, and cups my cheeks. "You have to understand what you're letting me do. Get into your mind willingly, into your most inner thoughts."

"I've been there before."

"Not with someone like me, with whom you started the legătură with. When I controlled your mind, before, you were not a participant in it. This time, you are. And it will cement our bond, Fiona. A bond you have denied, time and time again. Are you sure you're ready for that?"

The yearning in his voice gives me pause. I don't know what I expected, him to just take me at my word? But this is the first time I realize, truly realize, that Tytus' earlier broken promise has weighed heavily on him, too, not just on me. And it's the only reassurance I need.

"I know I'm willing to try."

He nods and then closes the remaining distance between us and grabs hold of my hands in his.

Chapter 19

Încredere
"Learn to trust the journey even when you do not understand it."
-Unknown-

Tytus

Does she realize she's trembling, her fingers jittery against mine? I squeeze them, waiting until she meets my eyes. "It'll be okay. I swear I'll protect you."

Fiona smiles. "I know."

I want to tell her how proud I am. How far she's come. How utterly strong and indestructible she is, despite everything she has been through. Even more, I wish I could convey with words the strength she gives me, of all people. Fiona doesn't need my validation, but I sure as hell want her to see herself through my eyes. She is anything but forgettable...

And once I get rid of Igor, I will do better than tell her. I will show her. For as long as she'll have me. *If* she'll have me.

One step at a time.

I focus on her hands. "Close your eyes. Feel me. Feel *us*. I'll do the rest."

When we flew together, me in my zmeu form, and we communicated, it was more of my mind picking up her thoughts aimed at me. I was always careful, always mindful not to accidentally cross the barrier of her defenses. Back then, I knew Declan had already done so multiple times, and Fiona deserved respect and protection.

Then I stupidly warped her thoughts and controlled them, pushing her away from the vasilisc so I would protect her. Not realizing the harm I was doing, even with my good intentions.

Now, I'm about to go against my every intuition. I'm specifically seeking to enter the private confines of her psyche. And when I do, I need to do so in a way it doesn't remind her of Declan.

Fuck. No pressure.

Yet it's specifically why Igor did this. With all the knowledge he has, and having screwed with both our heads enough, he assumed we could not get past this. That Fiona would never trust me, and I would have to kill her to win my escape. That choice was never given to me, but I have no doubt Igor, in his evil mind, planned much, much ahead.

Not that I ever would have given in. If anything, I would have taken advantage of Fiona's stubbornness and continued to convince her of my true love. For as long as it took, the world be damned.

Still… Sensing the trembling in her hands now, I am infinitely more aware of how precious this gift she is giving me is.

I close my eyes and ignore the weight in my chest. Then I reach out mentally and probe. The connection, her hand in mine, helps. I sense her hesitation, her fear, but also something else. Her love. No matter how much she wants to hide it, to protect it, it's there. And it makes my heart swell, and my grip on her tightens.

"Breathe, sweetling," I whisper.

I hear her gentle exhale and use that as my way in. Gently, I part the curtains of her mind. Multiple thoughts assail me at once, and I force my energy to remain smooth, gentle. Waiting. Just waiting for Fiona to get used to it, to *me*, to realize the choice has to come from her.

Inside me, I sense the burn. The zmeu. The need. The yearning for the connection to be fulfilled.

Outside me, the room grows cooler in contrast. Fiona gasps, but doesn't let go. Nor do her walls come back up. Instead, she lets me in....

And it is the most intimate, intrinsic connection. She is everywhere around me, physically and mentally, like we're two halves of the same whole. The warmth in me radiates through my palms and I open my eyes, only just noticing a steady flow of energy passing from me to her. It's red. It's flaming. But it's not... hurting her.

I dig deep into the corners of my mind, the corners I have not visited in so long.

"Come with me... I need to show you something."

Fiona hesitates, then follows in my mind, down the path I show her, to the memories passing by at whirlwind speed.

I'm following Alina in the woods. At first, when Declan first presented us, her sweetness overtook me. But a few months later, things started to bother me. It was more of an instinct, and I laid in wait, expecting something to happen.

It did. One night when I was staying over, Alina snuck out of the house. I waited for her to return, and when she did, she seemed afraid. Yet she only said she couldn't sleep, and that she normally takes walks in the middle of the night.

I was more careful, after. I started following her. This particular night in the memory, I use a rune to keep myself hidden, and maintain my footsteps light on the cool grass.

Ahead of me, despite her frail body, Alina makes as much noise as an elephant. Branches and twigs crack under her feet, and I'm not the only one who notices.

A big bulk of a man pops up in front of her. Rather than scream, she squeals joyfully and jumps in his arms.

"Lina," the giant mutters as he drops her down. "You must be more careful!"

"Of what?" She laughs, her tone filled with malice. "I have Declan wrapped around my pinkie, and he'll do anything I say."

And there it is. The truth, ugly as sin, laid out for all to see. Even me. How will I tell Declan of this betrayal, when he truly cares for this wench? It gives me no satisfaction to have been right. Absolutely none.

The giant is quiet for a bit, then nods. "Anything? Even invite you to their castle, their stronghold?"

"I do believe that is possible."

"Good. My brethren Serafim will be happy with the news. Come, let us catch up."

As they disappear further into the woods, I don't follow. I heard enough.

In the real world, I sense Fiona's urge to withdraw, to question what she has seen. I tug on her mind, pleading. *Wait. There is more.*

The next memory follows, this one in my own castle...

I'm returning to my bedroom from a hunt—or something. Blood is all over my clothes, and I head straight to the shower to wash off. When I return, something moves out of my periphery.

It's Alina.

"What are you doing here?"

"I came by to talk to my brother-in-law," she grins. "I thought this might be a good time to catch up."

"Perfect," I mutter, with no enthusiasm. "Why don't you wait for me in the dining room, and I'll join you after I get changed?"

"Or, I could wait here and watch you get changed."

I don't have a chance to take it all in before she throws herself at me. Kissing me, trying to shove her tongue in my mouth, plaster her body to mine—

I grip her waist and shove her away hard enough that she stumbles, nearly falling on her ass.

"What is wrong with you, wench?"

She tosses her head back. "Come now,

Tytus. There is something here, surely you sense it."

I can barely contain my growl. "The only thing I sense is your duplicity. Get out of my chambers, now."

Fiona's mind is in a daze, I feel it clear as day. I only hope she senses my honesty, and the truth of the memories I have shown her.

How? Her thought floats to me. How did Declan and Igor then think you were lovers?

Declan was under her spell. And Igor took advantage of it, probably showed him what he wanted. She was a Trojan horse from the Serafim, destined to infiltrate our ranks and ruin us. She did…. Only in a different way. She broke me and Declan apart.

There is a long silence as Fiona ponders all the different facets of the truth she has been fed. Then I sense acceptance dawn on her, even as we both come back to the present.

"Tytus?" Fiona's violet eyes hook mine.

"There's one more thing," I add. "I want you to see yourself, the way I do. So you never have to question my feelings for you, ever again. So you can understand, for real this time, that there is only honesty in all that I feel."

She hesitates, then nods slightly. I close my eyes this time and bring forth every memory I have with her from the very beginning. When I was searching for her, while she was captive, intending to find out what she knew about Declan. Our first interactions, and the grudging admiration I had for her survival skills, topped with a healthy dose of annoyance at my zmeu finding her attractive.

Further still, to our first one-on-one conversation in the woods, and her shy strength. The quiet understanding of what she went through, and the steel backbone I could sense in her.

And then I bring forth the other memories. Of the cavern, our getting acquainted. The admiration that turned into more, the pull of the bond that brought us closer. Back to the castle, to the protectiveness she raised in me, the fierce love. My awe of her ability to move past what life threw at her, to find light and joy.

I linger past the memory of the vasilisc, making her understand my reasoning. My fear for her life, my desperation to get her out of there. My shame that she might see me so weak, so close to death, and think me unable to protect her.

Deeper still I go into the nights we spent together. Her body against mine, the passion driving me—us—to the pinnacle of ecstasy. I let Fiona feel everything, every bit of it, until I open my eyes.

We stare at each other across the well of energy, and it is the closest I've ever been to her.

The energy from us expands, swirls like a myriad of flames, and then it shoots to the dome holding us hostage. A loud vibration starts and I hurl Fiona against my chest, willing to use my body to protect her, if need be. But I shouldn't have worried. The barrier cracks and falls like rain around us, a mix of fallen stars, disintegrating as they hit the ground and release us.

Fiona pulls away gently, looking around with wonder in her voice. "We're free."

I let go of her hands, only to cup her cheeks and move closer. My thumb traces her lower lip and I savor this moment between us. A moment of peace. Of quiet. Of connection.

Inch by inch, I lower my head until our mouths touch, fusing together with renewed passion. Fiona's hands thread through my hair, and I pull her even closer.

It's only a kiss–but it rocks me to my core. Whereas before the bond was present, now I feel tethered to Fiona, like we're both each other's satellites, orbiting around the sun of our love.

And when we pull away, it's all I can do to focus, albeit momentarily. The last thing I want is to fight Igor. Not because I'm a coward, but because she is the most precious thing to me right now. And fighting him means being away from her.

"I'll be fine," Fiona says, as if sensing my hesitation. "Thank you. For everything you've shown me. I was so, so wrong to doubt you, to doubt us."

When she touches me in return, caressing my cheek, a wave of calmness washes over me. And confidence. Her faith–in me.

"You know what this means?"

She nods. "Later. We'll have time."

With her hand in mine, I head out of the blasted tunnels and back to the surface. *Let us not be too late…*

Fiona

It's on shaky legs I move with Tytus. That connection, those moments when he was in my head… I'd been afraid, so afraid to be proven wrong, so afraid for him to do as his brother did.

But Tytus is nothing like Declan. He was gentle, and the way he allowed me time to let him in, despite being in a rush, only makes me love him more. My fears were unfounded, now and before. Knowing what he'd meant, with his persuasion skills, what he'd intended, it takes the sting out of the actions. Not that it means he was right to do so, but the remorse I felt in him more than makes up for it.

With Tytus, I will be safe. He will not

break down my walls, nor try to take over me. He does not intend our bond to tie me to him, to control me. He simply wants to love me. And in accepting I am deserving of that love, I can finally move forward with my life.

I sneak glances out of the corner of my eye at him—there's a new purpose to his stride, a glint in his eye that wasn't there before. And I put it there.

The knowledge warms something inside me, something that's been cold and lonely for too long. It's the dreary part of me, the miserable one—the one that always sought what it could never have.

But now I can.

I felt it in Tytus, when he let the barriers of his mind loose. I saw it in everything he showed me, in every emotion radiating from him. And I feel it now, walking by his side.

The connection between us is stronger, yes, just as he explained it would be. But *we* are also stronger, together.

¥

We emerge through the oak doors, Tytus ahead and blocking me with his body. His eyes immediately scan the skies, looking for Igor. The smell of sulfur has replaced the usual fresh air here, and I join him in the search.

"Is he gone?" Did we take too long?

Nothing around here is broken or destroyed. Outside the barrier, I see the bodies of the Serafim, the struggle of the battle. The ripped apart cars, and the scent of charred flesh. Tytus did all this–and rather than see him as the monster most would say he is, I know he was doing it to defend. Us, the castle, the world, even.

Yet if Igor is right, then that also means we paved the way for his plan.

Tytus' eyes narrow, then he slowly shakes his head. "No, he's there. Hidden by the clouds and… waiting. Not sure what for."

"Should we call the immortals?"

"No," Tytus says. "This is my fight, and mine alone." He turns to me, caressing my cheek before dropping a swift kiss on my fore-head. "Stay safe. He will use you against me if given half a chance, and I cannot lose you."

I nod, and it's with a heavy heart I watch him turn into his zmeu form, then fly into the skies. No sooner is he up there, that Igor bursts out of the clouds, and the fighting begins. I'm not sure how Igor fights blind, but he must have honed skills for it while underground. It's like he can tell everywhere Tytus will be, even before he goes there.

Tytus and Igor going at each other is like watching fire and darkness collide. Each with their own strengths, their own motivations. But where I thought Igor's bulk would work against him, I was mistaken. He is fast, and he is strong, and that tail of his keeps making Tytus bleed.

When Igor cuts a large gash in Tytus' back leg, I know it's time to reach out. If the immortals aren't answering, someone else could.

There's only one other person who can help Tytus out. And I loathe appealing to him, despite admitting to Tytus that I believe Declan is not inherently evil. Still, now that I am aware of the full story, even I have to risk it.

And for Tytus, I *will* risk it all.

So I drop the mental barrier I'd erected

around myself, close my eyes, and dig deep. Maybe, just maybe, he's still out there...

Declan

The tug in my mind is unexpected, especially when I realize who it's coming from. The little witch.

Bored without me already?

Her voice sounds panicked in my head. *This isn't about me, Declan. It's about your brother.*

He can die, for all I care.

You don't mean that. He's fighting Igor right now, and losing. I need you to help him!

Ah, so they found the balaur. I should be ecstatic, yet I am not. I blame the lack of reaction on the last visit I had with my little temptress, leaving my body satisfied beyond explanation. Who would have thought dreams have the power to heal the soul?

Still, I suppose even humans get deluded sometimes. Most times. Surely for Fiona to have reached out to her former captive, it shows her desperation.

You have lost your damned mind. When I try to set my head back on my paws, she keeps buzzing around my skull, like an incessant fly.

I won't let you sit by and do nothing! You have to help.

Do you forget I set all this in motion, little witch? There is nothing you can say that will make me change my mind. You had best leave before I use this link against you.

If you had wanted to, you would have already.

I glare at the cavern wall, not that it does anything. *What makes you think that?*

Alina.

The name she says freezes my entire body, including my breath. The leisurely afterglow in my body dissipates, instead replaced with anger–and pain. The agony is still as strong in my heart, despite the many centuries since her betrayal. Since her death.

Alina and my brother.

When I found out, when Igor showed me, I thought the world was ending. He convinced me of another way, a way to make them both pay. But her downfall at his hands didn't work, leaving me alone in despair and anger. Tytus only waltzed through life, unconcerned.

Uncaring.

NO! Is that really what you think happened?

Too late, I realize the witch followed my thoughts. I try to push her away, but her presence is relentless. Since when did she get so strong?

Listen to me, Declan. Igor fed me those same images!

Because they're true.

They are not. Tytus never betrayed you. When I accused him of the same thing, it confused him. I saw in his mind, Declan. I know what didn't happen, and that's him sleeping with Alina. The only human he's ever loved is... me.

Her revelation stuns me, and not in a good way. Followed by the thought of my brother happy again, while I'm here rotting, I cannot simply let it go.

You? What is lovable about you? For a zmeu, no less.

Your words don't hurt me anymore. I can feel your confusion, your doubt. Been through the rollercoaster of emotions myself, believe me. But I'm telling you, I saw it with my own eyes.

I do not believe you.

She's silent for so long, I think she finally gave up. Instead, she comes back stronger. *See into my mind, then. The truth is there.*

What does she know, I wonder, that makes her so sure of herself? Not even days ago, she was afraid whenever I contacted her. Then she kept me out, only for now to backtrack all those efforts? And all, what, to show me some deep truth about my ex-wife?

I have enough memories of Alina that haunt me. It takes much work to shut them up, to forget how much of a fool I'd been, trusting a human. And trusting that human, along with my brother. If I let myself think on it, the betrayal will sting like a real blow, driving my rage further and further on. With nowhere to go, given I am caught between four walls, with no escape.

Still, Fiona's offer is tempting. It will hurt to finally learn the depth of their betrayal, and assuredly only make me hate Tytus more. But in the end, if there is even a shred of information that will justify it, I would rather know than not.

Declan, please. See into my mind!

Well, she is relentless, I'll give her that... So if only to shut her up, I take the invitation and dive deep into our link. I see her and Tytus in the library underground, where Igor had been imprisoned. They are linking hands, and I sense the legătură cementing. Jealousy pushes through me, almost breaking the link, but I force myself to keep watching.

Fiona is allowed in Tytus' mind... As am I. And in there, I see everything she does. *Feel* everything she does. And witness my brother, pushing Alina away. His tracking of her, following her through days as she met with humans. No, worse. Not any humans– Cavaleri Serafim.

Alina was theirs, all along. And I was only a mission to her.

My nails dig into my palms, drawing

blood that trickles down my closed fists. I'm aware of it but make no move to heal it, instead staring at the wall, revisiting everything. All the memories I shut down, the love I had for Alina, the guilt at allowing her death as punishment, the weakness in me, from that love... The pain, that would never go away.

All of that. I felt *all* of that, and all along, she never reciprocated. My heartbeat increases, thumping into my ears, and all I sense is my zmeu's roar of agony, my own anger boiling, boiling to a blasting point.

That's... not possible. I pull back from Fiona, refusing to see any more.

Please, Declan. Deal with your shit after you help him. Igor will kill him! Do you really want his death on your conscience?

No, I do not. I spent millennia hating my brother, and I still am not a fan. He is still responsible for my original imprisonment. Though, if Ileana is to be believed, I cannot attribute even that to him.

Regardless. What Fiona showed me... Memories cannot be faked, not like that. And Tytus does not have the skill to fake them. But someone else did–Igor.

Rage fills me again, at being used, at having been someone's pawn. All along I thought I was leading the game, when in fact I was nothing but a tiny pawn being moved along for Igor's purposes.

And as the rage fills me, my zmeu reacts, rearing his head and sniffing for blood. I am, after all, a creature of pure impulse.

If I do this, I'll need you to keep the link between us open, since it was done willingly. The immortals have set in place various shields that will disconnect me from anything I take by force. Am I being clear?

Fiona's relief is palpable. *Yes, all right. Consider it done.*

She doesn't have to know I'm doing this out of a thirst for vengeance, more than a desire to save my brother. Either way, it will serve both our purposes. Still, I need to check one more time. For me to connect with Tytus long term, I have to push through this barrier. And he will only toss me away. Fiona's willing link will allow her to be a conduit between us, an unbreakable link until I choose to break it. It seems an odd risk to take, especially given our history.

Do you realize what you're offering me?

Yes. And I'll do it.

Who am I to contest it?

Tytus

I'm dragging my back leg, and Igor isn't giving up. His jets of flame keep hitting from above and below. For an older guy than me, he shouldn't be this fast. But he is. I underestimated him, thinking Declan was ruling him, and I was wrong.

Declan.

The name makes my gaze draw back to Fiona. I caught it before, the little tug in her mind. With our bond that much stronger, the whirlwind of her emotions was striking, and I know only one person could cause that in her.

Declan must be seeking to control her again.

Her hands are clenched by her side, her eyes tightly shut. Is she fighting him? Is she winning? And why is he attempting to take over her now, of all times?

My distraction costs me. Igor swoops in from above again, and this time his claws rip into the side of my head, nearly blinding me. With a screech of pain, I pull away, managing to hurt his wing in the process.

Latched onto one another, we tumble into the abyss below–then at the last possible moment, I escape his clutches and fly away. Despite the close call, I try to get a good read below, but it's hard to do. Fiona has become a blur in a sea of movement.

Shit.

Just as I hear an angry roar behind, a nudging in my mind pulls my attention. *Fiona?*

Not quite, frate.

Surprise makes me jerk mid-air, nearly losing altitude when I realize the source of the connection. I catch myself at the last possible minute. *Declan! What are you doing in her head?*

She invited me.

You lie!

If only. Your witch was quite persistent that you needed my help. And from what I can see, you do. Actively.

Flying above Fiona now, I peer below. Only it's not her violet eyes that catch mine, but golden ones. Declan really has hold of her now, more than before. I want to yell at him, to call him the evil monster I thought him to be, but I cannot. The words die in my throat, suppressed by the knowledge of Igor's machinations. And by the reality that Declan isn't, nor has he ever been, as evil as I gave him credit.

Leave her be, I end up pleading.

A sigh echoes in my head. *Frate, I cannot. She invited me, and she alone can release me. And she will not do so until I help. Stop being your usual stubborn self and let me.*

Before I do any of the like, I need to make sure he isn't in this to backstab me. I may know the truth, but if Declan doesn't... *Is this another trick to make me fall under Igor's grip?*

I assure you, it is not.

What guarantees me you are telling me the truth?

A pause. *Because Fiona told me. About Alina, and how Igor fooled both of us. And while that doesn't lessen my dislike of you, nor erase these millennia during which I was imprisoned, it makes me want revenge.*

On Igor?

Precisely.

I gaze around, hunting for our common enemy. He's using the clouds as cover again, and it won't be long before he attacks. There is a pattern to his attacks, only I cannot discern it. And with the darkness that suffuses his magical sweeps, I am always left catching up, on the defensive. It is not a situation I am used to.

How are you able to maintain the link?

Declan sighs, as if annoyed at my constant stream of questions. *You know the immortals are weakened. Igor's attacks on their prison have left me enough of an opening to reach out to someone. But it has to be someone who willingly lets me in. Fiona offered, and through her bond to you, I can now remain connected. Fully.*

And you think, what, that playing this little game we did as kids will help?

Declan's tone is more bored this time. *If you do not want my help, then tell your witch to release me. But we both know Igor is winning this particular fight, judging by your wounds.*

I want to tell him to fuck off. But then I glance at Fiona, and Igor in the sky, and I know I cannot. For the same reason she took this risk–because I have to protect her.

I accept. On the condition that as soon as his heart stops beating, you get out of Fiona's head.

If it's so important to you, then I shall. Something in his tone makes his next reply sound amused. *If she lets me.*

It's hard to ignore the bait, but I manage–barely. *What insight can you provide?*

Your immortal friend, Făt Frumos. His blade alone will kill the balaur. It is the same titanium that would kill us, and has taken the lives of many of our kin. Not to mention it is reinforced by the strongest primordial magic.

Perfect. All good to know… Only we have no immortals around, frate.

They will come. Their meddling nature will draw them as surely as flies to honey.

Charming picture. I'll make sure to let Ileana know.

I still need to subdue Igor, and we'll only have one shot at this.

Precisely, Declan says, following my thoughts. *Igor has a weakness. A lucky shot from a human messed up one of his scales. It's under his right wing, and he is completely vulnerable there. Thus, the plan is simple. Get as close as you can, and keep working that angle until he drops.*

He overpowers my strength.

Not anymore, he does not. I am with you in this, brother. Mind… and body. If you allow me.

Like when we were kids?

Exactly like that.

Memories of those simpler, less complicated times fill my mind. I don't know if they're mine, or Declan's, but I watch us soaring through the skies, chasing each other. Venturing well out of our lands, into new places, and dealing with the elders' wrath when we returned. I see us as brothers, as friends, backing each other up–not tearing each other down.

I want to refuse Declan's offer, I truly do. He is not that young child, and nothing tells me he won't try to take advantage of this situation for himself.

But this is about more than me, more than my familial quarrel with Declan. I have to defeat Igor if I'm to ever get Fiona back and try out the life we could have. When the balaur swoops down from the skies again, I run out of time to debate and instead beat my wings backwards, making him chase me.

All right. In that same instant, I open the gates of my mind, allowing Declan's being to merge with mine. Through this, we will each be navigating my zmeu, effectively lending strength to the other.

Never would have thought this old trick would help us.

Nor I, Ty.

Nostalgia tries to creep on me at the old nickname. Memories of the many times we

did this, the many moments we had together, threaten at the edges of my consciousness. And not all of them are mine–
Declan, too, is relieving them.

Like one body, one mind, we stop
running away and instead turn to face Igor.
He can't tell anything is wrong, and he
attacks as always. Only this time, my claws
rip through his chest, and when my body
smacks with his, it jolts him out of the sky
and backwards.

His head tilts to the side, assessing me
despite his blindness. I don't know if he
senses Declan in me, if he can feel it. But I
won't wait to find out. Instead, I roar and
attack.

Chapter 20

Speranţă
"Out of the mountain of despair, a stone of hope."
-Martin Luther King, Jr.-

Fiona

It's the oddest sensation, having Declan channel his communication with Tytus through me. I can see everything else, but Declan owns my body, my movements. And this time, it's on purpose. The odd thing is, there is no fear in me. I have no doubt I am mistress of my fate, if only in the passenger seat for the moment.

Through Declan's eyes, I look above, watching as Tytus gains on Igor. His attacks are more determined, less hesitant. There is new strength in the way he's aiming, and

Igor knows it. He's backing away, refusing to engage.

Tytus is not allowing it. Whatever Declan's doing, he's pushing forward. Together, the two brothers are unbeatable.

And through my connection to both, I sense them. Not like before, where it was abstract. But I can hear their thoughts, sense their intentions. Tytus' rage, his protectiveness of me. He's worried I'm so far away, and Declan is taking them further and further. He's worried he won't be around to help me.

I'll be fine. I try to send to him.

Focus, Tytus! Enough with the human. We both know she can take care of herself.

Declan's words would be harsh, but oddly they're not. He's.... At first, I think I'm losing my mind, but when I push deeper, I realize he's feeling less lonely. The rush of the hunt with Tytus reminds him of old times. Simpler times. He likes it. More than that–he *missed* it!

My realization must be too loud mentally or something because Declan focuses on me, pushing back. I toss my mental barriers up and nearly kill the connection in the process.

Stay out of my head, witch.

Leave her alone! Tytus yells just as loud, sensing Declan's focus shift.

In the skies, rather than fly, Tytus' zmeu form zig zags as if two drivers are fighting for control.

Shit.

"What the hell is going on?"

I jump and look behind, noticing Făt come out of a portal.

He frowns at me, sizing me up. "Fiona?"

"Yeah," I say, my voice deeper than normal. "I'm channeling Declan to help out Tytus."

He's on me in a second, his grip painful around my shoulders. "Why would you do that!"

I toss my head back. "Do you want to get better or not? Well, we figured out the reason."

I point up to the sky and Făt looks up. His jaw slackens, and he lets go of me, taking a few steps in Igor's direction.

"How...? A balaur!"

I nod at his back, focusing my attention on Tytus. That's when I see Igor zeroing in on us. Specifically, Făt. I remember what he said about the Underworld and Ileana having something precious hidden in there.

Oh, shit. The reason he's here is not because he's waiting for Tytus. He was waiting for the immortals!

TYTUS!

I only hope my mental yell jolts the brothers out of their ongoing argument. Not waiting to see if it does, I tackle Făt to the ground just as Igor passes over us, nearly scraping my backside.

Făt pushes me off him and stands in a crouch. He spares me a glance filled with surprise and gratitude, before focusing back on the enemy. Already his hand is glowing, and he pulls a sword out of thin air it seems–just like Tytus did. As if the air was a sheath and the sword just waited for its master.

Odd swirly symbols are etched on it, but he moves too fast for me to make them out. When Igor comes back, Făt rises and shoves the blade upwards, nicking part of his forepaw. Blood splatters everywhere around us and we move out of the way, even as Igor hides back into the skies.

Or, tries to. Tytus is waiting for him. It seems he and Declan finally got their shit together, and are acting as one, once more.

"You saved my life," Făt says, distracting me from the fight.

I turn to him. "You're welcome."

Just as I say the words, another portal opens and Ileana steps through.

Făt immediately goes to her. "Where were you? I thought the zmeu had called you."

"No, it was not him."

"Then who?"

The murmur of their voices ebbs and flows away, at least for a while. Until their tones rise in argument, distracting me once more from my search of the skies. Where the hell is Tytus?

"The wolves will be fine," Făt is saying.

Is he talking about the rogues back in Rockland Creek? Part of me cannot help but tune in, while still squinting at the clouds, trying to make out the battling shapes of the shifters.

"He ended up in the Underworld, Făt. Does that sound like they're doing all right?"

A quick glance over my shoulder shows them head to head. Then Făt glances above and sighs, stepping away. "I know you care for them. Go, draga mea. I will take care of this."

Ileana hesitates, as though she didn't expect the quick capitulation.

"Go," Făt repeats, and kisses her forehead softly. "With my blessing, and my heart."

Then he turns away from her, all softness replaced by determination. In his hands, the blade catches the sun's rays and glints harshly. Deadly.

Tytus

Watch your back!

A growl escapes me. *Will you let me lead, already?*

This was the one part of our trick that didn't always work. Declan and I never could share one zmeu body properly. Or weapons. Or food. Or, truly, anything that involved giving the other an advantage. It was one of our biggest drawbacks.

If only you would heed my warning! Igor is coming. Flip, now!

I listen to his instructions and shoot a jet of flames, scorching Igor's underbelly, already exposed by my previous scratches. He howls in pain and tries to move, but I follow him and fire at his back and wings.

Lightning is present in the air and I draw on it, focusing it toward Igor and letting Declan lead the strike. It hits Igor in the head and he freezes, as if dazed. Then his body drops altitude, but he catches himself, shaking his head and attempting to focus.

His head must be ringing.

Forget about that, Ty. Take the fucking shot!

I dive under Igor, using air and gravity so I'm as quiet as possible. When I'm under him, my attention zeroes in on his right wing, and the scale underneath. It is the area closest to his internal organs, and I know a blow there will toss him out of the skies, for good.

The zmeu I used to be might have

considered being merciful. But when I think of the pain he put my brother through, the machinations that tore us apart, and the agony Fiona survived because of him.... I cannot find a single shred of mercy in me.

I draw on lightning again, and Igor stops moving, trying to pinpoint where the noise is coming from. By the time he tilts his head beneath him, where we are, it's too late. The shot of lightning hits him straight under the wing, scorching it and travelling through his body, amplified by my rage.

Smoke escapes Igor and, unable to retaliate further, he drops from the sky.

We go after him as one mind, one body, one intent of vengeance. With a little nudge of air, Igor even loses control of his fall, and gravity takes over.

Igor doesn't land, he crashes. The ground shakes under him. Declan and I continue to draw on lightning, on air, pinning him so he's unable to move ahead or behind.

From afar, already I see Făt coming

closer. Something glints in his hand—a blade.

Good. At least he wasted no time.

Keep in mind whatever kills Igor can also kill you, Declan reminds me. *I would strongly suggest you stay the hell out of his reach after Igor is dead.*

I shall.

Igor stands, trying to move away. I drop on the ground next to him, expanding my wings and roaring, effectively cornering him. Făt approaches from behind, and Igor turns to take a bite out of him.

I move then, sinking my talons into his burned wing, shredding it to pieces. And as he bends over, slowed down by his agony, Făt moves in easily. The blade glints before sinking into Igor, straight where his heart would be.

Făt steps back, releasing it and watching the balaur. He never turns back to his human form. Instead he stumbles, then drops to the ground, his breathing growing heavier and heavier. The darkness holds him to the very end when he looks at me. Recognition flashes in his eyes, and he whispers one last threat.

"You think you have won, brothers? You have failed. What we began, cannot be stopped."

On a last exhale, he expires. Rather than see the soul leave as normal with a zmeu, his body shrivels into itself, curling up and burning until there is nothing left, except the sword.

Făt takes a step closer and grabs it, wiping it on his pants. I stay far out of its reach, recalling Declan's warning. But the immortal only spares us a glance.

"About time we eliminated this threat."

Vengeance does taste sweet, Declan says.

It does.

I transform back to human form, only afterwards realizing the shift must have broken the connection with Declan, since it cannot take place while I'm human. I push the thought aside, promising to deal with him, later.

Instead, I stride to Fiona, pulling her in my arms. "You were amazing."

"I know," she chuckles in my chest. The light in her eyes–violet, not golden–remains even as her tone changes. "But we have to talk about Declan–*to* Declan."

Her touch on my arm shimmers, and I sense her creating that connection once more.

Declan

With the link broken, I find myself back in the cave. Imprisoned and alone once more. With no way to escape. I've just helped my brother out and still am where I first started.

Worse, now I'm left with memories of what my ex-wife truly was, and how I got played by Igor. Looks like I'll have the next batch of centuries to reflect on my actions, whether I like it or not.

Damn it all to hell.

Before I can get as riled up as I'd like, I sense a prod into my mind. Thinking it's the witch again, I let her in.

What do you want?

To thank you.

I'm surprised to recognize my brother's energy instead.

How sanctimonious of you.

He snorts. *Don't start. I just thought you should know, I'm coming for you.*

More death threats?

No, brother. I'm not coming to hurt you. I will release you from under the immortals' thumbs, and then you and I are going to have a long, long talk about what happened eons ago.

He actually means it, the bastard. To hide my surprise, I revert to status quo.

Don't worry, frate. I make my own escape.

Chapter 21

Paradox
"I have found the paradox, that if you love until it
hurts, there can be no more hurt, only more love."
-Mother Theresa-

Tytus

Declan breaks the link this time, and I am left pondering his words. Fiona burrows further in my embrace, sighing happily.

"I love you."

My heartbeat stops for a second, then picks up at a racing pace. I push her away, just enough so I can tilt her chin and look into her eyes. "You don't know how long I've been waiting for those words."

She smiles and rises on her tiptoes to kiss me. It's only a small, swift press of her lips to mine, but my zmeu roars in victory, and I am very tempted to join him.

When Fiona sinks back into my arms, I wrap them tighter against her and simply hold her. Something in me soothes at having her safe, and sound, and close by. I'll have to ask her later why that chat with Declan was absolutely necessary now, but I am glad, in a way.

Never would I have thought I could forgive him. As it turns out, it is he who has to forgive me for everything I let happen without contest. Without trying, more.

As I promised him, that will be a later conversation. A *much* later one, given I have to let the immortals' guards drop first before I begin another war.

Having Fiona safe is all I care about, all I should care about right now. I've fought too hard to have her by my side, and my zmeu is too eager to finalize the deal.

But Făt and Ileana interrupt us, both looking much healthier than the last time we saw them.

"You look better," I tell Ileana.

She smiles. "With the balaur destroyed,

his enchantments have also died off."

I glance at what's left of Igor. Later, I'll return and wipe this entire area clean, but nothing can tear me from Fiona's side right now.

"Did you figure out what Declan's plan was, in its entirety?" Ileana asks.

I recall the promise I just made to my brother and try to answer honestly, but giving nothing away. "Da, we did. Igor wanted access to the–"

"Weapons in Tytus' castle, and his own mind," Fiona interrupts.

I attempt to keep my expression cool, but luckily the immortals are too focused on her to care about me.

"That makes no sense," Făt mutters. "Are you sure that's all it was?"

"Yes. Igor lost his mind in the dungeons." Fiona shrugs, as if lying is as easy as breathing for her. "When he had me down there, he told me everything."

"Right..."

Făt still doesn't seem convinced, but Fiona leans heavier against me, putting a hand up to her forehead as if she's about to faint. "I'm not feeling so great."

"It must be the strain of helping us." I tighten my hold on her, knowing full well through the bond that she's not sick, at all. Not that I'm about to argue against some alone time.

To the immortals, I ask, "I take it this concludes our business?"

"Da," Făt says. "For now."

He walks away without another word, opening a portal, but Ileana lingers behind. She glances between us, smiling. "Thank you, for all your help. I wish you both good luck."

I nod and she joins him, leaving us alone. As I would prefer it. Always.

Fiona

The moment the immortals are gone, Tytus walks us both back to his castle. He waits until we're inside to turn me in his arms, cupping my cheek and gazing into my eyes.

"Why did you lie to them, sweetling?"

I shake my head, not quite knowing the answer, either. "This will sound crazy, but I heard what Igor said at the last minute. Ileana and Făt have acted a bit odd throughout this whole thing, but what if it goes bigger than that? What if there's more than you and Declan, being affected? You are the last of your race, but there aren't that many immortals out there, either."

"You think it could be some kind of covert war?"

"Maybe. Either way, it's better to keep the cards close to our chest. At least until we get Declan out." Tytus' eyes widen, and I laugh.

"And you're all right with that prospect?"

Maybe. For now. Unless he shows he's a psycho again. I shrug. "He came to your defense, and I could control him in my mind. Things are changing, and not for the worst."

It's the truth, in as much as I can figure it out. We were all wrong, to some extent. Declan, the most, but Tytus, as well. And even me. We were played by forces out of our control, and whether we want to admit it or not, it created an understanding, of sorts, between us. A truce. As unlikely as it seems.

"Indeed," he says, and kisses me until

my toes curl and all I want is a bed. With him in it.

¥

I wake up to the light of the moon. A shadow by the window has me jerk awake, but it's only Tytus. His back is to me, and he's staring out, looking forlorn.

As if sensing I'm awake, he turns and smiles at me, moving closer to the bed. "You're awake."

"I am." I lick my dry lips, and hold out a hand to him. "And you're safe."

"I am." A pause follows as his expression grows more serious. "It was crazy, what you did. To allow Declan in like that..."

"Probably. But I needed to help you, and it was the best way I knew how."

He stares at me, finally saying what is on his mind. "Do you know why it worked, what you did?"

"Because Declan used me as a channel to this world."

"Not just to this world. To me, sweetling. He sensed the strength of our connection. Of our bond."

I try to read between his words. "You mean...?"

"Da. If you want it." He caresses my cheek. "What would you say to spending a lifetime by my side?"

"A human lifetime."

Tytus' eyes crinkle at the corners when he grins. "Not with zmeu magic, darling. When we join, when we truly *pair,* my zmeu essence will infuse you. It is a way for the zmeu to ensure his mate would be forever safe, forever protected. Our fates will be intertwined, and your life would be as long as mine. Do you think you could handle it?"

My heart melts at the hope, the slight quiver in his voice. "I can handle anything, if it's by your side."

"I was hoping you'd say that."

He bends his head to me, and our lips brush. At the contact, my entire body feels like it's on fire, and I grip his shoulders for support.

"Tytus?"

"Your acceptance started it," he whispers. "But don't worry, sweetling. I'll take care of you."

Tytus

Never in all my time on this earth did I ever consider mating. Mainly because of the dangers, but also because of what it implies. Tying one's immortal existence to someone else, forever, seems like a gamble. I warned Elisandra against it, too.

How fast some things change. Now, in bed, with Fiona in my arms and moonlight shining down on us, nothing has ever felt so right.

As we kiss, as she surrenders to me, my hands roam her body like it's the first time. Like it's the only time. Her breathing increases and unlike before, I don't have to guess or strain to figure out if she's turned on.

I feel it in my core.

And she does, too.

Her eyes open and latch onto mine, and her hands dig in my hair. "Is this how it's going to be?"

I chuckle against her neck. "I sure hope so."

And then I'm kissing her all over,

taking my sweet time. Savoring the eternity we have waiting for us. Savoring her surrender, and her little moans that tell me she's enjoying this.

My hands heat with inner fire, and when I thrust inside her, Fiona arches beneath me. I'm buried so deep in her, and she's so tight and warm around me, that it takes all of my control not to lose it then and there.

The steady thrum of my heartbeat increases. A pounding grows louder in my ears.

I intertwine our fingers, slowing my thrusts. Slower, slower, *slower*. And Fiona moans under me, clenching around me.

The heat in me permeates to her. Fire fills my belly and takes over my skin. Then hers. The same red haze from before surrounds us, and the bed itself gets surrounded by flames. Different shades of red, not burning the sheets or anything else. But focused on us–on our joining, our emotions.

Fiona opens her eyes, staring at me. The flames burn brighter now, around us and within us. Real, hot, licking flames.

Her skin glows beautifully in the orange light, and I let go and thrust deeper inside her, losing my last shred of sanity. Fiona shouts my name on a long moan, and it's the most at peace I've ever felt.

I fall asleep first, lulled by the beating of her heart.

Fiona

I wake up at daybreak and extricate myself from Tytus' arms. On tiptoes, I make my way to the library and the window giving onto the sunrise.

On my way there, my eyes linger on the journal I'd been reading. Igor had lied, it's true, but that journal... Determined to satisfy my curiosity and put the last piece of the puzzle in its place, I pick it up and flip all the way to the final entry.

December 17, 717 A.D.

Tytus walks around as if he owns the castle. As if I can forgive his betrayal, as if I do not know the truth. But I do. Igor was truthful, more honest with me than my brother ever could be.

And with his help, I will make sure Tytus pays. That they all pay—including the humans who thought it would be easy to kill a zmeu.

I have a new mission in life, and that is to eradicate them. Forever.

I close the book on a sigh, then place it back on the shelf. It was Declan—all along, *Declan* wrote that journal, not Tytus. And had I only flipped through all the entries, I would have saved myself a hell of a headache.

With hesitant steps, I head to the window and stare outside. The sky is painted in shades of pink, orange and purple, and I stare at it in amazement until my eyes burn and tears fall down my cheeks. Only their appearance on my hands makes me realize I'm crying.

An arm comes around my waist, and Tytus drops his forehead to my shoulder. "Why the tears, sweetling?"

"Cathartic." I turn in his arms. "It's nothing bad, I promise. I was just thinking how far I've come."

Pride shines in his eyes. "No one sees it more than I."

I allow the kiss until he's pressing me against the window, moving against me in a way that suggests we may be heading for bed once more.

"Now that we saved the world, what will we do?"

He shrugs, more interested in my neck–and, presumably, my response to said caress. "The world is our oyster," he says eventually. "After I renovate this place, I'll show you around the mountains. Plenty more villages to see."

"We should invite Elisandra and the other girls for a visit, no? They would enjoy it."

"Hmm. Later, yes. I do need to finish their training. But for now, I want you all to myself."

And then his mouth shuts up any further protests, and I give in to him. Not because I have to–but because I choose to. He has shown me my inner strength, and by so doing I was able to fight off my demons. And now, whatever else comes our way, we can fight it off... together.

Epilogue

Far from Tytus' castle, but closer than they would have admitted, Ileana and Făt were rejoined in the hot springs near a mountain.

Făt spoke first, shedding his suit jacket. "Are the wolves still doing all right?"

"Da. Better than ever, in fact."

"It has only been a few days since you last saw them."

Ileana shrugged. "And over time, I will learn distance. I am glad you came with me."

"Da, and I want to go back to our earlier conversation... You said something crazy then. About using Declan to get back our daughter."

Ileana watched as her consort dove deep into the hot water, then resurfaced and shook his head. Droplets of water flew all over the place, and his blue eyes settled on her.

"Have you thought more about it?" she asked.

"Yes."

"And?"

"I am of the same mind. With one caveat. After the stunt he pulled on us, even once he returns Constanza back to us, I will not release him."

"Good. Neither will I."

"Then you can speak to him, I give you my blessing."

Ileana smiled. "Perhaps we'll let him brood another night." Then she joined him in the hot waters, shedding her robe of flowers and enjoying the heat building into his gaze. When she came into his arms, she whispered, "Let us forget all of zmei and wolves for tonight, dragul meu."

"Da," he nuzzled her throat. "Let us only celebrate."

Ileana took him deep within her, then, and threw her head back. And as her eyes stayed locked on the stars, she knew without a doubt their journey was only getting better and better.

Igniting the Ice (Flaming Rogues, #2)

A *Moonlight Rogues* Spinoff

Declan

Something changed in the air. Unsure, yet intrigued, I lift my black muzzle off the ground and sniff. Nothing.

Perhaps I was mistaken.

Incredibly bored out of my mind, I drop my head back on the cave's cool ground and rest it on my front paws. One would think living permanently in my zmeu form would be comfortable, and offer heat, at least. And one would be correct.

Yet I also miss the human. See, as a Romanian dragon, I'm a shifter. Among many, *many* qualities, I can use elemental magic to the point of becoming a storm myself. And yet I have once more become imprisoned by a witch's hand, all thanks to my dear, fucking brother.

Tytus.

A growl escapes me, reverberating in the cavern. *Patience. Soon enough, they will figure out this prison will not last.* When I shift to a more comfortable position, the massive gold cuffs around my paws catch the dim light.

And then... It happens again. The air changes, and the scent of cinnamon permeates it fully. My eyes open once more, landing on my hated jailor.

What now?

Constanza

"Constanza!"

I cringe at the loud booming voice. Part of me wants to cower away, and the other part, well... I share a mischievous glance with my best friend, Persephone. "Oops."

She rolls her violet eyes and stands from the grass. We'd been fooling around in the gardens near Lethe–again. It was my idea, even knowing Hades hates it when we linger here, on account of the dangers of the river.

And, given I'm his long-standing guest, I really should pay more attention to his instructions. It's not like he's a control freak–much. Still, something about the silver river calls to me, and not in order to drink from it. It's just... pretty.

"Constanza!" He calls again, this time closer.

Persephone flicks a lock of her dark brown hair and winks at me. "I'll take care of this. But, umm, maybe go for a long walk, yeah?"

With a grin and an air-blown kiss, I take off under some bushes. Hades' voice echoes behind me, followed by Persephone's softer murmur as she calms him down. She knows he's afraid of losing her to the depths of the Underworld, that is all. Which, in a way, is super romantic – the fact he loves her enough not to let go, not the other part.

I wish I had someone like that.

The thought lingers, not unlike previous times. It's becoming more frequent lately. Mom and Dad leave me be, I mean after all I'm immortal and have the rest of eternity ahead of me to find someone.

But a girl has needs... And it's getting bad enough that I'm starting to have dreams.

Sexy, sexy dreams of a dark blond god with eyes of molten gold. I lick my lips at the reminder, and suddenly, I'm feeling like it's time for a nap.

Maybe I'll see him again. There's no harm in dreaming, right?

Author's Note & Acknowledgements

Wow. I didn't realize what a ride I was in for, when I decided to launch this duology. But Tytus and Declan were that addictive, so my hope is you'll get to enjoy them, too :)

If you're reading this first before my *Moonlight Rogues* series, have no fear. *Fanning the Flames* and *Igniting the Ice* are connected to the *Moonlight Rogues* universe, but they can be read apart. If you did want to read them chronologically, you'll want to start with my free short story collection, *Moonlight Rogues: Origins*, then make your way through books 1-3. Tytus' story picks up right after *Third to Tumble (Moonlight Rogues, Book 3)* and *Igniting the Ice* picks up after *Last to Love (Moonlight Rogues, Book 4).*

OR you can keep reading and enjoy the duology on its own :)

Now, a few thank yous are in order. First, to my husband and my furry doggos.

I was a tad more impossible to be around while wrapping this story up, and all kudos go to them for keeping my sanity and keeping me fed!

Huge thanks also go to the team behind this book, as well as to Candace for her love of this series and support of my never-ending brain waves coming up with stories. To Siobhan, for the wise advice and equally awesome sibling insights (and quotes!) provided.

Massive thanks to Y. Nikolova at Ammonia Book Covers for the epic covers <3 I adore them!

Huge thanks to one very awesome reader, Billie Wichkan. I was stuck on the name for the bad guys in this series, and my placeholder name kinda sucked (no, you don't get to find out, because it sucked :P) and Billie was awesome AND super fast in finding me an option that just **fit**. When ya know, ya know. Soooo whenever you see *Cavaleri Serafim* or *Order of Serafim* in here, you've got her to thank :)

About the Author

Alexa Whitewolf is a fiction writer, newspaper columnist of daily issues and author of the critically acclaimed *Moonlight Rogues* shifter series.

Alexa has been a lifelong writer and first began creating other worlds and characters at the ripe age of 12. Growing up in the Transylvania region surrounded by epic mountains and a never ending stream of legends and stories was bound to create an overactive imagination. This shines through Ms. Whitewolf's writing by creating worlds filled with unique folklore, life wisdom and plenty of furry creatures.

An avid traveler, Alexa writes under a penname and spends her days between an office job and writing in Canada's capital, when she's not flying somewhere with lush landscapes and plenty of hiking trails.

Her series focus on strong heroines, kind yet sexy men, fights of good and evil and the never-ending learning curve of humanity's strong – and weak – points. Romanian folklore is intertwined with her writing, more notably in her shifter romance series, the *Moonlight Rogues.* Her other series draw on world mythology, such as the Avalon myth and Arthurian legend (*The Avalon Chronicles*) and Ancient Egypt (*The Sage's Legacy*).

You can follow her blog at www.alexawhitewolf.com/blog or on social media. Her column in Observatorul also tackles various issues, including health, technology, and a writer's life.

If you want up to date releases, make sure you sign up for her newsletter. For new releases notifications, you can also follow her on Amazon and BookBub.

Also by the Author

The Avalon Chronicles series
Avalon Dreams
Avalon Wishes
Avalon Nightmares
Atrox – An Avalon Chronicles Novella
Exclusive inside look in the series

The Sage's Legacy – YA series
The Dragon Medallion
The Dragon Manuscript
Relics of the Underworld
Exclusive inside look in the series

Moonlight Rogues series
First to Fall
Second to Surrender
Third to Tumble
Last to Love
Moonlight Rogues: Origins
Exclusive inside look in the series

Flaming Rogues series

Fanning the Flames

Igniting the Ice

Exclusive inside look in the series

Standalone novels

Blood Ties, Love Binds

Unconditional Love

Blazing Ashes

More novels coming soon

www.ingramcontent.com/pod-product-compliance
Lightning Source LLC
Chambersburg PA
CBHW020246030726
47499CB00001B/78